BRIAN FI

COLD L

BRIAN FLYNN was born in 1885 in Leyton, Essex.
He won a scholarship to the City Of London School,
and from there went into the civil service. In World
War I he served as Special Constable on the Home
Front, also teaching "Accountancy, Languages, Maths
and Elocution to men, women, boys and girls" in the
evenings, and acting in his spare time.

It was a seaside family holiday that inspired Brian
Flynn to turn his hand to writing in the mid-twenties.
Finding most mystery novels of the time "mediocre in
the extreme", he decided to compose his own. Edith,
the author's wife, encouraged its completion, and
after a protracted period finding a publisher, it was
eventually released in 1927 by John Hamilton in the
UK and Macrae Smith in the U.S. as *The Billiard-
Room Mystery*.

The author died in 1958. In all, he wrote and published
57 mysteries, the vast majority featuring the super-
sleuth Antony Bathurst.

BRIAN FLYNN

COLD EVIL

With an introduction by
Steve Barge

DEAN STREET PRESS

Published by Dean Street Press 2021

Copyright © 1938 Brian Flynn

Introduction © 2021 Steve Barge

First published in 1938 by John Long

Cover by DSP

ISBN 978 1 914150 59 3

www.deanstreetpress.co.uk

INTRODUCTION

"I believe that the primary function of the mystery story is
to entertain; to stimulate the imagination and even, at times,
to supply humour. But it pleases the connoisseur most when
it presents – and reveals – genuine mystery. To reach its full
height, it has to offer an intellectual problem for the reader
to consider, measure and solve."

Brian Flynn, *Crime Book* magazine, 1948

BRIAN Flynn began his writing career with *The Billiard Room Mystery*
in 1927, primarily at the prompting of his wife Edith who had grown
tired of hearing him say how he could write a better mystery novel
than the ones he had been reading. Four more books followed under
his original publisher, John Hamilton, before he moved to John
Long, who would go on to publish the remaining forty-eight of his
Anthony Bathurst mysteries, along with his three Sebastian Stole
titles, released under the pseudonym Charles Wogan. Some of the
early books were released in the US, and there were also a small
number of translations of his mysteries into Swedish and German.
In the article from which the above quote is taken from, Brian also
claims that there were also French and Danish translations but to
date, I have not found a single piece of evidence for their existence.
The only translations that I have been able to find evidence of are
War Es Der Zahnarzt? and *Bathurst Greift Ein* in German – *The
Mystery of the Peacock's Eye*, retitled to the less dramatic "Was It
The Dentist?", and *The Horn* becoming "Bathurst Takes Action" –
and, in Swedish, *De 22 Svarta*, a more direct translation of *The Case
of the Black Twenty-Two*. There may well be more work to be done
finding these, but tracking down all of his books written in the original English has been challenging enough!

Reprints of Brian's books were rare. Four titles were released
as paperbacks as part of John Long's Four Square Thriller range in
the late 1930s, four more re-appeared during the war from Cherry
Tree Books and Mellifont Press, albeit abridged by at least a third,
and two others that I am aware of, *Such Bright Disguises* (1941)
and *Reverse the Charges* (1943), received a paperback release as

part of John Long's Pocket Edition range in the early 1950s – these were also possibly abridged, but only by about 10%. They were the exceptions, rather than the rule, however, and it was not until 2019, when Dean Street Press released his first ten titles, that his work was generally available again.

The question still persists as to why his work disappeared from the awareness of all but the most ardent collectors. As you may expect, when a title was only released once, back in the early 1930s, finding copies of the original text is not a straightforward matter – not even Brian's estate has a copy of every title. We are particularly grateful to one particular collector for providing *The Edge of Terror*, Brian's first serial killer tale, and another for *The Ebony Stag* and *The Grim Maiden*. With these, the reader can breathe a sigh of relief as a copy of every one of Brian's books has now been located – it only took about five years . . .

One of Brian's strengths was the variety of stories that he was willing to tell. Despite, under his own name at least, never straying from involving Anthony Bathurst in his novels – technically he doesn't appear in the non-series *Tragedy at Trinket*, although he gets a name-check from the sleuth of that tale who happens to be his nephew – it is fair to say that it was rare that two consecutive books ever followed the same structure. Some stories are narrated by a Watson-esque character, although never the same person twice, and others are written by Bathurst's "chronicler". The books sometimes focus on just Bathurst and his investigation but sometimes we get to see the events occurring to the whole cast of characters. On occasion, Bathurst himself will "write" the final chapter, just to make sure his chronicler has got the details correct. The murderer may be an opportunist or they may have a convoluted (and, on occasion, a somewhat over-the-top) plan. They may be working for personal gain or as part of a criminal enterprise or society. Compare for example, *The League of Matthias* and *The Horn* – consecutive releases but were it not for Bathurst's involvement, and a similar sense of humour underlying Brian's writing, you could easily believe that they were from the pen of different writers.

Brian seems to have been determined to keep stretching himself with his writing as he continued Bathurst's adventures, and the ten books starting with *Cold Evil* show him still trying new things. Two of the books are inverted mysteries – where we know who the killer is, and we follow their attempts to commit the crime and/or escape justice and also, in some cases, the detective's attempt to bring them to justice. That description doesn't do justice to either *Black Edged* or *Such Bright Disguises*, as there is more revealed in the finale than the reader might expect . . . There is one particular innovation in *The Grim Maiden*, namely the introduction of a female officer at Scotland Yard.

Helen Repton, an officer from "the woman's side of the Yard" is recruited in that book, as Bathurst's plan require an undercover officer in a cinema. This is her first appearance, despite the text implying that Bathurst has met her before, but it is notable as the narrative spends a little time apart from Bathurst. It follows Helen Repton's investigations based on superb initiative, which generates some leads in the case. At this point in crime fiction, there have been few, if any, serious depictions of a female police detective – the primary example would be Mrs Pym from the pen of Nigel Morland, but she (not just the only female detective at the Yard, but the Assistant Deputy Commissioner no less) would seem to be something of a caricature. Helen would go on to become a semi-regular character in the series, and there are certainly hints of a romantic connection between her and Bathurst.

It is often interesting to see how crime writers tackled the Second World War in their writing. Some brought the ongoing conflict into their writing – John Rhode (and his pseudonym Miles Burton) wrote several titles set in England during the conflict, as did others such as E.C.R. Lorac, Christopher Bush, Gladys Mitchell and many others. Other writers chose not to include the War in their tales – Agatha Christie had ten books published in the war years, yet only *N or M?* uses it as a subject.

Brian only uses the war as a backdrop in one title, *Glittering Prizes*, the story of a possible plan to undermine the Empire. It illustrates the problem of writing when the outcome of the conflict was unknown – it was written presumably in 1941 – where there seems little sign of life in England of the war going on, one character states that he has fought in the conflict, but messages are sent from Nazi conspirators, ending *"Heil Hitler!"*. Brian had good reason for not wanting to write about the conflict in detail, though, as he had immediate family involved in the fighting and it is quite understandable to see writing as a distraction from that.

While Brian had until recently been all but forgotten, there are some mentions for Brian's work in some studies of the genre – Sutherland Scott in *Blood in their Ink* praises *The Mystery of the Peacock's Eye* as containing "one of the ablest pieces of misdirection" before promptly spoiling that misdirection a few pages later, and John Dickson Carr similarly spoils the ending of *The Billiard Room Mystery* in his famous essay "The Grandest Game In The World". One should also include in this list Barzun and Taylor's entry in their *Catalog of Crime* where they attempted to cover Brian by looking at a single title – the somewhat odd *Conspiracy at Angel* (1947) – and summarising it as "Straight tripe and savorless. It is doubtful, on the evidence, if any of his others would be different." Judging an author based on a single title seems desperately unfair – how many people have given up on Agatha Christie after only reading *Postern Of Fate*, for example – but at least that misjudgement is being rectified now.

Contemporary reviews of Brian's work were much more favourable, although as John Long were publishing his work for a library market, not all of his titles garnered attention. At this point in his writing career – 1938 to 1944 – a number of his books won reviews in the national press, most of which were positive. Maurice Richardson in the *Observer* commented that "Brian Flynn balances his ingredients with considerable skill" when reviewing *The Ebony Stag* and praised *Such Bright Disguises* as a "suburban horror melodrama" with an "ingenious final solution". "Suspense is well maintained until the end" in *The Case of the Faithful Heart*, and the protagonist's narration in *Black Edged* in "impressively nightmarish".

It is quite possible that Brian's harshest critic, though, was himself. In the *Crime Book* magazine, he wrote about how, when reading the current output of detective fiction "I delight in the dazzling erudition that has come to grace and decorate the craft of the *'roman policier'*." He then goes on to say "At the same time, however, I feel my own comparative unworthiness for the fire and burden of the competition." Such a feeling may well be the reason why he never made significant inroads into the social side of crime-writing, such as the Detection Club or the Crime Writers Association. Thankfully, he uses this sense of unworthiness as inspiration, concluding "The stars, though, have always been the most desired of all goals, so I allow exultation and determination to take the place of that but temporary dismay."

In Anthony Bathurst, Flynn created a sleuth that shared a number of traits with Holmes but was hardly a carbon-copy. Bathurst is a polymath and gentleman sleuth, a man of contradictions whose background is never made clear to the reader. He clearly has money, as he has his own rooms in London with a pair of servants on call and went to public school (Uppingham) and university (Oxford). He is a follower of all things that fall under the banner of sport, in particular horse racing and cricket, the latter being a sport that he could, allegedly, have represented England at. He is also a bit of a show-off, littering his speech (at times) with classical quotes, the obscurer the better, provided by the copies of the *Oxford Diction-ary of Quotations* and *Brewer's Dictionary of Phrase & Fable* that Flynn kept by his writing desk, although Bathurst generally restrains himself to only doing this with people who would appreciate it or to annoy the local constabulary. He is fond of amateur dramatics (as was Flynn, a well-regarded amateur thespian who appeared in at least one self-penned play, *Blue Murder*), having been a member of OUDS, the Oxford University Dramatic Society. General information about his background is light on the ground. His parents were Irish, but he doesn't have an accent – see *The Spiked Lion* (1933) – and his eyes are grey. Despite the fact that he is an incredibly charming and handsome individual, we learn in *The Orange Axe* that he doesn't pursue romantic relationships due to a bad experience in his first romance. We find out more about that relationship and the woman involved in *The Edge of Terror*, and soon thereafter he falls head over heels in love in *Fear and Trembling*, although we never hear of that young lady again. After that, there are eventual hints of an attraction between Helen Repton, but nothing more. That doesn't stop women falling head over heels for Bathurst – as he departs her company in *The Padded Door*, one character muses "What other man could she ever love . . . after this secret idolatry?"

As we reach the halfway point in Anthony's career, his companions have somewhat stablised, with Chief Inspector Andrew MacMorran now his near-constant junior partner in investigation. The friendship with MacMorran is a highlight (despite MacMorran always calling him "Mr. Bathurst") with the sparring between them always a delight to read. MacMorran's junior officers, notably Superintendent Hemingway and Sergeant Chatterton, are frequently recurring characters. The notion of the local constabulary calling in help from Scotland Yard enables cases to be set around the country while still maintaining the same central cast (along with a local bobby or two).

Cold Evil (1938), the twenty-first Bathurst mystery, finally pins down Bathurst's age, and we find that in *The Billiard Room Mystery* (1927), his first outing, he was a fresh-faced Bright Young Thing of twenty-two. How he can survive with his own rooms, at least two servants, and no noticeable source of income remains a mystery. One can also ask at what point in his life he travelled the world, as he has, at least, been to Bangkok at some point. It is, perhaps, best not to analyse Bathurst's past too carefully . . .

"Judging from the correspondence my books have excited it seems I have managed to achieve some measure of success, for my faithful readers comprise a circle in which high dignitaries of the Church rub shoulders with their brothers and sisters of the common touch."

For someone who wrote to entertain, such correspondence would have delighted Brian, and I wish he were around to see how many people have enjoyed the reprints of his work so far. *The Mystery of the Peacock's Eye* (1928) won Cross Examining Crime's Reprint Of The Year award for 2019, with *Tread Softly* garnering second place the following year. His family are delighted with the reactions that people have passed on, and I hope that this set of books will delight just as much.

Steve Barge

CHAPTER I

FRIDAY, DECEMBER 2ND, 10.20 P.M.

IT WILL be as well, I think, if I go back to the evening when it all
started. As Martin Burke finished his story, I can remember that
Chinnery laughed uneasily. The laugh, too, was accompanied by a
quick furtive glance over his shoulder in the direction of the door.
Verschoyle smiled a thin, dry-lipped smile as befitted his cloth and
his calling. Only the Squire, of all the party, seemed absolutely the
same man when Burke's story ended. Burke looked round at the
various members of the company. To see the different effects, probably, that his recital had had upon each one of us. First of all, his
eyes challenged mine.

"Well, Clyst, what about you—don't you believe me?" he
questioned.

I shrugged my shoulders.

"Why pick on me?" I countered.

"Why not?" He gave the question back to me immediately.

Verschoyle then came into the conversation. He was our host
that evening, and on this account, I think, felt the position somewhat more keenly than the others. The conversation after dinner had
taken such an unusual turn, and this so surprisingly, that Burke's
contribution was but a natural conclusion to it; when one drags in
the occult and the weird, it's ten to one that, from then onwards, no
other topic will get a show. Verschoyle became pedantic. He seldom
was able to avoid the temptation.

"The chimaera, which Burke tells us actually came to life in this
Chinese village where he was located for a month, took its name from
the volcano 'Chimaera', in Lycia."

Chinnery touched his brow with a finger-tip.

"Am I quite mad, or have I dreamt it? Wasn't there some connection, too, with the city of Belfast? Or am I thinking of . . . ?"

Verschoyle nodded. "You're neither mad nor dream-laden, Chinnery. You refer, of course, to the city arms of Belfast. There you find
a sea-horse . . . that is to say, a combination of horse and fish. The
same form also appears on the arms of Oliver Cromwell."

Burke showed signs of impatience.

"But look here, Edward, I don't know that you're—"

Verschoyle held up his hand and stopped him. "Just a minute, Martin. I've digressed, possibly, from the main avenue, but all the time I've been perfectly well aware of it. I think I can tell you what you were about to say. Let me extricate myself."

"Go ahead, then," smiled Major Burke encouragingly.

At that precise moment, I leant forward and threw a log on the fire. There was a swirling white mist outside and the chill of the air was beginning to invade the room.

"Thank you, Clyst." Verschoyle waved his appreciation of my services and went on.

"The chimaera, of course, was not a sea-horse but a fabled fire-breathing monster. The Greeks found this word for it. It was a combination of lion, goat, and serpent. That right, Burke?"

Burke nodded his lean dark head. "Take a hundred per cent, Edward. Lion's head, goat's body, and serpent's tail. Quite true. Sometimes, though, the serpent was more like a dragon. Mine was."

Squire Copeland roared. His huge shoulders rocked the gusts of his laughter.

"Martin, Martin, I'll wager that you'd emptied the bottle that night! Why, man, my own brother used to see worse things every night that was, than the one that you've just described! Pink rats, my boy, and even snakes. Man alive, why don't you admit it?"

Burke ignored the interruption. He took a deal of shaking off, did Major Martin Burke, when he saw his course clearly in front of him. Verschoyle came in again, quietly and steadily.

"After its first representations, the chimaera used to be portrayed as a lion, with the head of a goat protruding from its back. Sometimes, even, it was depicted as having three heads, those of a lion, goat, and serpent. The volcano, Chimaera, that is to say the crater at the top of it, was inhabited by lions and goats, and the base by serpents. I will admit at the same time, though, that the swan, the crocodile, and the cuttle-fish are all associated in mythology with the forms of fabulous monsters."

"Fantastic," growled Copeland, "utterly fantastic."

"Very true," returned Verschoyle, courteously. "So fantastic, indeed, that the term 'chimaera' has come to be used to denote not only any fantastic beast or monster, but a wild fury, a delusion, or even an incongruous medley of spirits. Your remark is really a tribute, Copeland."

Verschoyle's reply had no effect.

The merriment still showed in Copeland's eyes. Verschoyle continued:

"None the less acceptable, however, by reason of its being unintentional."

There was a hush. Then Chinnery's high-pitched voice broke in.

"Did anybody else see the thing besides you, Burke?"

"Oh, yes! Plenty of people. The affair was talked about for days afterwards. On account of the deaths, of course."

"How do you explain it yourself?" I asked.

"Frankly," said Burke, "I can't."

I persisted. "You admit that you have—?"

"No explanation at all," Burke answered me gravely. "If I gave one to you, you wouldn't believe it."

Verschoyle intervened quietly. "On the other hand, Major Burke, I should be most interested to hear it."

Burke pursed his lips. Copeland, ever practical, poured out a stiff peg of whisky. The fire still burned high with its crackling logs and the Rectory of St. Crayle was snug and warm again no matter what the elements were like outside. Chinnery had his pale-blue watery eyes fixed on Burke, who, conscious that he was the cynosure of all, laughed a trifle nervously.

"My explanation is probably even more fantastic than the Thing itself. But the East is the East, and banal though that statement may be, I don't know that I can think of a better. I tell you that I saw this 'Thing' rush madly down the quaint Eastern street. I heard its cry. I saw the three dead bodies afterwards, as they lay in the gutter. All you could say about them was that they lay inanimate—and I can only offer one explanation." Burke broke off a little lamely.

"Yes?" came Verschoyle's gentle prompting question.

"I believe," said Burke very quietly, "but I don't ask you to join in that belief, that the three men who died in the way that I have described, were murdered."

Verschoyle nodded his head. Once, twice, several times. As though the idea that Burke had put forward had found favour with him.

"Murdered?" cried Chinnery tremulously. "How?"

Copeland boomed scepticism. "Yes, by which of your animals, Burke? By the lion, by the goat, or by the serpent? Personally, my money's on the latter. I loathe the things. What's lower than a snake's bite?" He laughed contemptuously.

Again Burke paid him no heed. Instead, he answered Chinnery's question. "Although there wasn't anything in the nature of a wound on any one of those three bodies, I believe that the men were murdered just as clearly as if they had been stabbed to the heart with a knife. The only sign that they bore was a dull red mark . . . something like a burn, behind the ears. But there was no puncture of the skin and poison was out of the question." He paused and then continued: "They were killed, in my opinion, or were the victims, rather—let me put it like that, it's better—of a most advanced form of hypnosis."

Verschoyle nodded. "Just what I expected you to say. Another form, you mean, of the idea behind the Indian rope-trick?"

"Exactly." Burke's tone was quiet, but emphatic.

"I think I get your meaning," volunteered Chinnery—"but go on with your explanation."

Copeland looked at me and winked. Burke continued: "I mean nothing more and nothing less than this: that in some way, which we Western people don't understand yet, these Indian and Chinese 'mystics' can project what I will call an individual 'power'. They *will* things to happen, and then those things that are *willed* to happen, *do* actually happen! Call it hypnotism—call it what you like. Even to a subtle form of murder. The three victims, I suggest, had offended one of these so-called 'holy' men. They were *willed* to die. Therefore, as a sequel, they died in the way that was selected for them. I, fortunately, was on the mere fringe of the affair. With others. But inasmuch as the projection, or the emanation of the evil, was not directed against me, I came through the experience unscathed.

I was, if you like, near enough to be an interested spectator—but no more beyond that."

Burke paused and shrugged his shoulders. It seemed that he was half apologetic for the position that he had taken up. Yet, at the same time, he appeared not to care how we treated his explanation. Chinnery again sought the sensation of detail.

"You say you heard this 'Thing' cry?"

Burke faced him steadily. "Yes."

"What was the cry like?" Even Copeland had forced himself to ask the question.

"Like the cry of a stuck pig. Or at least as much like that as anything."

"Horrible, then?"

"Definitely." Burke was desperately grave. Chinnery shivered and looked at me. He was a solicitor and the blood in his veins was therefore thin.

"Clyst," he said, "does Burke realize that you and I have to walk home tonight? Across Constanton Moor?"

Burke reacted to the statement. "I'm sorry, Chinnery. You shouldn't ply me with questions." Verschoyle sought further information. "When this visitation, I like to call it that, came to you, did you have any particular *personal* sensations? I confess that I'd like to know that. You see, Burke, whatever you may have done for these people here, you've definitely set me thinking."

The Rector smiled as he finished his sentence. Burke's face showed signs of weariness. He tossed away the burning stub of his cigarette. I noticed that it went right into the centre of the fire.

"Yes, as a matter of fact, I *can* understand your asking that question, because something of that sort undoubtedly did happen to me. For instance, my eyes were affected."

"In what way?" asked the Rector.

"Well, it's difficult to explain. But I was conscious, first of all, of a series of what I will describe as 'luminous points'. These points gradually merged into a transfused radiance. This radiance was intensely brilliant, but never glaring or trying to the eyes. Tall fountains of light seemed to swim into the air like volcanoes of living flame. Cataracts flowed in streams of rippling light and the whole turned to blood-red against the sky. Other people to whom I spoke—and who had been near—remarked on having experienced much the same sensation."

Verschoyle's eyes sparkled with interest, but on Copeland's face there showed rank incredulity.

"And this," he said, "this freak of nature and this Brock's benefit affair that you have so beautifully described are all, according to your idea, part and parcel of a scheme of murder? Do I get you right, Burke?"

Burke kept his temper admirably under the onslaught.

"Yes, that's what I think. But, of course, I have no proof. There is no evidence to offer you, no data of any kind, I realize that fully. There is little doubt, however, that many of the tricks that are regularly practised by the genuine fakirs have their basis in hypnotism of a sort. In this way. The minds of the onlookers are dominated by the mind of the fakir. He makes them think that something is happening, whereas, actually, nothing whatever is taking place."

"Don't get the idea at all," said the Squire. "You don't really explain anything. You leave everything stone cold. If what you say holds water, how did your three people die? I mean this: when a human being dies—or anything come to that—there must be a *cause* of death. What was it?"

"Fright," answered Burke curtly. "Sheer fright. Fear—if you prefer the word. Stark abject fear! The fear that paralyses, the fear that kills. They were *willed* to die. They died! Their hearts, if you will allow me to put it in this way, were choked with fear."

"What were the red marks, then?"

"Don't know. Wish I did. Call them the sign of the evil."

I'm certain that I heard Chinnery's teeth chattering. I'm positive that his body shook in a shiver. He wasn't of the sort to take part in such conversation. Especially at this time of night!

"Well," remarked Verschoyle, a smile again playing round the corners of his mouth, "what do you say to it all now, Copeland?"

Copeland laughed boisterously.

"Why! That one thing emerges from it clearly."

"What?"

"Well, why not call it a boon to intending murderers? You want somebody out of the way to suit a purpose of your own—and you just 'will' it! If Burke's theory is to be believed! Sort of 'Monkey's Paw' business. Why use poison and be hanged when you can do the job so much more easily? Look at it for yourself, Verschoyle."

Here Burke interposed.

"Yes, that's all very well, but—" He paused.

"But what?" queried Copeland curiously.

I listened intently for Burke's answer. It seemed to me that so much at this moment depended on it. Burke showed unmistakable signs of impatience.

"Well, Squire, as I explained to you before, it's all a question of *power*. You either have it or you haven't. If you *have* this power—well and good."

"No. Ill and bad," whispered Verschoyle.

Burke went on, heedless of the Rector's comment: "If you haven't—well, you're just 'powerless'. That's the real word that one should use. Personally, I think that the influence definitely belongs to the East. There is little doubt that, much as we vaunt our culture and civilization, in many directions we're miles behind them."

"Thundering good job, too, I should say," declared Copeland, "if that's the sort of thing they put over on innocent people. Give me a good sock in the jaw and 'shake-hands' afterwards."

Burke lit another cigarette.

"Yes, in some ways, perhaps. But it's difficult to generalize fairly over matters like this."

Verschoyle left his chair by the fire and came and stood by Chinnery's shoulder. This change of position brought him face to face with Burke.

"Tell me, Martin," he said gently, "have you ever experienced anything of the kind since? Anything in any way at all like it?"

Burke hesitated before replying. "I'm rather sorry that you've asked me that question," he replied eventually, "but since you *have* asked it I'll endeavour to answer it. Yes, I have. Once!"

"What were the circumstances?"

Burke answered with steady composure. "When that poor fellow fell into the sea from the end of St. Crayle harbour . . . a fortnight ago. You remember that we were powerless to help him in that sea and that he drowned before our eyes."

Verschoyle nodded. His face was set. "Yes, I do remember very well. But I wasn't conscious of anything such as you've described. To me, it was just an ordinary accident that might have occurred in any place of that kind. The man slipped, fell into the sea and was drowned."

Copeland came in again. "Do you mean that you saw the lights and your three-headed monster on St. Crayle harbour on a November afternoon? Come, come, Burke . . . I really can't accept that."

"No," said Burke, calmly, "I don't mean that . . . altogether. I simply mean that I was sensitive to a projection of evil. Evil that was close to me. *Cold* evil. Callous evil. I felt evil around me. When he asked me the question, Verschoyle used the term 'anything at all like it'. I'm right there, am I not, Verschoyle?"

The Rector nodded. "Yes, Martin. They were the words I used. And I understand you, I think. 'Cold evil'! Yes. That would describe it excellently. And I've heard of something of the kind before. From people . . . or from the published stories of people . . . who had spent a night in a house that had had the reputation of being haunted. The coming of the evil spirit has been constantly described by them as preceded by a cold gust of air . . . or a chilling current of wind. . . . 'A deathly chill pervaded the room' is quite a common sentence used by those people who have suffered the experience of which I speak. So that it is eminently reasonable to suppose that something of the kind happened to you."

Copeland turned to me. "You've said very little during all this, Clyst. Neither on my side nor on Burke's. You aren't usually so reticent. Rather the reverse, in fact. How have you been reacting to all this?"

I didn't quite know how to reply to him. You see, I liked Martin Burke, and I knew that he always meant what he said. *Believed* in it! Whereas, on the other hand, Dick Copeland was of the unimaginative type. Unless you could give him chapter and verse, as he called it, for everything that you put in front of him, he was nearly always out for its utter rejection. Each of them was years my senior, but to us who lived in and around this village of St. Crayle these age discrepancies made but little difference to the condition of our companionship.

"I'm interested," I returned curtly, "but you speak as though you and Burke were in deadly opposition to each other. At least, that's the impression any outsider would get from listening to you. Let Burke tell us some more."

Chinnery smiled a sickly smile.

"Glad you fellows like all this. Blessed if I do."

Verschoyle, the perfect host, filled the whisky glasses. That was one indication of the secret of his unusual popularity. He never pushed his cloth at you, and never attempted to ram his ideas down your throat. He was a man first and a sky pilot afterwards. Chinnery took a stiff peg. I watched his face carefully. The muscles of it were twitching convulsively and his hands, as well, were tremulous. There wasn't the slightest doubt that he was badly rattled. I fancied, too, that Verschoyle had noticed his condition and was worried about him. Verschoyle always prided himself on being the host *par excellence*. It was, perhaps, his one little vanity. Burke had lapsed into silence. Copeland broke the lull.

"Half past ten, you chaps. Time I was getting." He rose from the deep armchair that his big body had filled so well. He looked significantly at Chinnery and me. "Coming my way?" he asked. "I know the Major isn't."

I glanced at Chinnery interrogatively. He was just draining his whisky.

"What do you say, Clyst?"

"Kind of Copeland," I returned, "but it's not a lot of good to me. He'll have to drop me unless I take him some distance out of his way." Copeland's place was four miles odd from the Rectory.

"You'll take your usual short cut, I suppose, across Constanton Moor?" said Copeland.

"Yes. I thought so. It was my intention. What do you say, Chinnery?" I appealed to him. He looked thin and cold as he replied:

"If I go with Dick," he said, with a sickly smile, "I've a mile and a half on my own. If I come with you, Clyst, I've only about half a mile on my lonesome. Think, if you don't mind—I'll come with you."

Copeland turned away. "That's all right, then. I understand how you feel. Good night, Burke. Good night, Verschoyle. Thanks awfully for the evening. Night night, you two. I'll go and see what the weather's doing. Hope to God my engine isn't cold."

"You covered it, didn't you?" said Verschoyle.

"Rather, you don't catch me like that. I'll buzz round to the garage and get it going. Cheero."

Verschoyle went to the door with him and Chinnery and I followed them. Burke remained where he was. A few minutes afterwards, we saw Copeland's car back slowly round to the front door of the Rectory. There came another chorus of "good nights" and Copeland's car purred down the gravel of the Rectory drive. Chinnery and I walked behind it steadily until we lost sight of it in the darkness. The white mist was getting thicker and we had walked but a few yards when the rime began to settle on our hats and on our clothes. But we walked steadily on and the last view that I had of the scene that we had left behind us was of Martin Burke standing in the glare of the swinging light of the Rectory porch. The cold was intense and folded itself round our ribs as though an icy giant were wrestling with us and held us tightly in his grip. Chinnery began to cough. It was a harsh cough. It irritated me.

CHAPTER II
SATURDAY, DECEMBER 3RD, 2.22 P.M.

I WAS on the point of going out on the following afternoon, when Sybil Burke came from the line of elms that skirted my garden and up the garden path. I don't think that I had ever seen her look lovelier. Her furs were tucked right to the tip of her tilted chin, the little hat that she wore suited her better than perfectly, and Winter had touched her cheeks with that sparkle that is his only of the seasons of the calendar. For the time of the year it was a supremely glorious day—sun and crystal-clear air. Had she arrived a moment later, I should have been gone and she would have missed me. She waved to me and the contemplation of her delicious loveliness almost made me catch my breath.

With my hands in the big pockets of my overcoat and a stick crooked over the left wrist I walked down the garden to meet her abreast of the rockery that separated the garden from the farm proper.

I had known her three years and I hadn't yet discovered whether she was in love with her husband or not. I would have given a lot to have known for certain. I was an architect, professionally, before I took up farming and my training had taught me that I liked my lines hard and clear.

"Hallo, Sybil," I said, "gladsome of you to come over. I shiver to think how nearly you missed me."

Her eyes sparkled—every bit of the deep violet of them. Lucky Martin Burke!

"Or because of how nearly *you* missed me. Confess now."

I laughed.

"You're a dear, Jack, but your drawing-room manners want taking down and dusting now and then, you know."

"What are we doing?" I asked her.

"A walk, I think, most definitely," she answered. "This is an afternoon off the top shelf. There may not be another like it for months. Let's walk up to Hawthorns. We might be in time for the second half . . . or part of it."

"Who is it?"

"There isn't a club game. 'Probables' *v.* 'Possibles'—or something. It's a county trial."

"Right-o," I returned. "I'm on. Half a second to fill my pipe, and I'll be with you."

For a few minutes we walked in silence. The ground was hard—rutted and furrowed with the cold.

"Almost too much hoar on the ground for Rugger," I remarked. "No joke to fall today with half a dozen hefty forwards on top of you. Shouldn't be surprised if they call it off."

She nodded, but there was a far-away look in her eyes and I could have sworn that there was more behind her call on me than she had so far indicated. But she swung along at my side with the ease and grace of the true walker and I was well content to stride along with her and to watch her. After a time I teased her with a verse with which I knew I could always annoy her.

"When we were a soft Amoeba in ages past and gone,
Ere you were Queen of Sheba and I King Solomon,

Alone and undivided we led a life of sloth.

Whatever *you* did, I did. One dinner did for both.

At length came Separation. By passion and divorce.

And a lonely pseudopodium, I wandered on my course."

She frowned—as she always did when I recited this to her.

"Horrible! I don't mind you as a 'pseudopodium'—but as an Amoeba—ugh! Beastly!"

I corrected her gently. "A *soft* Amoeba, Sybil. Keep the party clean."

"Where did you say that came from?"

"Cambridge, my pet. That university in whose monotonous success over a certain course from Putney to Mortlake you used to take such an unholy annual delight. But you wait, my lady!"

"What for?"

"The swing of the pendulum."

"What's that?"

"Glory knows, but I know that one always waits for it and takes it into one's calculations."

"You mutt, Jack."

"Tell me," I said to her, "when were you married?"

"Why, what on earth . . ." Her eyes smiled at me and her lips were half parted.

"What month, I mean?"

"March! All on a wild March morning."

"I was afraid so," I remarked sententiously. "The character of a March bride is that she is a frivolous chatter-mag, much given to quarrelling and domestic strife."

"Been reading 'Old Moore'?"

"Stages higher than that," I replied contemptuously.

"But you don't really believe what you said?" She seemed anxious.

"I don't know," I replied playfully. "I don't think Martin's been looking his best of late, by any means. What have you been doing to him?"

She made no answer, but walked on thoughtfully. Our steps rang on the anvil of the frosty ground that still and chill December had chosen to give to us.

"It's rather odd that you should have said that, Jack, because that's really the reason why I walked over to see you."

"Carry on, Sybil. What's the trouble?"

She shook her head. "Don't know—quite! It's a perfectly hackneyed thing to say, I know, but he's just 'not himself'. Doesn't tell you much, does it?"

"Not a lot. Anything tangible? In the way of symptoms?"

"Preoccupied! Moody! Worried, almost. Gives the idea, to me at least who am living with him, that he's afraid of something—of something happening. That he's anxiously waiting for it, and won't be himself again until it's all over."

We came to the edge of Constanton Moor and turned towards St. Roseworthy, that is to say in the opposite direction to St. Crayle. Down on the hillside, the tombstones in the churchyard looked like broken teeth in a giant's jaw. For a time I didn't reply. I thought this—that the more I could learn from her about Martin's condition, the better, possibly, I could serve her and him.

"H'm," I said, eventually. "All pretty vague, Sybil Burke! How long has this been going on?"

"Some time now, Jack." She thought hard. "Eighteen months, perhaps. Certainly a year. But all the time there has been a gradual development of the condition. I mean by that, progressiveness all the time. It has steadily become more noticeable to me." She turned suddenly, and as she did so I remember that a powerful car flashed by us travelling in the direction of St. Crayle.

"You were with him last night at the Rectory, Jack. What did you think of him yourself? Tell me. I want to know."

"I thought he was in top-hole form, if that will satisfy you. He fascinated me and the Rector too, I fancy. In fact, he reduced Chinnery to the level of a human blancmange."

"Stories of Indo-China?" she queried.

"H'm-mm!"

She nodded. "I thought so. I've heard 'em all, I expect."

"He tells 'em well, Sybil. Must give the dear old devil his due."

"Very, that's why one is so impressed. What was their theme-song?"

"Well, that's a bit difficult to answer. How shall I put it? Murder by 'the projection of evil!' In other words, my dear Sybil, the perfectly undetectable crime. To kill by thoughts rather than by deeds. What time did he eventually crawl home to you, Sybil?"

"Late, very late. Why?"

"Thought he'd be in late. Chinnery and I left him there at the Rectory with Verschoyle. Copeland went before us. I should come home to you quicker than Martin does, Sybil."

She smiled beautifully. She took little notice of my foolery. I liked her all the more for that.

"Would you really? Well—never mind that, now, it's beside the point. What I'm trying to tell you is that I'm worried, *desperately* worried, about Martin."

"What's he doing this afternoon?"

"I don't know, Jack. He's scarcely said a word all the morning. When I suggested a walk he simply said 'Nothing doing, old girl'—so I came along to you."

I frowned at her. "Second-best! The rôle I always have to play."

She accepted my raillery in the spirit in which it was given and for a time we walked in silence. Then I thought of something.

"Has Martin ever been like this before? Or is it his first attack?"

"Oh, the first, Jack. Since he came home from abroad the last time, he's been quite a cheery soul."

"So he ought to be, with a wife like you!"

"You don't know, Jack! You haven't lived with me. I'm not a hag, I know, but you can't be certain that I'm not the shrewest of shrews—now, can you?"

"No, Sybil, but I'd chance it. Courage has always been a Clyst quality."

"That brings me to something else. How's your cousin these days?" she asked.

"Anthony?"

"Yes. Hasn't been down for ages, has he?"

"No. Think he's had a spot of work to do, for a change. Probably pretty hectic while it lasts. Generally is so with him. Last time I heard of him he was at work on the Merivale case."

"Hark!" she said, stopping with her finger raised. "Hear it. The thud of the ball! They're playing, then, despite your forebodings re the ground."

"Good! We'll stay half an hour or so, and then stroll back. Unless somebody's there who'll give you a lift."

"I think I'd sooner walk, Jack, if it's all the same to you. There'll be a crush of cars, too, at the end of the game."

We got into the ground and made our way to the back of the old-fashioned wooden grandstand. That moment I regard as the last really *decent* moment of my life—because, since then, nothing has ever been the same. I can definitely mark it down as the boundary-stone of Time when I walked from one existence that was moderately happy into another that, for what seemed an interminable time, was one of dark horror and brooding suspense. A few seconds after our arrival Surtees came bustling up. He's a doctor . . . *the* doctor, I suppose, of the St. Crayle and St. Roseworthy area. Big bug in his way . . . you know the idea—been there years . . . J.P. and all that. Knew everybody round about. I'm a liker or a disliker, and I can't say that I cared a lot for him. Could never let you alone and usually had a rare mouthful to say, which you became heartily sick of long before he'd got it off his chest.

He was a Charing Cross man and we all understood that he had made something of a name up there. Had written a brochure or something of the sort on the various causes of Progressive Muscular Atrophy. He was a florid, square-faced, deep-chested man, with glasses, the centre-piece of which always left a reddish ridge on the top of his nose. As I said, he "bustled" up to Sybil and me. He always "bustled" up to people. Any other manner of approach to men and women on his part would have been a physical impossibility.

"Afternoon, Mrs. Burke! Afternoon, Clyst. You're very welcome. There are no two people in the world whom I'd sooner see."

Before I could reply or launch a word of inquiry, he had taken more breath and was off again.

"I say, have you heard about Chinnery?"

"No," I replied. "What about him?"

"The beggar's missing. According to Mrs. Chinnery, who rang me up about eleven o'clock this morning—he hasn't been home all night!"

You may believe it or not—but the news stunned me—and I couldn't find words in which to reply to him. I was completely nonplussed. I saw Sybil furrow her brows and give me a sideways glance. Surtees again continued:

"I didn't know what to say to her, Clyst. 'Pon my soul, I didn't. Dashed awkward, you know—a moment of that kind. Especially with a woman like Mrs. C."

"Yes," I replied drily. "They were well-matched."

Sybil turned to me. "Mr. Chinnery was all right last night when you left him, wasn't he, Jack?"

I nodded. "Well . . . yes . . . I suppose you'd call it all right." I could have wished Sybil miles away. Surtees instantly pounced on my remark like a cross-examining counsel.

"How do you mean, Clyst? Were you with him? Where was this?"

"We walked home together, a part of the way, that is, from the Rectory. We'd had dinner with Edward Verschoyle. That was the reason why we were together. Nothing ulterior about it."

My reply didn't satisfy him. He regarded me almost suspiciously.

"You seemed a little doubtful, I thought, just now, about him being all right. What was the idea?"

His tone annoyed me intensely. "Oh, the mist and the darkness and the loneliness had got him down a bit. But, good Lord, he'd walked that bit of the moor alone thousands of times in the past. Must have done!"

"Which bit?"

"From the edge of the moor to his own place. But look here, Surtees, I've had enough of this. I didn't bring Mrs. Burke here for an inquisition on Chinnery's nocturnal habits. We came for the game—or part of it." I turned away and was about to take Sybil by the arm. But Surtees refused to be denied. I might have known it.

"I'm afraid it's more serious than you think, Clyst. Your attitude won't do at all. Mrs. C. has gone to the police." My facial expression provoked him still further.

I spoke quietly. "My dear chap—who shall blame her?"

"I don't mind telling you that at the back of my mind there's an idea that the police suspect foul play."

"They would," I replied, "but if a chap were really murdered they'd argue that he fell off a wheelbarrow."

Dr. Surtees shrugged his fleshy shoulders. I could see that he was becoming impatient with me. He delivered a broadside.

"Well, chance it, Colonel Blount's here now. Mrs. C. got in touch with him and he came over to see if he could pick up anything." Colonel Blount, let it be remarked, was the Chief Constable of Glebeshire.

"Well, I'm here if he wants me," I said resolutely; "rest assured, doctor, that I shan't run away."

The fool took me seriously and puffed out his plump cheeks like a frog. This was enough—more than enough—and Sybil and I walked away from him. As we made our way along the rows of seats I caught sight of the lean-jawed Blount whom I had met once or twice before at social crushes in the district. He had a knot of men round him, two of whom were in police uniform. Blount was talking earnestly, as though endeavouring to drive certain points home to the selected audience whom he had with him. Sybil caught me by the arm as we sat down.

"Was Mr. Chinnery all right when he left you, Jack? I mean—you didn't keep anything back from Dr. Surtees purposely, did you? You worried me. I wasn't too sure about it."

"Yes, my dear," I replied, "as a matter of fact, I did."

"Why?" she interrupted.

"Oh, just devilment," I returned. "He's a pompous old ass whom I'm beginning to dislike most heartily. He can't keep his nose out of anything, which is a trait in people that I positively loathe. When I get a chance of kicking their pants, I always take it with both hands. Feet, I mean."

Sybil shook her head decisively.

"Very likely, Jack. I can understand it. I know how you feel. But this may be a serious matter. Then there will *have* to be inquiries. And it won't be any good your being obstinate. How should I feel if Martin didn't come home, and there was no word of him from anywhere? I should at once imagine all sorts of dreadful things, now, shouldn't I?"

I winced at her words. Because, I suppose, they were so undeniably true.

"Let's watch the game, Sybil," I said casually.

"O.K.," she said, rather surprisingly, "and while we're watching it tell me as quietly as you can what you didn't want to tell Dr. Surtees." She gave a glance round the area of our immediate neighbours. "There's nobody near whom you need worry about."

I laughed at her projected precautions. "You seem determined on 'mystery', Sybil. This is a side of your character I didn't know and hadn't suspected. What other surprises have you in store for me?"

But my light-heartedness drew no similar response from her. The crowd round us was roaring to the men on the field, but Sybil, in some strange way, kept herself aloof and apart from them—and not only herself—me as well.

"Tell me, Jack," she said quietly, "I must know before it's too late."

Somehow, I felt myself surrendering to her mood.

"There isn't a great deal to tell, and really, you're getting all worked up over nothing. Chinnery had been very nervous during the evening."

"Why?"—she cut in like a razor.

"Oh—no particular reason that I can remember. Oh, well tackled, sir! Did you see that, Sybil? Carr pulled Flowers down a foot from the line. I'd have given twenty to one that he was over—almost under the posts too."

"Never mind." She pressed my arm. "Now about Chinnery. This is more important than any football. Try to remember what had made him so nervous. Please!"

"Well," I urged, "the general conversation round the room as much as anything else."

"Whose?"

"Oh—generally—as I said."

"No, Jack. It won't do! You gave away too much coming along. You're not going to put me off as easily as you imagine. Martin's?"

"Martin took part, naturally. Knowing Martin, you can almost take that for granted."

"What was Martin's especial contribution? Don't forget what you told me coming along, before Dr. Surtees spoke to you. You said that he fascinated the Rector and got Chinnery down. You see you had already told me that, and you can't go back on it. Now—why? What induced Martin to start talking along those lines . . . 'Murder by a projection of evil'? There must have been a definite reason for it. I wish I didn't know these expressions so well." She sighed.

"I don't think that I could honestly say, Sybil. You know what a 'stag-party' is. One thing brings up another. Who can say, even half an hour afterwards, 'who' amongst the party brought up 'which'? With any certainty, that is? Boil it all down to this. We talked about strange happenings, sudden deaths, and such-like. What more natural than Martin jumping in with all his vast store of experience?"

"Agreed, then, that there was nothing more to it than that." She turned on her seat suddenly and her eyes sought my face as she spoke to me. She went on: "You aren't frightened about Chinnery?"

"Frightened? Lord, no, why should I be?" As the words left my lips I *knew*, in spite of the strength of my denials, that I *was* afraid. That is to say—afraid of something to which I should have found it impossible to put a name. Sybil refused to be put off, however.

"You don't really think that anything has happened to him?"

"No, of course not. How could it?"

"That isn't the point. And you're very silly to ask it. You can't get away from one thing. If nothing has happened to him, why hasn't he gone home in the usual way?"

"Probably for a reason that we know nothing about, but which, when we *do* hear it, will prove to be an excessively simple one."

She nodded. "Yes—that's fair. I realize that it's fair. But, all the same 'possibly' would have been a much better word than 'probably'. Constanton Moor and its vicinity are hardly the places in which one would choose to spend a December night, now, are they? What time *about* did you leave Chinnery, Jack?"

I made a rapid calculation. As a matter of fact I checked up on a previous calculation I had made, knowing full well that I should be asked about it.

"About twenty-two minutes past eleven."

A sudden burst of cheering announced to me that the game was over. There came a rush from the people all round us. It was growing dusk, too, and I shivered as I realized that the short December day was nearly dead. I rose from my seat and Sybil rose with me. There was a strange light shining in her eyes. She caught and held me by the sleeve of my overcoat.

"Do you realize that you may have been the last person, Jack, to see Chinnery alive?"

I did—but I wasn't going to let her think so. At any rate, not quite so easily.

"Do you mean," I said to her, as we made our way along the line of seats, "that Chinnery's dead body is lying out on the moor somewhere? Stark and cold?" A shudder went through her frame and I saw her close her eyes.

"Don't, please, Jack! Death is horrible, and the moor at night is horrible, and the two things together make a complete coward of me. I've always thought, from the very first moment that I came here, that the moor was a place of evil. Now I'm nearly sure of it."

"Nice afternoon we're having," I declared. "So bright and cheery." As I spoke I saw Blount and Surtees coming towards me. From their glances in my direction, their purpose was obvious. So Surtees had told Blount that I was here. Silly old fool! What interfering busybodies some men were, to be sure! I strode forward, grasping my stick firmly. Sybil was hard put to it to keep pace with me. Near me a man coughed. The cough was just like Chinnery's.

CHAPTER III
SATURDAY, DECEMBER 3RD, 4.30 P.M.

BLOUNT'S lean jaw looked leaner than ever when he came close to me and thrust it near my face.

"Good afternoon, Mr. Clyst."

"Good afternoon," I returned, with little show of cordiality.

When he saw Sybil, his eyebrows lifted a little.

"This is Mrs. Burke," I said curtly. "I think you've met Major Burke. This is Colonel Blount, Sybil—the Chief Constable."

Blount bowed to her. I'll say this for Blount. He wasted no time in window-dressing.

"You can probably guess what I wanted to speak to you about. Dr. Surtees tells me that he mentioned it to you earlier in the afternoon."

"Chinnery?"

"Yes . . . Chinnery." Blount spoke the last two words very slowly.

"Right-o. I'm ready. Go ahead."

He seemed a trifle disconcerted at my curtness. "Well, it's like this, Clyst. Mrs. Chinnery has reported that her husband has disappeared. According to her story he hasn't been home all night."

"So I hear. I understood Dr. Surtees to say pretty much the same thing. Well, what of it?"

"Yes, I believe Dr. Surtees did tell you. Well, I've had a posse of men out searching the moor and its vicinity, but up to the time that I came away this afternoon they'd reported no success."

"Success?" I eyed him. People of his sort undeniably get my back up. It's because of their insufferable self-satisfaction.

"Well—you know what I mean. Up to the moment, they've come across nothing. There's not a sign of Chinnery anywhere round about, or of anything connected with Chinnery."

"It's remarkable," I admitted.

Blount came to grips.

"I understand that you and he were together last evening, Mr. Clyst?"

"That's so." By this time the crowd had dispersed and the four of us stood by ourselves.

"Would you tell us what you know?"

"Certainly. It won't take long."

"What time did you leave him?"

"About 11.22. I'm exact, you see. But don't regard the fact as suspicious. I was prepared for it. Mrs. Burke happened to ask me the same question some little time ago."

"Oh, why was that?"

"Why did you, Sybil? The Colonel wants to know." I gave the question straight back to her.

Sybil looked annoyed at my tactics. "Hearing what Dr. Surtees had to say, I was naturally interested. I had no other reason for asking you."

"H'm," grunted Blount, discourteously. He turned his attention to me again.

"How was Chinnery when you left him?"

"All right. As far as I could tell, that is. We said 'good night' to each other and he walked away in the direction of his home. Nothing remarkable about the parting, I assure you. Just about as commonplace as parting your hair."

He frowned at me. "Anybody else about? Did you pass anybody, for instance, when you were walking? Coming from the Rectory, weren't you?"

The words were ominous to me. He had evidently already been making routine inquiries.

"Yes. I didn't notice anybody. Certainly nobody passed us."

"Dinner with the Rector, wasn't it?"

"Yes, very good dinner, too. Verschoyle does you very well."

He frowned again, but I didn't care two hoots what he did, or what he said.

"Why didn't you accept the Squire's offer and go home in his car?"

'Hallo?' This to myself. 'Inquiries pretty thorough at this stage of the affair!' "I preferred to walk."

"Chinnery likewise?"

"Apparently. At any rate he chose to come with me rather than to ride with Copeland. But don't ask me why—because I can't answer it. He had his reasons, doubtless."

More frowns from Blount.

"Amazing thing, " he commented. "A man to vanish into thin air. This place isn't like Piccadilly Circus exactly."

"No," I said. "I thoroughly agree with you. Very cold to-day, isn't it?"

Blount grunted impatiently and old Surtees looked at me as though he would have liked to eat me.

"You can't help me, then?" persisted the Colonel.

"No more than I have," I replied. "I've told you all that I possibly can. I expect when we get home this afternoon you'll find that he's turned up all right. You mustn't meet trouble half way."

Blount shook his head.

"I can't see that a man would go off across Constanton Moor at half-past eleven on a winter's night to stay out until the following afternoon. Doesn't make sense. Not exactly a joy-ride. It's bitterly cold here now—let alone what it was like last night on the Moor. Sorry, Clyst, but I can't share your optimism."

"You don't know that he did," I responded.

"You almost suggested it."

"No. Not for a moment. He may *not* have stayed out all night."

Blount stared at me curiously and Surtees hunched a shoulder in my direction that showed conclusively that he shared the Colonel's curiosity.

"What do you mean, Clyst, exactly?" queried Blount. "Don't beat about the bush."

I shrugged my shoulders carelessly. "Well, here's one to go on with—*cherchez la femme*. Heard it before, haven't you?"

He stared at me. "Do you seriously mean that?"

"It's always a pretty safe card to play, don't you think?"

Blount's gaze wandered from me towards Sybil Burke. I smiled and let her see the smile. The lines of the darling's mouth were set in resolute determination. Surtees switched the conversation on to practical issues.

"Your main trouble, Colonel, as I see it, is that the moor isn't a park. If anything has happened to Chinnery it might be the devil's own job to find him."

"And *he's* not in the police service," I contributed joyfully. "At least he has no official appointment."

I saw anxiety come into Sybil's eyes. Blount replied to Dr. Surtees.

"Yes. That's just it. Like looking for a needle in a haystack. A body might lie in certain parts and be undiscovered for a week or more. Ah, well—we needn't detain Clyst any longer, for the time being, that is. We can always get into touch with him, if such a procedure should be necessary."

I was secretly amused at the pompous old idiot. He turned to Sybil and raised his hat. Remembered his manners at last.

"Sorry, Mrs. Burke, to have kept you standing in the cold like this—but as Mr. Clyst was here it saved me the trouble of going over to his place to have a chat with him. Good-bye, Mrs. Burke." He bowed to her and Sybil made her acknowledgment. "Afternoon, Clyst."

"Good afternoon, Colonel Blount. Good afternoon, doctor." I raised my hat in the return courtesy. The four of us paired off. Sybil came with me, while the doctor and Colonel Blount made their way towards the other gate.

For some distance along the road Sybil walked with me in silence. It was already nearly dark. The branches of the trees and the twigs of the bushes that we passed had already begun to look ghostly in the waning light. Our steps rang out sharply on the frosty earth. I cast a quick glance down into Sybil's face. It was set and strained.

"The arms of the Medici," I commenced gravely, "were originally eleven balls. But they have undergone many changes." I saw Sybil look up at me. I continued: "It has been suggested by more than one authority that these balls represented pills—a punning allusion to their name, and there is also the story that Averardo de Medici, a follower of Charlemagne, slew a giant named Magello, whose weapon was a club to which were attached six iron balls."

Sybil stopped in her stride and put her hand on my sleeve. "What on earth are you talking about, Jack?"

"The Medici," I returned—"their reputation, you know, was somewhat similar to that of the Borgias. You see—I know all about these things. You have to—if you want to be on top of your job. Regard me as their legitimate successor. Because I'm certain that Blount and Surtees do."

Sybil suddenly saw the drift of my remarks and a smile lit up her eyes. "Jack, you're an idiot."

I shook my head with mock solemnity. "A quarter of an hour ago I made sure that Blount was on the point of producing a pair of handcuffs. He looked at me very much as a stoat regards a rabbit. Say what you like about it—I mean what I say."

Sybil's lighter mood vanished as quickly as it had appeared. "I can't bring myself to joke about it, Jack," she said. "I don't know why. I can't explain anything, but there it is. I feel that I must get back to Martin as soon as I can."

"We're going back," I returned. "Though quite frankly I don't see what Martin can do to ease the situation."

"Jack, I'm going to ask you a plain question. Do you think that Mr. Chinnery is all right? Tell me now, honestly."

I hedged. "I don't see why he shouldn't be! Who the devil would want to bump off Chinnery? Now—I ask you, Sybil?"

She replied in low tones. "I must be 'fey', I think, but I'm dreadfully worried. I feel that there's a sort of blanket of evil that's descending on us. When I came out this afternoon, I felt it. And then I knew nothing of the trouble about Mr. Chinnery. So you see that, in a way, I was right in thinking as I did."

I made no reply. I didn't see what I could say to her that would be anything like adequate. Thus we walked until we came to the home of Martin and Sybil Burke.

Martin had evidently been watching for us, for he was out to meet and greet us like a shot as we unlatched the gate.

"I was wondering what time you were coming home, Sybil," he opened. "Hallo, Clyst—how are you?—pleased to see you."

I nodded.

"We've been up to the Rugger trial, Martin," declared Sybil—"I went up to Jack's place and asked him to take me up there. I felt that I must have companionship."

"Thank you, Clyst," said Martin Burke—"very decent of you. Much obliged. I'd have gone up to Hawthorns myself, but I had a special job of work that's been hanging about for some time and which I wanted to get shot of. Coming in for a cup of tea?"

I accepted the invitation and followed them into the house. Sybil pulled off her gloves and removed her hat and coat. I saw her turn quietly towards her husband.

"Martin," I heard her say, "have you heard any news this afternoon?"

He seemed puzzled at her words. "No—what do you mean, Sybil?"

"I only wondered. Jack will tell you what I mean." She turned to me. "Do you mind, Jack? I think that Martin should know."

There was a mute appeal to me in her eyes.

"Not a bit," I returned. I looked straight at Martin. "Chinnery's missing. That's what Sybil wants me to tell you."

Martin paled at my statement.

"Missing? Chinnery missing? How do you mean?"

"He hasn't been home all night. Mrs. Chinnery is already in touch with the police, and the police have already been in touch with me. You see, he walked home with me from the Rectory last night, and has since vanished into thin air, which fact evidently places me within the area of violent suspicion."

I shall never forget the look of strained emotion that showed on Martin Burke's face. It was as though I had caught a momentary glimpse of a tortured soul. There came seconds of silence. Burke seemed to be trying desperately to understand something. I use the word 'desperately' deliberately, because I sensed acutely an atmosphere of hopelessness in his mental effort.

"Tell me, Clyst," he said, eventually, "all that you know. Because this news worries me."

I told him how I had walked with Chinnery until we had come to the parting of our respective ways, how Chinnery had waved 'good night' to me and started off towards his own house. Through my words came the stir of Sybil's movements with the tea-things.

"What time exactly did you part from Chinnery?"

"As nearly as possible—twenty-two minutes past eleven."

I'll swear that Burke made a mental calculation as I gave him this information.

"Well, it's all very mysterious, Clyst," he said, "and I'll tell you frankly, I don't like it. I don't like it a little bit." He shook his head gravely as he spoke.

I saw Sybil give him a sideways glance, but she said nothing.

"Old Surtees was on the ground with Blount, you say?"

"Oh—quite. As big as bull beef. Doing his best to look like a police doctor of sensational fiction. You know—all blowing out cheeks. He puffed and he puffed and didn't blow the house down. I formed the impression—I told Sybil coming along—that both he and Blount would have liked to have hanged me on the spot, in order that justice might be summarily executed."

Burke gave an impatient movement of his head.

"Chinnery's wife must be frightfully worried, poor soul. Down here in this wildish country isn't like being in a London suburb."

"You aren't even being original," I murmured. "Blount was most insistent on pointing that out."

"What's he done so far—did he tell you?"

"Sent the usual men out. Sort of informal search-parties all over the moor. But nothing doing! The next step will be 'blood-hounds'.

And then I expect that Chinnery will stroll in, looking perfectly unconcerned and say that he had an attack of nasal haemorrhage or something innocuous like that, and the momentary sensation will slump into the mists of oblivion."

"No, Clyst. You're wrong. I'm sorely afraid that we are in deep waters."

Burke's face was white and strained.

"I knew you'd say that. But even if we may be, for heaven's sake, let's wait until we're moderately certain about it."

"Well, *everybody* can't be inactive while Chinnery is missing! Your policy of aloofness, this splendid isolation, if I may use such a term in connection therewith, isn't practicable, Clyst. Have a heart, man! Blount must do something, if only to justify his job. Surely you can see that?"

"Quite," I returned coolly; "all that I've been trying to say is that it's pretty feeble to start screaming 'wolf' before you've any real data to work on. I may have expressed myself somewhat crudely, but that's the sum total of what I've been endeavouring to say."

There was an awkward pause, which was broken by Sybil's invitation to us. "Tea's ready, you two. Take the two chairs by the fire, will you, and I'll sit here in the middle?"

She drew the tea-waggon towards the blaze. The flames flickered hungrily on the low hearth. Almost instinctively, I thought of Chinnery out there on the moor. Out there on the moor, *perhaps*. Why did all these people unite in a common purpose? Why were they all so seemingly certain that something like the worst had happened? It was far more sensible surely to refuse to consider the worst until sheer necessity made you do so. Good Lord, where would you ultimately get to, if you went through life consistently apprehending the worst? There was reason on my side, too, because I had been the last person to see Chinnery alive. No—I shouldn't say that. It presumed far too much.

Sybil handed me my tea. "I've remembered this time, Jack. Strange that neither you nor Martin should take sugar. I can't think how you can enjoy tea that tastes as bitter as yours must do."

"Bitterness, my dear Sybil," I remarked ironically, "is my lot in life. It surrounds my shoulders as a natural cloak."

Martin Burke smiled his slow, heavy smile. "Say that you don't know, Jack. If I'm any judge of things you're a particularly lucky devil."

"Why, to be sure?"

He countered: "Why not? What's your trouble, at any rate?"

I purposely crossed swords with him. "A man doesn't need to have definite trouble to embrace bitterness. Hopes unachieved, little personal discredits and failures, may cause it. Life-disappointments may be his and all these things stored within a man's soul may make him feel bitter."

Martin smiled again. "Only for a time, my boy. Purely temporary and transitory. They pass all right. Here today, but gone tomorrow, so to speak. You and your cloak of bitterness! It would have done you good to have put in a spot of work with me in Indo-China. No time for self-pity there, I can tell you. Thank you, Sybil. Pass Clyst the cake. The cherry cake. Sweeten him up a bit."

"Don't tease him, Martin. Teasing doesn't mix, somehow, with the events of the day."

He put his arm on her shoulder with a gesture of proprietorial protection that I more than disliked. I knew what Sybil meant.

"Curious, you know," I said, "that this Chinnery business should have come on the heels of last night's dinner conversation."

I knew, directly I had finished speaking, that Sybil's nerves had tightened. I remembered how she had questioned me as we walked to Hawthorns earlier in the afternoon. Burke took some time to reply.

"I don't know that I altogether agree with you, Clyst. It might appear to be curious and yet it might not be. What appears to be a coincidence worthy of remark is often due to the natural sequence of events. Dreams, I think, which are so frequently regarded by the dreamers as amazing and utterly unexplainable, may be logically placed within the same category. That is to say, definitely suggested by something which has gone before, but which the brain has glossed over and, because of that, received no vivid impression. For instance, we see or read a certain name, of a person, or maybe of a place. At that time of primary reception, we hardly noticed that the brain which we are using has taken in the information. But it *has*, and in its own time it *reproduces* it. *In its own time*, mind you! In a form which we then do not recognize and, as a result, are unable to trace the connection. Do you see what I mean?"

"Yes, perhaps I do. Who started that conversation last night? I've been trying to remember, but I can't pick up the thread."

"About the uncanny, do you mean?"

"Yes." I could see from the corner of my eye that Sybil was listening intently.

"Let me think. It started with the astral bell business, didn't it?"

I thought over his question. "Not quite sure. But the 'astral bell' was early on the scene, certainly. I'll give you that."

"Copeland, I fancy, was the initiator," returned Martin Burke. "Didn't he tell the story of the ape-man of the secret passage-way in the house of the Scottish nobleman? About cannibalism being much more practised than people ever dreamt of, and the man-eating alderman of Trentside? But I'm not certain of it being Copeland who actually started it, now that I think again. We all took it up, I fancy, much about the same time, and it wasn't long before we were all well in our stride."

I intervened.

"I'll tell you this, though. I can say with certainty that it was your story which first made Chinnery nervous. Because I noticed it."

Burke shook his head. "I don't think so. It was Verschoyle did that. When he got on to those Kobolds of his and those fiery vampires that saddened even kings with the thoughts of their impending doom. That was immediately preceding my yarn of the Chimaera."

Sybil took my cup to refill. "Martin," she said, "did you tell them your story of the château of Ghismondo? Your favourite horror-effort?"

He shook his head and a frown passed over his features. I read annoyance in that frown.

"What's this?" I asked. "I haven't heard this one, and I don't want to miss any. Spin it."

Burke demurred. "No. Not now."

I persisted.

"Why not?"

"Oh—I'd rather not. That's all."

I worried him for the yarn. Taunted him almost. He gave way. I dragged it out of him.

"It's pretty foul, Clyst. Always gives Sybil the creeps when she hears it. This particular château of Ghismondo was reputed to be the place of the Devil. But, although so unholy, it was always the scene of strange festivities on Christmas Eve. Brilliant lights illuminated its many windows. These lights caused great consternation in the neighbouring farms and villages. Travellers, who were courageous enough to pass under the walls and near the windows, told weird stories of hearing strange inhuman voices and singing of an extraordinary kind. The story grew, until all believed that it traced back to a bestial murder that had been committed within the chateau many years before. A Seigneur of Ghismondo had hacked his young bride to pieces with a butcher's cleaver. Well, eventually the explanation that came to be accepted by the villagers was this. The bride came direct from Purgatory and the Seigneur came from hell every Christmas Eve to join her and hold high revel in the château. The Seigneur was accompanied by no less a personage than the Devil himself and also by a squad of specially selected evil spirits."

He paused. I couldn't resist temptation.

"The Frying Squad! That's not too bad," I rejoined. "I've heard much worse than that."

"Wait until you hear the end," put in Sybil ominously. "Martin hasn't finished yet."

Martin Burke went on. "One Christmas Eve, an intrepid young farmer who lived in the district broke into the château swearing to put an end to these diabolical ceremonies that usually disturbed the neighbourhood. He was armed with a scythe. He rushed up to the murdering Seigneur, and swung the scythe. A jet of blood was projected from the body and this blood began to drip slowly to the floor. Simultaneously, the same thing happened to all the other flitting figures, although—mark you—the intending avenger hadn't moved another, step. Drip, drip, drip! So it went on. Dripping blood from rolling bodies. The young farmer, with a wild shriek of despair, dashed madly from the horror-haunted place and hanged himself on the first tree that he could find. There you are. That's the bundle!"

Sybil shuddered. I shuddered. Martin Burke smiled grimly, and went to the door. He opened it. "I think I'll use the 'phone. There may be some news of Chinnery."

Burke opened the door.

"What's that noise?" I cried fearfully. Sybil's hand went to her mouth.

"I can hear it too," she whispered. We heard Martin Burke's footsteps going away from us. Neither of us spoke. Burke returned, with a mocking smile playing round the corners of his mouth.

"It was the cold-water tap dripping in the kitchen sink. I heard it too. You hadn't turned it off properly, Sybil. That's a habit of yours. I've told you about it before." Her eyes looked at him appealingly. He smiled slightly and went to the telephone in the hall. Sybil rose and closed the door behind him, before returning to my side before the fire. Again, neither of us spoke. We looked into the red depths of the forest of flames. I began to count the queerest misshapen figures that my eyes could fashion in the fire. The door opened again. Martin came back. His words cut icily across the room.

"There is no news of Chinnery," he said.

I saw Sybil clench her hands and then slowly lift her eyes to mine.

"Whom did you 'phone?" I asked.

"Blount," he replied. "I thought that if anybody had had news, he would have had."

Sybil stared once again into the heart of the flames. Either consciously or unconsciously, she repeated the words that Martin Burke had used when he had entered the room. "There is no news of Chinnery."

Outside, the wind howled so that the windows shook, and I fancied that I could still hear Chinnery . . . coughing. . . .

CHAPTER IV
SATURDAY, DECEMBER 3RD, 10 P.M.

WHEN I got home to my own place that evening, I couldn't rest. Try as I would, no employment or diversion seemed to satisfy me.

Reading palled and the programme that was offered me by the radio was, if possible, worse than usual. Ten o'clock struck and as I heard the strokes of the St. Crayle church-clock sounding the hour, I went to the window of my cosy dining-room and looked out into a world of darkness and chill. As I looked I shivered. 'Curse Martin and his spooky stories,' I said savagely to myself. 'He and they are getting on my nerves.'

Then an idea came to me. I would go out. I would far rather be out in the open, active, than stuck here in this frowsty room, a prey to fears and forebodings. So I put on my heavy overcoat, found a cap and gloves, took a stick and set out. I intended to walk to that point of Constanton Moor where I had parted company with Chinnery the evening before. I should probably find some of Blount's flat-footed auxiliaries lolling about, but what the merry hell did that matter? There was no reason, that I could see, why I shouldn't stand as much chance of running across Chinnery—if he were there—as any of them! In fact the chances were, I considered, that I should have a distinctly better opportunity. Again, it was a horribly cold night. Colder than the afternoon had promised and considerably colder than even the night that had preceded it. The mist that curled away from the dark-brown stretch of moorland was wispy and wraith-like. Little yellow clouds of it floated towards me, almost challengingly—inquisitive. They seemed to roll forward as though desirous of testing my intentions in travelling abroad on such a night. My eyes smarted and my scarf took the damp and wetted the edges of my cheeks, but I strode onward.

Half an hour's brisk walking brought me to the edge of the moor. To the spot where Chinnery and I had parted company less than twenty-four hours previously. I gave a glance across my shoulder back at the road which I was leaving behind me, and put my foot resolutely on the dried hard frosted grass of the brown moorland. I knew, within a little, which way Chinnery had taken. I had seen him walk along the track across the moor many times in the past. I had even watched him upon occasions, and I knew that by cutting off a corner of the moorland he came out right against the house where he lived, the lights of which would be visible to him before he came to it.

When I had gone about two hundred and fifty yards, I saw the figure of a man silhouetted against the skyline. In a vague way, the figure seemed familiar to me, but I guessed that it couldn't be anybody I knew and that it must be one of Blount's posse that was still searching the moor in this particular direction for traces of the missing man. I kept on my way for some distance, and much to my relief left the main moorland track and came to the side track for which I had been looking. This must be the way that Chinnery had trodden of habit, and those pin-points of light that I could now see, the lights from his home. I kept my eyes open in all directions. Then the thought came to me that I wished I had come out earlier or alternatively brought an electric torch with me. It would have been such a help as to the examination of the ground that I was covering. I walked on for a distance again.

Suddenly, and a chill went right through me coincidentally, I heard the faint sound of footsteps. They were faint, as I have said, but nevertheless unmistakable. They seemed, in the judgment of my ear, to be coming from my left. But strain my eyes as I might, I was able to see nobody. I stopped. The footsteps stopped. The absolute synchronizing of the cessations was uncanny. I determined to test the matter more thoroughly. I commenced walking again. The footsteps started too. There was only one conclusion to which I could come. I was being followed, and yet I was unable to see any pursuer or even the direction from which he or she was coming. I stopped yet again. The footsteps ceased simultaneously. I stood there and listened intently. Yes, as it had been with my initial idea, if anything, they seemed to come from my left. I turned and peered through the darkness to see if I could detect any form or figure coming towards me. Again—I could see nothing. As far as I could tell from where I stood, I was the only living person there on the moor. The situation was both puzzling and eerie. I thought of Chinnery and of Burke's words to his wife and me some hours previously. "There is no news of Chinnery."

I suppose that I must have stood there, my eyes straining into the yellowish mist, for a minute at least. Suddenly I turned again. I was conscious in the most weird, inexplicable way that I was not alone on the moor. A man stood beside me. A man with a hawk-like face, a jutting nose, two fierce black eyes, and wide sweep of jaw. As I turned, I felt the warm breath of him on my cheek. I suppose that recent events had made me jumpy, for I recoiled quickly with that unspeakable feeling that runs through one when a spider's web breaks on one's face in the dark, and the foul filaments of it are left on one's cheeks.

"Who are you? What do you want?" I challenged him.

"Come to that," he said, aggressively, "what do you want out here at this time of night?"

"I am walking," I returned. "Anything wrong with that?"

Suspicion of me blazed from his eyes. Then I saw him change curiously as though he at last had recognized me.

"Mr. Clyst, isn't it?" he said, "of Scarpe Farm?"

"Quite right. I don't know, though, that I have the pleasure of your acquaintance. But we live and learn, to be sure."

He smiled broadly. The smile transformed his face. The lean hard look of it gave place to something warmer and kindlier and the fierceness in the eyes softened.

"I'm attached to the police," he informed me. "At St. Roseworthy. Name of Foxon. There are three of us out tonight. Colonel Blount's orders."

"Oh, yes, I can guess why. Any news of Mr. Chinnery come through?"

His face went back to the normal again. "Not a word, sir. As far as I know, that is. If there's any news at all, it's been picked up since I came out and by somebody else. You going far, Mr. Clyst?" He stuck his face close to mine.

I shook my head at him. Something had just occurred to me that had made me wonder more and more. "I never heard you come up tonight, Foxon. You seemed to spring from nowhere."

He smiled again. "That's my job, sir. If I may say so. Rubber-soled boots. I put 'em on a-purpose. In case there were things knockin' about on the moor that needed a bit of lookin' into. Gives me a bit of an advantage, you see, sir."

Directly he spoke, a chill came to my heart. Those footsteps that I had heard then had not been the steps of this man, Foxon! There was no gainsaying that! I determined to test him on the matter, as much for my own satisfaction as for any other purpose.

"How long had you been watching me before you spoke to me?"

His reply was evasive. "Oh, I can't answer that exactly. A matter of a few minutes, perhaps." He paused and then flung a question at me. "Why do you ask, Mr. Clyst? What's the point?"

I looked him steadily between the eyes. "I'll tell you why, Foxon. As I came across here, I'll swear that somebody was following me. I heard footsteps most distinctly. Footsteps that were so attuned to mine that there wasn't the slightest doubt in my mind that they were connected with my movements. Away over there," I pointed. "But you must have heard them as distinctly as I did."

He shook his head decisively, and there was something in the gesture that made me think that he disbelieved my statement.

"No, sir, I didn't hear anything of the sort. And I didn't see anybody either. I think I should have been bound to see anybody who was coming up behind you. What about you, sir?"

"Do you mean did I see anybody? I'll answer that at once. I didn't! The fact was so surprising to me that I mentioned it to you."

He shook his head again—but slowly this time.

"It's a bit misty, I know, but visibility's not too bad, considering, and I think you're wrong, sir. If you'll pardon me saying so. You were mistaken."

"You can think what you damned well like, Foxon. It makes no difference to me. I know what I heard. There was somebody following me for some reason that isn't known to me at the moment. I couldn't see who it was. It was uncanny. All of it. Well, I think I'll be getting on a bit further. Good night, Foxon. Best of luck to your search-party." I turned on my heel, and as I did so he brought his hand to his cap smartly in a salute.

I stepped out briskly and then, just as suddenly stopped again. Those uncanny footsteps were coming again! More audible than ever on the chill December air. Triumphantly I turned again in my tracks and hailed Foxon from the few yards' distance that I had been able to make from him. He answered my hail and came running up noiselessly.

"Well, Foxon!" I cried, almost provocatively. "What do you make of that? Did you hear it?"

"I wasn't sure, Mr. Clyst. I heard your own foot-steps as you walked away from me . . . and I couldn't be certain whether there were others or not."

I came to an immediate decision. "Here—come with me for a little way, Foxon. We'll see what happens to us. It'll be your judgment then as well as mine."

"But where are you going to, sir?" he demurred.

"Does that matter?" I returned testily. "I might find Chinnery, for all you know."

He looked at me curiously and then rubbed the edge of his jaw.

"All right," he returned at length, "you win—I'll come."

"Right," I returned.

We strode out. To my utter relief, but a few seconds' walking were sufficient to prove the truth of my contention. There was no mistaking the sounds that came to us.

"Look," whispered Foxon, pointing to a line of dark bushes away to the left of us. "Behind there! I think I saw the shadow of something in that patch of scrub. With me, Mr. Clyst, quickly! At the double."

I needed no second bidding. In my case, action of any kind has always been preferable to passivity. Foxon and I raced across the moor towards the bushes which Foxon had indicated. As I ran, I clutched my stick defensively. But the bushes, when we came to them, held nobody. Either in them or behind them. I looked at Foxon. Foxon looked at me.

"I don't like it," I said. "I don't like it a little bit. I'm going home."

"I don't like it either," returned the plain-clothes man who had shared my night adventure, "but I'm staying here. Not from choice, though. You see, Mr. Clyst, I can't go home. I'm under orders."

"Worse luck for you," I replied. "Good night." I put my hand to my scarf. It was almost saturated!

CHAPTER V
SATURDAY, DECEMBER 10TH, 4 P.M.

DURING the week that went by after my adventure on Constanton Moor, the rigours of the weather increased, and at last the country-side lay in the relentless grip of a hard, cruel frost. One of the worst, from the point of view of duration of the severity, that England had ever known. There were occasional bursts of sunshine, it is true, but gradually companion fog took a sinister hand in the game and few there were who were sufficiently attracted by the conditions to venture very far afield. All the 'Rugger' that was scheduled to be played was abandoned owing to the state of the ground. Straw was laid at Hawthorns in the hope that this protection would render the ground playable, but the effort made proved to be in vain. The frost had taken too firm a grip, and when at length the fog joined forces with it, the combination was too strong for man to cope with it.

Of Chinnery, there had come no news at all. He had, so it seemed, completely disappeared. Without the slightest trace. Search-par-ties, trebled in strength of number, had traversed every inch of the moor. The fact that the man was missing had been broadcast across the world. It was as though an invisible, but omnipotent, hand had plucked him from the bed of the living and annihilated him completely. Just as a weed is pulled from a garden and trans-ported to oblivion. Strange to relate, too, nobody came forward and claimed to have seen him! Let me explain what I mean by that. I do not refer only to people who had been intimate with him or had lived moderately close to him. My statement is intended to be compre-hensive. Not a soul in any part of the country, north, south, east, or west, came forward and stated that Chinnery had made contact with him, or her, since the time of his first disappearance.

Colonel Blount, as a result of this utter silence, had come to his wits' end, short though the journey may have been. Dr. Surtees found great difficulty in being decently civil to me. Copeland drove over to Scarpe Farm to have a chat with me, and, for once, I found his presence unusually welcome. Although I had never liked him particularly—by no means, for instance, as much as I liked Verschoyle and Martin Burke, I found him, on the occasion of this visit, a much more attractive companion than I had ever done before. Soon after his arrival, he began to speak of Chinnery. The cigar that he held trembled in his fingers. The ash must fall from it before long.

"Clyst," he said to me, "what's your real opinion of this Chinnery disappearance? I'd value your opinion if you'd give it to me."

"In what way?" I asked him.

"Well, what do you think has really happened to him?"

I chose the words of my reply deliberately.

"If you want my opinion, Squire, and without any beating about the bush, I've at length been converted to pessimism. I think that Chinnery is dead."

Down went the ash from the cigar.

"Don't say that! It's too horrible. It's only just over a week since you and I dined with him. Just think of it!"

I shrugged my shoulders.

"Can't see myself what difference that makes. The Rector didn't hand out insurance coupons, we didn't sit down thirteen at table, and as far as I know, Chinnery didn't spill the salt."

"No, Clyst. I know all about that. But if Chinnery's dead, how did he die?"

"Ah—that's a much more difficult question to answer. Let's say that he was first chloroformed, then banged on the head, and finally his body thrown down one of the small ravines of which there are so many on the moor."

Copeland drained his whisky and soda. He stared at me.

"Why! What for?"

"Motive—do you mean?"

"Yes! How about motive, my dear Clyst? People aren't murdered for the fun of the thing."

"Well—let's say robbery. That should do as well as any."

"Robbery!" Copeland's tone showed unmistakably what he thought of my theory. "What do you mean by robbery? Do you suggest that Chinnery was carrying the Crown Jewels?"

I looked him straight between the eyes.

"I don't know what he was carrying. And neither do you. So that speculation on the point is absolutely idle."

He gestured hopelessly towards me. "I don't think that you quite understand me, Clyst. This affair has shocked me. It has disturbed me tremendously. I don't mind admitting it. It's so close to us. It's only when things like this happen close to us that we get a proper idea of their perspective. When they touch other people, we disregard them. That's human nature. Every morning when I wake, I think of Chinnery and wonder what has become of him. And then I say to myself, it might have been Verschoyle, or Clyst, or Burke, or myself." He almost whispered the last words and his powerful shoulders seemed to sag as he sat in the chair. I leant over towards him.

"You aren't shocked, Copeland, you've got cold feet. That's what's the matter with you. Your diagnosis was wrong. Pull yourself together, man. You won't frighten me—but in this mood, you'd give some people the 'Willys'."

"Yes," he whispered, "perhaps you're right. It's cold in here, now, isn't it? Can't you feel it? Give that fire a stir."

I grinned. To see the big blustering Copeland in this condition was a new experience. Funny—Chinnery's affair getting him down like this! The fire blazed and I'll admit that I felt the grateful difference of the added heat as Copeland did.

"Remember those blue eyes of Chinnery's, Clyst? They were watery blue eyes. It's awful to me to think that he may be lying out there somewhere . . . dying . . . or dead! Supposing—" He broke off suddenly.

"Supposing what?" I pressed him.

"Oh, this is on my nerves, Clyst, I'll frankly admit it. But supposing Chinnery was on his way home across that little strip of the moor that he used to walk and he saw something! Have *you* thought of that?"

His eyes fascinated me. Copeland was dead scared and no mistake. I thought that I understood the direction in which he was heading.

"Something?" I asked him, "or SOME THING? Which do you mean?"

He nodded vigorously.

"Yes. You've caught my meaning. Burke! Remember what he told us? The thing that ran down the street and cried like a stuck pig. And the strange lights that Burke said he saw? Clyst!" He leant over towards me and put his hand on my knee. "*I've* seen strange lights, strange dancing lights on Constanton Moor! This very week!"

"Somebody going along in the fog," I told him. "Using a torch." But I scarcely believed in my own contention.

"Do you think so, Clyst? I wish I could."

I made no reply.

"Tell me, Clyst," he went on, "do you really think, in your heart of hearts, that we shall ever hear any more of Chinnery? Because I feel certain that we *shan't*. I feel as though he's just been—how shall I put it?—'removed'."

I temporized. "Well, Squire, people have vanished in the past, and never been heard of again, but it's long odds, I should say, against that happening in these days. And there may be an angle of the case that we haven't yet considered."

I watched him curiously as he looked up at me. "What? Don't add any more horrors."

"No. Nothing to do with 'horrors' of any kind. Why should we always look for explanations of these disappearances, from the unreal? Most solutions, when all is said and done, are to be found in ordinary, normal happenings. Supposing, for instance, that Chinnery *wanted* to disappear! That he *elected* to disappear in that way?"

"What on earth for?"

I spread out my hands. "Well—does that matter? I merely project the possibility. Were I forced to natural suggestions, I could nominate one or two. I might even lisp to one or two companions of the earth earthy—'*cherchez la femme*'. It's usually a fairly safe card to play when a married man walks over the edge of the world into space."

Copeland found spirits enough to laugh.

"Chinnery? Not on your life. Kit Chinnery was the wrong side of fifty-five. No red blood in his body. Only ink! Done and finished with all that sort of thing."

"Well, I can try again. Here goes! He was a solicitor, wasn't he? Misappropriation of private funds! Auditor due to appear on Monday. Defalcations bound to be discovered. No hope of evasion. Exit Chinnery! Gone to start life again under a new name and with a fresh identity, at Chorlton-on-Medlock. With, probably, a ginger moustache."

Copeland stared at me.

"Why Chorlton-on-Medlock?"

"Why—oh, I saw the name in the *ABC* the other day. Rather picturesque, don't you think?"

But Copeland was in no mood for my badinage. He still harped on the subject that was uppermost in his mind. "Burke's story the other night took me back to a similar yarn that I heard many years ago, Clyst."

"Oh, what was that?"

He darted uneasy glances round the room. "A man spent the night in a room where a dreadful murder had been committed some years before. The room had been left exactly as it had been at the time of the murder. Nothing touched or moved. Nothing happened for some while and eventually he went off to sleep. About half past two in the morning, he was awakened by an icy draught blowing through the room. Just as if, by some invisible or ghostly agency, all the windows and doors of the room had been simultaneously flung wide open. A shadowy figure crossed the room towards the bed where the man was lying. When it came nearer, he saw that it wore a yellow shroud. Its teeth were bared to the gums and in the eye-sockets of the skull were points of green fire which grew to the flicker of flame. It came close to the bed and pulled the bed-clothes from the terrified man. All the time that this was happening, it gibbered. When the man was uncovered, the apparition laid an icy hand on the sole of his foot. He shrieked with horror and, hearing the noise, the spook disappeared. In the morning, on the sole of the foot that the icy hand had pressed was a scarlet hand-print—faithfully reproduced. Burke's story, or was it Verschoyle's, the other evening, reminded me of it."

"Forget it," I said laconically. "All those stories are complete 'punk'. All sheer imagination. You're working yourself into a highly nervous condition. There have always been these stock 'spook' stories. Of icy hands and walking phantoms. There always will be. Morbid people love to hear them. They trot 'em out every Christmas. Turn the lights out when they tell 'em. If any harm has befallen Chinnery, which we don't *know* yet, I'll bet confidently that it didn't come from any so-called ghost. A tramp with a cudgel would put a man out much more effectively than a gibbering skull dressed in a shroud. And you can take that from me."

Copeland nodded eagerly.

"A week ago I should have said exactly the same thing. Look how sceptical I was at the Rectory when Burke and Verschoyle were backing each other up! But somehow, this uncanny business of Chinnery has affected me. Got me rattled. It's made me change my mind. I'd be the first to admit it. As I said just now, it's when things come home to roost close *to* you that you sit up and take notice."

He rose from his chair and walked to the window. Everything was still in the relentless grip of the fierce frost.

"Should be skating this time, Clyst, if we're lucky. And before very long, too! It must be years since I got my skates out. By Jove, yes, years. . . ."

I nodded. Then I walked over to the window and stood at his side. The trees looked like naked giants with gaunt extended limbs. Copeland pointed to the ominous greyness of the sky.

"Snow-clouds, Clyst. Over there. Look at 'em. Heavy with snow, if I'm any judge. We're in for it. Before morning, too. I loathe it. I think that I even prefer fog to snow. It's all right when it's on the ground doing its Christmas-card stuff, but when the inevitable thaw sets in—my God! Ugh—that squelching wet that rots the sides of your shoes and gives you those icy feet—that forerun pneumonia."

"Icy feet?" I grinned at him.

He turned to me.

"For goodness' sake don't talk about icy feet. Anything but that. I shall think of that creeping ghost again."

I looked out of the window, up at the ugly grey clouds, which Copeland had pointed out to me. The Squire seemed to interpret my thoughts with uncanny exactness.

"If Chinnery's body is out there on the moor somewhere, and heavy snow comes down and lies for some considerable time—" He broke off and shrugged his broad shoulders.

"You mean?"

"I mean that it might be weeks before—"

"Before?"

"Before we could establish anything definite. Terrible! Imagine—a frozen corpse."

I shook my head.

"For the wife. Just think of her. Poor creature! I haven't had the heart to call on her yet. Two or three times I've thought of doing so. Just fancy what it might mean for her. Weeks of anxiety and suspense."

"Let's hope it won't come to that, Squire. There may be good news before long."

I turned from where we had been watching at the window and strolled back towards the fire. Before I reached my armchair at the side of the fire-place, the bell of the telephone purred and rang. I walked into the hall and picked up the receiver almost mechanically, for I knew that my mind was miles away. It was Sybil Burke who was ringing me.

"Is that you, Jack?"

I replied suitably and listened to her. And although her message was pregnant with meaning, my brain reacted to it almost as though it had been trivial or meaningless.

"Thank you, Sybil," I said dully, when she had finished speaking. "It was kind of you to ring me. I'll be here, tell Martin, when you arrive. I can't—I can't quite take it all in. I want time. But I won't say any more now. You know what I mean, don't you?"

I replaced the receiver as quietly as I knew how and stood there for a second or two. Then I walked back to Copeland. He turned, and his eyes held a question. I answered it.

"Chinnery's body has been found, Squire. This afternoon. On the moor. Just by the old quarry. Right away from the path that he would have taken on his way home."

Copeland stared at me. His lips moved tremulously. Neither of us spoke.

A piece of burnt-out coal fell suddenly into ash. I flinched at the noise.

Chapter VI
SATURDAY, DECEMBER 10TH, 7 P.M.

THE Squire had been gone about three-quarters of an hour when Martin and Sybil Burke arrived. Sybil's face was twisted with emotion, but Martin looked as though he had been racking his brain over something. To me, their coming was both opportune and welcome. I mixed Martin a spot of whisky directly he came in, but Sybil refused to have anything. After that, I wheeled an extra chair into the circle of the fire and took it for myself. Sybil sat on my left and Martin on my right. I made no reference whatever to Chinnery. I knew that any news they had for me would be forthcoming in due season. Sybil held her hands to the blaze. Time after time she did this. She must have felt very cold. The firelight lit up her features and once again I thought what a lucky man Martin Burke was. Martin drank and put down his glass.

"Fill up," I said.

He nodded his acceptance. "Thanks, Clyst. Good of you. You as well?"

"Please." I held out my glass to him. There were minutes of silence. I watched the face of Martin Burke. Sybil shivered, and pressed forward even more closely to the fire. "Shall I make a bigger fire for you?" I asked her.

"No, thank you, Jack," she replied. "It's me. I feel that I shall never be warm again. That not only is my body chilled through and through, but something else. My soul, perhaps."

"It's something to have one, Sybil. These days. Don't think everybody has."

"Sometimes, Jack, I don't feel too certain that it's an advantage."

Martin started to speak. The vital news was coming at last.

"We heard the news, Clyst, from Verschoyle. He had it to-night from Blount."

I nodded. "What time did they find him?"

"About four o'clock this afternoon."

Funny, I thought. That would have been about the time that Copeland and I had been discussing the very possibility of such an event.

"How did he die? Any idea?"

Burke hesitated. "I'm not too sure on that point. Surtees has given Blount some sort of report, but from what Verschoyle has told me, Blount is waiting for more details. But there's no—"

Burke paused. He seemed uncertain as to how to go on.

"No what?" I put my curiosity into words.

"No wound of any kind on Chinnery's body. He wasn't shot, for instance. Or stabbed. Or knocked on the head."

"No?"

"No. So there may be no question of foul play, after all. See my point? We mustn't jump to conclusions."

I raised my eyebrows. "But there must be a credible explanation, surely? Death must have been caused in some way."

Martin Burke was silent. Sybil looked across at me. Her eyes held an unmistakable appeal. Something which I had not yet appreciated was troubling her. I persisted with Burke.

"Why don't you answer? That must be so, mustn't it?"

"There is such a thing as natural causes."

"Is that an explanation that satisfies you?"

He shrugged his shoulders.

"Give me time. I haven't all the data yet. And I'm not an expert."

"Who found him?"

"One of Blount's men. He's had men working in search-parties across the moor all the week. Two of them were out with bloodhounds on Wednesday and Thursday. I think the man who found Chinnery this afternoon was a local man. I fancy that's what the Rector said. Luke Foxon."

I remembered my walk across the moor of a week ago. By a miracle, I had been within a hundred yards of this spot known to the villagers as the "Old Quarry", where Chinnery's body had evidently been found. Or sometimes "Priestley's Quarry". Why hadn't I gone a hundred yards further? Priestley had made his money and retired, and the quarry, like so many of its kind these days, had fallen into disuse. Priestley lived at St. Roseworthy, and although accused by many of the local "cognoscenti" as having a somewhat "murky" past, had achieved local honours and was now a County Councillor and a

Justice of the Peace. Verschoyle and Copeland knew him well, but neither, I believed, liked him overmuch.

"Priestley's Quarry?" I said aloud, giving it the local name.

Burke nodded.

"Yes. Chinnery's body was lying just across that ledge where the ground begins to dip."

"How do you know that, Martin?" Sybil's question was spoken in a low voice.

"Verschoyle told me. He had asked Blount several questions—so he said. That happened to be one of them."

Burke coughed, and there was a look in his eyes that I had never seen there before. An idea seized my imagination.

"Martin," I said, compellingly, "are you keeping anything back from Sybil and me?"

"Perhaps!"

"What the hell do you mean—perhaps?"

"Very well, then. Yes!"

"You *are*! You admit it! Why—what's the big idea?"

Martin Burke's cold blue eyes held mine steadily.

"I might have more than one reason. I might have one special, particular reason."

"Such as?"

"I *might* be frightened."

"You!" I gave it back to him instantaneously with a shake of my head. "*You*—of all people, frightened! I find that difficult to believe, old man."

"And yet—why should you? I am but an ordinary man. Not different from any other. Of like passions and frailties with all the rest of us. I don't suppose that my personal supply of courage is any greater than yours, Clyst. All that may be said of me in that direction is that I've possibly had more experience of tight corners, and, therefore, might be expected to prove more than ordinarily useful in a rough house. There it ends."

"You're modest, Martin. *Are* you frightened?" Burke glanced at his wife before he replied.

"Yes."

"What of? What of, *particularly*?"

He smiled rather whimsically. "Not of death, Clyst. Don't think that for a minute. However clever or stuffed with courage any of us may be, we are none of us able to avoid that. I don't know, either, that in the end I shall desire to. Many lives that come to four score years are, as the Psalmist said, but labour and sorrow. No. It's just this, I'm frightened of things *that I cannot understand*."

I understood him. "You know more than you've told us. You've admitted as much. The more that you know is that part of it all which you can't understand. Now, what is it?"

"Are you prepared for *anything*?"

He watched me intensely for my answer. There was something in his tone that partly quelled my eagerness for knowledge, but I threw the doubt over my shoulder.

"I must be."

"Surtees can't explain something about Chinnery. Which was perhaps the chief reason why Verschoyle was so prompt to pass the news on to me. *There are reddish marks behind Chinnery's ears.* According to Surtees' description of them, 'they look as much like burns as anything else'. *Now* do you realize why I admit to being frightened?"

I sat there absolutely dumbfounded. I am not often at a complete loss for words, but that was, most assuredly, my condition on this occasion. Martin's statement had knocked me right back. Sybil sat bolt upright in her chair. Her hands gripped the sides of it and her knuckles showed white where the flesh was drawn taut.

"Well, Clyst," queried Burke, "do you realize the importance of *all* that I have said to you?"

I nodded. Weakly, I'm afraid.

"The East is not St. Crayle, Burke! For God's sake—for all our sakes—don't attempt to prove that it is. East is East and—"

Burke made an impatient gesture with his head. "Oh, cut it, Clyst. It's not my pigeon. I've told you what Dr. Surtees has reported to Blount, who has passed it on to Verschoyle, who relayed it to me, who have told you. And I told my story at Verschoyle's, Clyst, the other night, because I was afraid *then*. I find fear, you see, in two places. And I'm frightened that I shall find it . . . before we've finished, in *more* than two."

"Fear? Of *what*?" I cried wildly. "Put it into words."

"*Evil*, Clyst. Powerful, destroying evil."

"Intelligent anticipation on your part."

"Not altogether."

"Why? How do you mean?"

"It's difficult to explain. But when there's evil about, that is to say 'native' evil, I react to it. Where another person wouldn't. I've a gift that way, you see. Like mental telepathy. I'm mediumistic, I suppose. I just can't explain it. So don't ask me. Sybil here could explain it better than I can, probably. It's her bad luck, you see, to live with the creature, and bear his name." He turned to his wife, "Tell Clyst what I mean, Syb. You know my moods and their 'whys' and 'wherefores' better than anybody."

"I know that you've been worried and anxious for weeks now, Martin, if that's what you mean. I know that you've *felt* in your own queer way that things haven't been as they should be. But I know no more than that."

The vagueness of it all irritated me. "Things!" I repeated the word after her. "What on earth do you mean by 'things'?"

Sybil took my bad manners in good part. She endeavoured quietly to amplify her explanation.

"Conditions. Conditions round about. In the neighbourhood, if you like. Martin responds to these influences when he senses them around him. Let me put it like this. His soul recognizes the forces and the powers of evil. Do you remember when the woman touched the hem of Christ's garment? Our Lord knew that 'virtue had gone out of him'. It's *something* like that. Martin knows when evil is *near* him. Call it a sixth sense. Have I helped you at all to understand?"

Again I saw appeal in her eyes. But I did see too, to a certain extent, what she had meant me to see.

"Yes," I returned. "But I can't understand *how* he does it."

"Of course you can't. Neither can I. We are different from him. Something in him responds to it. Take the instance of the water-diviners. The 'dowsers', as they are called. How do they find water as they do? But they do find it, by passing over it, and Martin is able to detect the presence of evil in much the same way."

"I'm afraid that Clyst isn't convinced, Syb. Not that I can blame him. It isn't normal, everyday stuff that you're giving him. And in justice to Clyst, many people would take it a great deal more sceptically than he does. We can't all be Verschoyles."

I raised my eyebrows. What was the hidden meaning here?

"Verschoyles?"

Martin Burke inclined his head.

"Yes. Verschoyle understands. Me! My power! Everything! He understood that story I told you when we were all up at his place. He's different from you others. He had studied the chimaera, no doubt, in his classical reading, but there was understanding as well as knowledge in what he contributed to our discussion. But you must have noticed that for yourself."

There came remonstrance from Sybil. "Doesn't it all resolve itself into this? We can't *undo* what has already been done. But what are we going to *do*?"

I was puzzled. "In what way?"

"Sybil means with regard to the business of Chinnery."

"Well—what *can* we do?"

"I don't know, Clyst. I must hear more details about Chinnery's death before I trust myself to the expression of any definite opinion. But I've let you see how I feel about it all. I told Sybil, when the news came through, that I must walk over and see you. I feel considerably better now. I feel that I've shifted something off my chest."

He rose to go. For the life of me I didn't know how to reply to him. Sybil rose to follow her husband. She came up to me and held the two lapels of my coat.

"Jack," she said, "promise that you'll do something for me. For us. For all of us."

I smiled down at her. "What can I do, my dear?"

"Just a minute, Sybil." The intervention came from Martin Burke.

"What, my dear?"

"Well, just this. Before you get Clyst here to come over all Sir Galahad and promise you the moon plus the stars, take a good look at the general position. I don't know what's passing through your mind, I'll grant you that, but whatever it is, look before you leap, old lady."

She shook her head. "Don't worry, Martin. Mine is going to be only a simple request. I'm only going to ask Jack for help."

"Help of what sort?"

"To get at the truth of what's happened."

Martin Burke shrugged his shoulders. "Something of a tall order, isn't it?"

She went to him and placed her hand on his arm. "Will *you* tell me the truth, Martin, if I ask it of you?"

"Depends."

"On what, pray?"

"Well—if I can, or not!"

"You'll have no difficulty in answering the question I'm going to ask you now."

"Right-o, then. Fire away."

"You've talked of 'evil'. You have tried to explain to us how you feel. I have no desire to be melodramatic, but you've almost drawn a picture in our minds of evil stalking abroad. Will you admit that?"

"Ye-es. Something of the kind. I'll pass that description. Well—what about it?"

"Do you anticipate that this evil will end, or the power of this malevolence will finish, with the death of poor Mr. Chinnery?"

Martin's face registered signs of disturbance at the question.

"I was afraid that you were going to ask me that."

"Why 'afraid', Martin?"

"Well, if you must have it, I *don't* think that Chinnery's death *will complete* the spell."

Sybil set her lips. "I knew it," she said with an ominous quietness. "That was why I asked you the question and why, too, I asked Jack here if he could see his way to help us." She turned to me. "Well, Jack! You see how things are. You've heard Martin's opinion. What do you say?"

I always find Sybil difficult to resist, and I couldn't refuse her now.

"What do you want me to do?"

There came a half smile into her eyes. "Perhaps you won't like my suggestion when you hear what it is. You won't feel flattered enough."

"More than likely. Still, bring it up for judgment. Can't jump on it till we know what it is."

"Ask your cousin to come down to St. Crayle to help us."

"Anthony Bathurst?"

"Yes. Who better?"

I shook my head at her. "Easier said than done, Sybil. For one thing, I don't know where the beggar is."

"But you can easily find out—surely?"

Sybil, pleading, made resistance more difficult than ever.

"And if I find out where he is and sound him on the subject, I don't know that he'd be able to come, do I?"

"I expect he would. He's pretty wonderful," said Sybil Burke simply.

I had no reply to that. Because there wasn't any. Anthony was one out of the basket—there was no denying it. One from the top branch. All the same, I wasn't any too keen on his coming. I thought that Sybil wasn't only rushing her own fences but attempting to rush ours as well. Also, they had no proof, *we* had no proof yet, that Chinnery *had* been murdered. I shrugged my shoulders. Sybil saw the gesture and came to me again.

"Well, Jack?"

I looked across at Martin, but he made a hopeless movement and turned away.

"Won't you do this for me, Jack? Please do! I can't explain why, but I feel that we simply *must* have Anthony Bathurst. I'm sure that we shall save other lives if we can persuade him to come to us. Don't you agree with me, Jack?"

"I don't see why it should make all the difference," I replied, rather surlily. "A.L.B.'s a great scout, but he's only human, and that means he isn't infallible."

"I don't know that I ever suggested that he was," replied Sybil.

There ensued an awkward silence. Martin held aloof and offered me no help. In the end I accepted the situation with the best grace possible. I walked to the telephone.

"Give me Trunks, please." I heard the girl's voice at the end. I settled down in the chair by the telephone table and waited patiently.

*

When I returned to Martin and his wife, I was again conscious of that same atmosphere of strained silence. Sybil broke it by coming to greet me.

"Well, Jack, what luck? Any?"

"Yes," I replied to her simply. "He will be here tomorrow morning."

"Thank God for that," I heard Sybil Burke whisper almost to herself. "That levels matters up. We have a chance now. Those others . . . won't have it . . . all their own way."

CHAPTER VII
SUNDAY, DECEMBER 11TH, NOON

IT WOULD be as well, I think, if at this stage I described my cousin, Anthony Lotherington Bathurst, as he was when he came to St. Crayle to investigate the strange death of Christopher Chinnery. Aged thirty-two at this time. A remarkable man in many ways, who had already made a big reputation as a criminal investigator. He had always possessed an extraordinary knack of drawing order from confusion; of separating complexity into its native elements. He was the keenest of critics. His grey eyes, always absorbed, took you in completely, at their first glimpse of you, and placed you forever into the scheme of things. Perhaps it would be truer to say, into *his* scheme of things. His power of analysis was unimpeachable. His cheerful candour turned you cold. He theorized concerning everything to be found in nature and society. If he had, as he always said, enough data. His knowledge of almost everything under the sun was immense.

Truly could it be said of him that he knew something of everything and everything of something. His memory powers were prodigious. When he was at Oxford he had seethed with anarchy. Would have deposed monarchs and deleted dynasties with no more ado than he would toss away the stub of a smoked cigarette. He gave every woman whom he met the feeling that he adored her, had been waiting for her coming since the beginning of Time, and, having found her, would idolize her for all eternity. He achieved this happy condition by placing her on his own level, which standard was indubitably high. He never, in the accepted sense, made love to any one of them, for, always excessively serious, he had no tricks of conquest or frills of flirtation. He had read everything from the Bible to Ruff's Guide. Physically, he was equally rare.

When he had come down from the Varsity, about ten years before this story opened, he described himself, after a tilt at both the Vice-Chancellor and the High Steward, as entirely naked and utterly unashamed. All animals worshipped him. All children loved him. Old people, flung on life's banks, felt warmed and comforted by his presence. His long, thin, tapering hands and fingers were as marvellously eloquent as his tongue. His courage might have come from lions. Thus Anthony Lotherington Bathurst, poet, athlete, and detective, when he came to St. Crayle on Sunday the eleventh day of December.

I have never been sure that he liked me! I am his cousin, you see. He despised me for many of my creeds and crudities, I am certain, for I was as heaviness to him who was garmented in light. He had met my little crowd at St. Crayle two or three times in the past, when he had spent parts of holidays with me at Scarpe. With Blount he had become fairly friendly, and the thought of this condition gave me a certain amount of hope for the future.

As we walked that Sunday morning, after putting up his car and enjoying a spot of lunch, there was still frost in the air. Over the sea lay the calmness of death. The movement of the waves was almost imperceptible. There was scarcely a breath that came from us that didn't steam from our mouths. Anthony Bathurst looked across at the countryside and quoted John Maxwell Senhouse.

"Fields of England, Jack. Elysian fields. Why don't we leave all behind us and take to them? Shades of the prison-house! Why do we earn, and sweat and save? Directly we do any of these things we drive a peg through our feet into the ground and there we rot. Lord, Jack—what utterly scheming fools we are! And what's at the end of everything? Death, laddie! Friendly Death with his warming-pan. For king and peasant alike. As your friend Chinnery found a day or so ago." He turned to me with a gleam in his grey eyes. "How far have we to go now, Jack?"

"Five to ten minutes' walk. No more. The spot where Chinnery's body was discovered is just by the old quarry. Priestley's Quarry. You'll recognize the place. You've been there with me before."

"I'd like to have a look at it. You said that you told Blount I was coming down?"

"Yes, this morning."

"How did the old boy take it? Did it brighten his existence?"

"Oh—all right. No hint of stuffiness . . . you're pretty well in with him, you know. Just as well, on the whole. For me, too, perhaps. As you know, from what I've already told you, I appear to be the last person to have seen Chinnery alive."

"And when you 'phoned me I was overhauling my tattered classics, choosing Epictetus and the tonic common sense of the free slave. A strange world, Jack, my son."

We had by this time reached the spot where the man Foxon had come up behind me. My cousin yielded to quotation.

"How shouldst thou have aught in common with Socrates, dying as he died, living as he lived?"

I made no reply. Eventually we came to the ledge of the quarry where I understood, from Martin Burke's story, that Chinnery had been found.

"Here?" queried Bathurst.

"Just there, so I believe." I pointed to the ledge where the ground began to dip.

"H'm. Pretty close to the moorland track. Notice that, Jack?"

I nodded. "Yes."

"Distinct possibilities there. See what I mean?"

Before I could answer him, I turned at the sound of footsteps behind us. As I had half anticipated, they belonged to Colonel Blount and Dr. Surtees. Each of them gave me the curtest of nods. My lip curled as I watched them. I couldn't help it. Anthony's grey eyes almost mocked them.

"Matters sweep swiftly to a climax," he said softly. "Afternoon, Colonel—afternoon, doctor. How did you guess that I was here?"

"Psychology," returned old Surtees with a smile that showed his irregular teeth. "You mustn't think that you've a monopoly of it, Bathurst. Despite your many successes."

"I don't," returned Anthony. "Monopolies are anathema to me. I have no desire for the State to become the Selfridges of England, I assure you. Well, how are you? Both of you." He shook hands with the pair of them.

I knew beyond the shadow of a doubt that both Blount and the doctor wished me anywhere but where I was. So I asserted myself. Deliberately!

"Good afternoon, Colonel Blount. How are you, doctor?" I held out my right hand to each of them, and forced them to grasp it. They muttered common-places which I acidly returned to them. Bathurst, as usual with him, went straight to his objective.

"Would you mind showing me, Colonel Blount, the exact spot where your fellow picked up the body?"

Blount took a stride forward. "Certainly. Just here. By this tussock of grass."

"H'm. Dead bracken and flat leaves. What a marvellous moorland. Pan is still with us and nymphs, for our delight. Just here, you said?"

"That's right. Lying lengthways, stretched to the full, that is."

Anthony nodded.

"Head here, and feet there. That it?" He pointed to the two places of his selection.

"Yes, quite correct," returned Dr. Surtees.

My cousin challenged Blount. "You'll be a sport and let me butt in on it, won't you?"

Blount grinned. "To a point, you can go as you please. Let me know, though, how we stand always. I must insist on that."

"Of course. You know me, don't you?"

"He's thinking of me, Anthony," I said. "I'm your poor relation, you see. We approach Crisis."

Blount attempted to laugh things off, but old Surtees gave me the benefit of one of his large-sized glares. A.L.B. came to the point again.

"Cause of death, Dr. Surtees? Satisfied yourself?" Surtees grinned. There wasn't a doubt about it. He didn't smile. He grinned. There were those teeth of his, all outside his face.

"Natural causes."

Bathurst drew back a pace. "Here—what's this? Natural causes?"

"Ay! If you'd like it given with greater attention to detail, Chinnery died through exposure. Exposure to the elements. Let me be telling you that it's been a wee bit cold down in these parts for the last day or so. We've all needed our 'winter woollies'."

"You mean that he lay out here on the moor and the cold killed him?"

"I couldn't have explained myself better."

"But *why*, man? Why in the name of Almighty Goodness did he lie out here all that time?"

"I'm not Chinnery, Bathurst."

"Was he taken ill, or anything, on his way home that night? Any indication of such a thing having happened?"

"There are *no* signs of such a thing having happened, Mr. Bathurst. His heart was perfectly healthy as far as I can tell from what I have seen of him."

"There will be a P.M., of course?"

"As soon as possible."

"Good. Best for everybody all round."

Surtees came a step nearer.

"Frankly, Bathurst, I am a bit puzzled, I admit. In short, the case is rather beyond me."

Open goal! "That's not surprising," I said.

Anthony intervened.

"Jack tells me that there are red marks behind his ears."

"That is so. But—how did you know, Clyst?" Surtees glared at me again.

"Burke told me. Sorry."

"Burke!" Surtees turned to Blount with unspoken interrogation.

"Don't ask me," interjected the latter.

"I can explain," I said sweetly. "You told the Rector, the Rector told Burke, Burke told me. I told my cousin. A vicious succession! Question—who is the criminal? Pick where you like and pay up if you're wrong."

"Red marks," muttered Anthony to himself. "Can you help me, doctor?"

"Well—as much like burns as anything. Nothing about them to indicate, as far as I can see, that they could have been in any way the cause of Chinnery's death."

"The thunder of her wings, eh? Foretold in Prometheus. Where's the body, Colonel? Far away?"

"No. In the mortuary at St. Roseworthy. Why? Want to see it?"

"Oh, I say, could I? Wouldn't it be presuming too much on—?"

Colonel Blount replied simply. "No. I'll make arrangements for you to visit the mortuary. I shall be grateful for any help."

"I'll take Clyst along, too, if you don't mind. Yes?"

"I've no objection," returned Blount coldly. "I shall come along with you. This evening suit you?" Anthony glanced at me. I nodded my agreement. He took it.

"Good," he said, "We'll pick you up when we get there. Clyst can pilot me." He walked over to Blount so that he might speak to him the more intimately. "Mrs. Chinnery? Anything to be picked up there?"

"Not a hope. Tried it myself. Knows nothing. Can explain nothing. They seem to have been a couple who were absolutely wrapped up in each other. As a solicitor, Chinnery had a good position and but few outside interests. He was a County Councillor and also a Justice of the Peace who sat on the bench at St. Roseworthy. Not an enemy in the world. Many friends. *Not* a woman's man. Not strongly a man's man. But a decent honest-to-goodness sort, who was ordinary and normal in everything he did or undertook. His career was his career and his home was his home and he appreciated both."

"I see. By Jove—the dawn must be a wonderful sight here! In Spring, an eternal wonder. The sun rising out of that sea, miles away in the distance, and the air then most marvellously mild. Why didn't Chinnery die in the Spring? When all the waves would be fire-edged. And Eos with fingers pink-tipped new out of bed, restful after her dreams. Aurora, goddess of the dawn. . . . Marsh-cotton and samphire! Chinnery was quite normal, you say? Pity. Might have picked up a thread of something if he hadn't been. Yes—pity! Hear that, Jack?"

I nodded.

"You know, Colonel," went on Anthony, "this is all very well in its way, but there must have been a reason! To keep a man from a warm bed and chained to the moor at night. And in a drear-nighted

December, at that. Oh, what would I give to know the thing that took him from his way?"

Surtees tried his hand. "Although I can't explain certain things, I'm almost positive that he died a natural death. That we're bothering our heads in futility."

Anthony froze him. "I never bother my head, Dr. Surtees, as you put it, and Chinnery did not die a natural death. He was murdered!" He spoke curtly, but with perfect and studied seriousness. Surtees snapped his teeth together and flung away impatiently, but Blount's eyes were grave and questioning. I thought that he seemed dismayed.

"Why be so hyperdramatic about it?" spat Surtees.

"Oh—help! Why shut one's eyes to the truth? The latter would surely be the greater fault." Bathurst's voice was tinged with annoyance. Blount endeavoured to produce the oil for the troubled waters.

"What time shall we meet you this evening, Bathurst? Seven suit you?"

"Rather early. There's dinner, you know. Must take dinner seriously. Can you make it eight?"

"Yes. If that's more convenient for you. Easily."

"Very well. Eight will suit me better than seven. And what suits me, I know will suit Jack."

"That's arranged then. Dr. Surtees and I will meet you there."

Blount nodded.

"Could I meet the man Foxon? The chap who found the body?"

"Yes. I'll arrange that for you, too."

Colonel Blount and the doctor turned on their heels and left us.

"So that's that, Jack," said my cousin. "Do you know," he continued, "the moment that you turn poetry into prose you commence to lie? We haven't done with Christianity very much but harm. We should have done a great deal better probably with our Thor, Wotan, and Frey. Life and death. What are they? Fine, moving, quick-fluttering flesh and then the putrefaction of death. I don't fear death, Jack, but I positively hate the idea of not being able to take that breath which would have been the one after my last. Lord—that's Irish, if you like. Know what I mean?"

"Yes. Of course I do. But it doesn't worry me that way. I haven't been blessed, or cursed, with your gift of imagination. That's where I score over you."

"I wonder if you do—when all's said and done. Or are you really clogged by petty things around your feet? Have you lived so long on lies that the truth fails to find you? Foxon! I could bear to know what sort of a bloke is this Foxon. Reliable fellow, would you say?"

"I should think so. But I've met him only once." Without entering into details, I told him of my encounter with Foxon. He listened to me with interest. "Just here, you say?"

"Almost. Over there, to be more exact. A few yards behind where we are now, away to the left."

He turned and measured the distance with his eyes. "H'm! I suppose it was all right? Blount *did* have his men out that night?"

"Oh, yes, I should say so. Why?"

"Well, if Foxon found the body of Chinnery on that ledge in Priestley's Quarry yesterday afternoon, why wasn't he a bright boy on the night that he met you? Or on any of the other murky nights that came between your good-bye to Chinnery and yesterday's discovery? Eh, Jack? Work that one out, old son."

"Well," I said, hesitatingly, "how the hell *can* you explain these things? Foxon found Chinnery yesterday. That's all there is to it. He had to find him some time, or somebody had to, and it happened to be yesterday. He just didn't find him before. It's not the slightest use arguing about why it didn't happen the day before or even the day before that. You could keep that game up *ad infinitum*."

The grey eyes gleamed. "Don't talk tripe, Jack. For heaven's sake use your intelligence. *Foxon was looking for Chinnery's body*, wasn't he? Or supposed to be! He wasn't on the moor for a breath of fresh air and he didn't stumble on the body by accident. Can't you see that *that* makes all the difference?"

I was dogged, however, and stuck to my point.

"Agreed. But he was looking for a body over miles of moorland. He wasn't playing hot boiled beans and bacon in a small living-room."

"Oh, all right," laughed Anthony, "have it your own way. There are none so deaf as those that won't hear. Come along, Didymus. I've seen all that I want to see here."

We turned to walk home to Scarpe. The wind was in our faces now and stung our cheeks. And there was winter in that wind. Merciless winter! That gives no quarter to the aged or the weak. The death of the year!

CHAPTER VIII
SUNDAY, DECEMBER 11TH, 8 P.M.

THE threatened snowfall had kept off. Blount and Dr. Surtees met us in the narrow High Street of St. Roseworthy, outside the door of the local undertaker's, within whose gloomy premises was the room which did duty as parish mortuary. Surtees, fussily impatient, led the way. We hadn't far to go. I looked at Bathurst as we passed into the little chamber where was the slab on which lay the body of Chinnery. My cousin's face was flushed and the veins stood out prominently at the side of his forehead. I knew the sign. He was excessively anxious to find out something. But what that something was, I wasn't sure. His eyes almost danced as he approached the body. I ranged myself at his side. Blount and Surtees stood at the head of the long, low slab. Bathurst made immediate enquiries of them.

"His pockets, Colonel? And clothes generally? Personal possessions, and so on? Anything significant to tell me?"

Colonel Blount shook his head decisively.

"Everything in order, Bathurst. Mrs. Chinnery has checked up satisfactorily on everything. Nothing taken. Nothing missing. Nothing interfered with. Money, papers, little private belongings, all of 'em all right. And no marks whatever on the clothes."

"Thanks. That's just what I wanted to know. Show me the marks behind the ears, doctor, do you mind?"

Dr. Surtees beckoned to him. "Come up here."

Anthony walked to the head of the slab and I followed him. The light wasn't too good in the corner. Surtees used a pocket-torch to obtain a better sight of things.

"There you are," he said gloomily. "Behind each ear. See them? Look! As though burned on to the flesh by the touch of red-hot tongues or a flaming stick."

I saw my cousin scrutinize the two marks with the utmost care. Chinnery, the man who had dined and talked and walked with me, looked to my lay eyes as though he were but asleep. Except for the change of colour there was little in this death upon which I gazed to distinguish it from sleep. Evidently Bathurst thought much as I did. I heard him say, "How like they are," and then excessively softly, "Thy brother Death came and cried, wouldst thou me? Thy sweet child, Sleep, the filmy-eyed, murmured like a noon-tide bee. Shall I nestle near thy side?" He jerked his head towards Surtees. "Burns, eh? Like burns! And yet he died from exposure to the cold and damp? Murdered by frost and fog? I wonder!" His eye rested on Surtees and he spoke deliberately. "When's your P.M., doctor? Fixed it yet?"

"Tomorrow. I've remembered the Sabbath Day to keep it holy. My father used to be a member of the Lord's Day Observance Society." Surtees scratched his head. He gave me the idea that he thought he'd given A.L.B. not only a poser, but also a piece of his mind.

"Let me know what you find?"

"Candidly, I don't expect to find anything. That man there died from the cold. Nothing else. The skin is pale and corrugated. The pupils of the eyes were dilated. He probably walked about the moor before he died, raving and wandering in delirium."

Bathurst pursed his lips. "I see. Any signs of frost-bite?"

Surtees stared at him. Anthony continued:

"Any discoloured parts on the body? Any blisters with fluid? Any purplish patches? Any contracted or shrivelled conditions where a part has died and dropped from the body with a red line of demarcation marking the separation between the dead flesh and the living? That is to say, the part separated by gangrene?"

Surtees rubbed his top lip just below his nose.

Blount's eyes were all screwed up.

"Tell me," persisted Anthony. "I'd love to know. Were any efforts made towards restoration?"

"No. Of course not. It was no use. Anybody could see that. When he was picked up the man had been dead some time."

"Oh—how long?"

"It would be impossible for me to say, with anything like accuracy, about a body found in the condition that this was. But you can take it from me that when he was found he was dead. Not unconscious. Dead." True to habit, Surtees snapped his teeth together.

Anthony pressed him. "Just a minute, Dr. Surtees. Do you know anything of the experiments made by Pflueger, the German psychologist, in this direction? Or the difference between slow and rapid warmings after a body has been subjected to an intense degree of cold?"

I was delighted to see the doctor redden. Anthony had struck a shrewd blow—that was evident.

"Not a great deal, I'm afraid. But I would point out, my friend, that Pflueger is far removed from being a modern authority. At the present day he would hardly—"

"Perhaps not. I can take that. But Pflueger's idea is, at any rate, worth remembering. It was that, if *rapid* thawing takes place, the waters of the tissue separate out, as it were, and the tissues are left in a moist, dead state, whereas if the process of thawing be accomplished *slowly* enough, the water is taken up and organically incorporated with the reviving tissues. That is why a person who has been exposed to the cold, as Chinnery must have been, lying there on the moor, should, if he were still 'not dead' when discovered, have been encouraged, directly the exercise became humanly possible, to move actively about. Alcoholic stimulants, for example, should *not* be administered immediately to him."

"Why not?" enquired Colonel Blount.

Anthony answered him. "They are more harmful than useful, sir. They tend to accelerate the loss of heat from the body by dilating the blood-vessels of the skin."

"It's extraordinarily good of Dr. Bathurst to give us this lecture. I regret that I didn't bring my note-book with me." Sarcasm from Surtees!

Anthony grinned at him good-humouredly. His grey eyes showed a satisfaction that he obviously found impossible to conceal. "You see," he went on, "this Chinnery was a thin, spare man. The thin man will, all other matters being more or less equal, succumb to intense cold long before the fat man. As a protection against external cold,

nothing is equal to a fair quantity of fat in and underneath the skin."
He suddenly swung round. To Surtees of all people. "Doctor, although
you are, unhappily, minus your note-book, as you pointed out, can
you help me? When this body was found, was it stiff and hard, like
a board, shall we say?"

"Yes. That's just what it was like. As Foxon, the man who found
him, put it, 'The bloke's frozen stiff, doctor.' I have quoted the man's
actual words."

Anthony drooped an eyelid in my direction.

"Good. Do you know, that information rather suits me! Where is
this man Foxon, by the way? Shouldn't he be here by now, Colonel?"

"He's here already, Bathurst. Awaiting your convenience. I told
him to stay in the outhouse at the back until I sent for him. Shall I
send for him?"

Anthony nodded. "If you don't mind, Colonel. Many thanks. There
are one or two things that I would like to ask him."

Blount walked away and only a few seconds elapsed before he
returned with Foxon. The latter touched his forehead again. Anthony
smiled at Foxon and I saw that the man took to him at once. The
condition of mutual trust and understanding had been immediately
established.

"What time did you find the body, Foxon?"

"At twenty-two minutes past three, sir. I looked at my watch at
the time. You see, I expected that I should almost certainly be asked
the question."

"And how was the body lying?"

"On the second and lower ledge of the old quarry. It's all over-
grown by grass now, but there's a ledge there all right if you take the
time and trouble to clear away the grass."

"Where was the head?"

"Towards the higher ground."

"Any signs of a struggle?"

"None at all, sir. But the ground's frozen hard, sir, you must
remember."

"How did you come to spot the body?"

Foxon wrinkled his brows. "You couldn't very well miss it, sir, if
you looked down from the higher ground."

"That being so, and I'm perfectly prepared to accept it, how do you account for the fact that the body hadn't been noticed before? This search for the missing man had been going on for a week, remember. And you, I believe, had taken part in it during all that period."

Foxon was far from being nonplussed by my cousin's challenge.

"Yes, sir, that's very true, and a fair question to ask. I can't be certain of what I'm about to say and the Colonel told me just now that I must be. So that it's only a matter of my opinion. Get that, sir, won't you? But I'll give it to you, if you still want it."

"I'd love to hear it, Foxon."

"You would, sir? Then you shall." Foxon paused and gave half a glance in the direction of Colonel Blount. That gentleman gave no sign from which Foxon was able to gather any confidence. Foxon coughed and then essayed a look across at me. I'm afraid that I smiled at him. I am equally afraid that the smile was provocative. Foxon was game, however, and disregarded it.

"My opinion is, sir," he said to Anthony, "that the body of Mr. Chinnery wasn't on the ledge before. And that's the reason why none of us found it."

Anthony Bathurst stared at him in surprise.

"You mean that it was brought to the moor some time on the Saturday and laid there?"

Foxon thought for a moment. "Yes, sir. Brought there, either very late on the Friday night or in the early hours of Saturday morning." Foxon tossed his head. "And I'd bet on that, sir, I would really. And I'm not a rich man, either."

"Any comments on that statement?" The question was from Anthony to Blount.

"Only this. I had men searching the moor from the time that Chinnery's disappearance was reported until the time that the body was found. Up to yesterday afternoon all the reports were negative. Which supports Foxon, you see."

"Did you actually cover all the ground of Priestley's Quarry, Foxon?"

"I wouldn't say that, sir. What I would say, though, is this. That if the body had been where I found it, *all the time*, I couldn't have missed finding it beforehand. Neither I nor any of our men who were on the job with me. Wouldn't have been possible, sir."

"He seems pretty sure of himself," I contributed. "And I can vouch for his zeal, I assure you."

Blount was on me like a flash. "How's that, Clyst?"

I grinned as he swallowed the bait that I had dangled in front of him. For swallow it he had. Hook, line, and sinker!

"I met Foxon on the moor one night last week. No—today's Sunday, isn't it? One night during the week before last. Now, when was it? Oh, I know. It was the night after Chinnery had disappeared."

"What time was this?"

"Between half past ten and eleven, I should think."

"What were you doing on the moor at that time of night, Clyst?"

"Just admiring the landscape."

"Don't be absurd."

"And don't you be absurd either, Colonel Blount. What do you think an ordinary man does on the moor? I went for a walk. Although you may find that difficult to understand, I believe in miracles, and sometimes I see one when I'm out walking."

"Certainly," added my cousin in my support. "You can't help seeing them all round you. Sunrise. The moon over the sea. The opening rose. The wind in the pine-trees. The abiding glory and splendour of the world. Don't grudge Jack Clyst his link with the things that matter, otherwise I shall be a disappointed man, and lose interest in the murder of Christopher Chinnery."

Blount frowned heavily. But the combination of Clyst and Bathurst quite vanquished him. Although his heart refused to burst! He addressed himself to Surtees, who was standing there looking far from pleased.

"Need we stay here any longer, doctor? I can conceive of cosier places where to spend a Sunday evening."

Anthony Bathurst rallied him. The imp of mischief gambolled in his eyes.

"Oh, come, Colonel, I regard you almost as my host. Forget the rendezvous and remember, rather, those who have gathered to it. What is one without the other? People make places, you know."

"I will take your word for that," returned Blount, pompously.

"Of course, that's sporting of you. 'I am no sapling, chance-sown by the fountain. I am moored to the rifted rock and proof to the tempest's shock.' I tell you—we Bathursts count."

Surtees laughed. For a wonder, knowing him as I did, he had caught and understand the humour that was in my cousin's tone. That laugh of his seemed to break the tension as a stick is snapped in two, and shortly afterwards we filed out of the mortuary into the little winding street. Surtees came last and locked the door behind us.

"To satisfy all of you, I'll start on the P.M. early tomorrow morning. The sooner I get that job behind me, the better." Anthony and I wished them good night and started to walk back to Scarpe.

"I trust," he said, "that the estimable Polglose will have a meal ready for us when we get in."

Mrs. Polglose, let it be said, was the widow who 'did' for me.

"Have no fear," I replied. "The Polglose is as near the impeccable as you will find. The meal will be ready for you and worthy of you. I cannot fault her. I would as soon lay lovers' hands on the Madonna."

"What's that?" he queried, turning on me suddenly.

I repeated the words.

"Do you know, Jack," he said solemnly, turning again to look at me more closely, "that shows me a side of you that I have never seen before. One, almost, that I had never even suspected."

I made no reply and we walked on to Scarpe in silence. Why should Anthony Bathurst have a monopoly of the things in life that counted?

CHAPTER IX
SUNDAY, DECEMBER 11TH, 11 P.M.

A.L.B. looked at me through the smoke-haze of our pipes.

"Psychologies, Jack! Please! I feel receptive. There are things of these parts that I feel I must know before I proceed any farther."

I smoked on steadily. "All right. Tell me what you want to know. Perhaps if you're feeling receptive I'm feeling communicative. Mutual telepathy. Example to be pointed—the dual art of conversation. Speaking and listening. One futile minus the other. Where do you start?"

"At that dinner-party of yours, about which you began to tell me this morning. At the Rectory. Home of the Rev. Edward Verschoyle. Give me as many details of it as you can remember, will you? I've a shrewd idea that they'll come in useful."

"Don't quite understand how."

"Never mind about that. You stick to your job and I'll stick to mine. And your job at the present moment is to provide me with facts. We are agreed on that, cousin o' mine?"

"Suits me. I'll tell you everything that's good for you to know. But first of all, I'll make up the fire and fill the glasses. There's nothing like starting properly. The cold of this place gets into my bones. It's never very warm at this time of the year, but this bundle's beyond a joke. This is the worst spell that we've had since I've been living here."

I found four sawn elm-logs for the fire and then mixed a couple of stiff pegs of Scotch. We drew our armchairs nearer to the blaze; even then I shivered as I took my seat in mine. After I had drunk I told my story of the various incidents that had happened at Verschoyle's dinner-party, slowly and deliberately. Anthony punctuated my recital with a succession of nods.

"It was Burke, you say, who told the story of the chimaera?"

"That's so."

"And then followed it up with the yarn of the three dead men?"

"Yes."

"Tell me the exact words that he used to describe the marks on the bodies. The *exact* words, Jack, if possible. I have a special reason for asking."

I puckered my brows in thought. "Something like this. 'The only sign on the bodies was a dull red mark behind the ears; something similar to a burn'."

He nodded sharply.

"Good for you, Jack. That's splendid. You're a bloke that a 'tec ought to take round with him always and make life one grand sweet song."

"You wait," I declared, discouragingly. "I've only just started. Perhaps I shan't be able to answer anything more."

"Gertcher! Now the point that Burke made, you say, was that the three men were 'willed' to die and died as the result of a 'projection of evil'. That the idea?"

"That's it. Just as you say."

"H'm. I've heard something of the sort before, but, of course, we're in England down here. Not in Indo-China. Makes a difference, Jack, you know. Can't tell you why—but it does. Can't help thinking that. Some of those fellows over there have forgotten more than we shall ever know."

"You really accept that?"

"Oh, unreservedly. Not a doubt of it. I must. There is so much evidence in favour of it. A wise man never allows himself to be blinded by prejudice. When he gets definite facts placed in front of him he's a fool if he deliberately shuts his eyes to them."

"Oh—I grant all that. But, after all, what are facts? Falsehood can be dressed in the garb of fact. Very often is, or so it seems to me."

Anthony shook his head. "You won't get out of it like that, Jack. Now—back to the night of the party at the Rectory. I want to hear about individual reactions. First of all—tell me about this poor devil, Chinnery, himself. How did he shape at things?"

I had no hesitation in answering that. "Scared stiff. But there were reasons. He was running true to form. Chinnery was no 'tough guy'. Never was. Never could be. His feet were stone cold long before we packed up at the Rector's."

"Yet he walked home alone?"

"Well, did he? Sounds all right—but no more. I was with him nearly all the way—remember. After he and I parted he hadn't a great way to go. Not much more than half a mile. You see—whichever way he went from the Rectory he had to walk part of it. Copeland offered him his car for a lift, but if he'd accepted that offer he'd have had about three times as far to walk when Copeland dropped him than he would have had if he came with me."

"I see. Now let's have a look at Copeland, shall we? That's Squire Copeland, of course?"

"That's the chap."

"How did he react to the weird stuff when it was shoved over?"

"Frankly and uncompromisingly sceptical."

"Wouldn't buy it at any price?"

"You've got it."

"Guessed I should do that. I know the bulletheaded English type as well as the next man. Better, I think. And Dick Copeland's one."

"All the same—" I paused.

"What were you going to say, Jack?"

"Chinnery's disappearance has poked the wind up him. He's by no means as cocksure of everything as he was, I assure you. There's nothing like so much of the hard-boiled about him now as there was. You know what I mean? The attitude that he adopted at Verschoyle's. 'If I can't see it, it can't be there.'"

"Came all over St. Thomas—eh! Are you certain of this change in him?"

"Entirely. He's talked to me about things since; in my opinion, Chinnery's death, when the various details become generally known, will make him worse. He'll take a wallop on the chin over it. Shan't grieve personally. He often annoys me no end."

"Ah, well, it won't do him any harm if it shakes his self-satisfaction a bit. Do him good, in fact. Now we come to Burke himself. How did he finish up?"

"On a subdued note. Not a doubt of it. As a matter of fact, Sybil Burke tells me that he's been far from himself for some time now."

Anthony looked at me with interest.

"How do you mean?"

"Says he's worried. Anxious. Gave his wife the undoubted impression that he expected the heavens (or something else) to fall on him at any moment. And what's more—she's let *him* worry *her*. Got him on her nerves. Badly."

"H'm. You surprise me. Extraordinary business. Don't know what to think about any of it. Those marks behind the ears are so damned eloquent. Don't see quite where to start. Now let's come to the Rector himself. Your host. Verschoyle. How did he react to it all?"

"Definitely sympathetic. Ranged himself on Burke's side. Appreciatively and unequivocally. Said in as many words—'There are more things in Heaven and Earth, Horatio, and all you other fellows, than are dreamt of in our philosophy.' Marvellous chap, you know, Verschoyle! So quietly confident and assured of all that he says and does."

"Yes, I know. That's how he struck me when I was down here before. I've a tremendous opinion and appreciation of Edward Verschoyle."

Then I thought of something. Something that had been away wandering, returned, as it were, to the courts of my memory-mind. Something that Martin Burke had said on the evening of Verschoyle's dinner. My cousin must have noticed the working of my face. He came across with a question.

"What's bitten you, Jack?"

"Why, a curious remark that I heard Burke make after that dinner at the Rectory."

He looked at me steadily. "Oh—what was that?"

"I'm just trying to remember. Exactly what it was, I mean. About somebody being drowned. Give me a moment or so, and it will all come back to me."

I thought hard. Anthony stayed silent. "I've got it. Burke had been talking about this theory of evil being 'projected'. Verschoyle asked him if he had ever run across anything of the kind *since* those actual stories of which he had been telling us. Burke said that he had. Verschoyle then asked him when and where. You know the idea. Full circumstances and so on. Burke's reply astounded me. It was so ordinary! So prosaic in the extreme. A simple yarn of a man falling into the sea from St. Crayle harbour, and being drowned before their eyes. Curious that, don't you think, old man?"

Anthony smoked on steadily. "Before *their* eyes? Who were *they*? I thought that only Martin Burke was telling the story. Who was with him on the harbour?"

"Blest if I'm sure of that. So many people were chipping into the conversation at odd times. Wait a minute. The Rector! The Rector himself. It happens that he had been with Burke on the harbour when the accident happened. Yes, that's right. I remember now. It's all coming back to me. Verschoyle described how the fellow slipped and fell into the sea."

"H'm. Did the Rector admit to feeling pretty much the same emotions that Burke felt? Did *he* feel, too, this 'projection' of the power of evil?"

Again I taxed my brain for remembrance with regard to that particular occasion. "I think not. At any rate, I can't recall that he told us he did."

Anthony Bathurst knocked the burned tobacco from the bowl of his pipe. "Strange! The whole business is strange. Or rather—stranger. And thanks to you, you old death's head, I can't see much sign of getting it cleared up. You keep telling me things that I don't particularly want to hear."

"Can't help that, old son. It's your own fault, not mine. You want the best truth. I have it."

"Let's hope that goes for all the time, Jack. In those circumstances, I shall find you more than ordinarily useful."

He refilled the pipe, pressing the tobacco into the bowl, methodically, with the tips of his long fingers. I noticed the quickness of those fingers, and recollected how he "picked 'em up" at first slip. His eyes were as fascinating as a pretty girl's. A.L.B. almost chuckled at times with his eyes. I have never met a man so deft with his fingers, or so light and graceful on his feet. In those fingers were both strength and gentleness.

"You know, Jack, you can't shred people's characters by blowing their neighbours up. You can only do that to their morals. What's gone wrong in this peaceful hamlet of St. Crayle, in the county of Glebeshire? The trouble is that the classes have got mixed up. Wondering what I mean?"

"Yes, I think I am."

"I'll explain to you. As far as men go, there are only two classes. You can include women in that, too. There are the men who can behave, and there are the men who can't. And it's going to be my job to sort 'em out." He frowned at me quizzically. "And you'll have to help me, Jack. Do you know what I always school myself to remember when I start on an investigation? That the cleverest man I ever knew in real life was a chair-caner. It helps to give me a better idea of proportion. They called him Daft Fred, but his brain was a burning flame of sheer wisdom. He used to lie in front of an old tent. Full length upon his stomach. His crooked elbows supported his old wrinkled face between his hands. He wore an old grey sweater, but when he talked! Oh, boy—when he talked, Jack, I listened, and behold Anthony Bathurst!"

I nodded. My cousin was one of the few men whose talk never wearied me.

"You know, Jack," he went on again, his eyes holding mine through the clouds of curling smoke that surrounded him, "I am a Pagan suckled in an outworn creed. Safely weaned, I grant you, but the memory of my early days remains. Tell me of Chinnery again. All that you know."

I complied with the request. At times he stopped me.

"So he's on the Bench? Or was! How long has he served? Any idea?"

"Years. He was made a J.P. soon after he came and settled down here. That was one of the reasons that made him so pally with Copeland and Verschoyle and a few others."

"Naturally. Besides, professional men invariably gravitate towards other professional men. There's a certain subtle sense of freemasonry among them that brings it about. I've noticed it hundreds of times. Now tell me this. Who's Burke's intimate friend? His bosom crony?"

"That's more than I can do. He hasn't one. Burke's not an ordinary fellow, by any means. We all like him. I don't think anybody would deny the truth of that, but he has no special friendship with anybody."

"What does he do?"

"For a living, do you mean?"

"Yes."

"Has a private income, I fancy, and scribbles a bit to supplement it. A thoroughly nice fellow with a charming wife, as you've probably guessed by now. I envy him meeting her before I did. No sense ever in hiding things. May as well be candid about it. Sybil Burke's a peach."

"Hello! Anybody else think as you do, Jack?"

"Why?"

"Why? Because all knowledge, my lad, is useful. Especially when it comes to you for the first time. You yourself can do the sifting of it afterwards. Come on now, out with it. What do you know?"

"Not a thing. Sybil's all right, don't you worry."

"I'll take your word for that. But don't get all hot and bothered when I ask you awkward questions. You can bet your life I shall ask you a lot more before I'm through with you, so don't get all shy at the start."

"I'm very fond of Sybil, and that's all there is to it. So you can shut up."

Bathurst frowned and went off in another direction. "What did you think of Foxon tonight? In the mortuary?"

"All right. I've a spot of admiration for Foxon. Almost against my will, if you know what I mean. Sporty sort of chap."

"I agree. He impressed me considerably. Much more than old Surtees did. Frowsty old owl, and a hundred years behind the times. Yes, good scout, Foxon. Sort of bloke you could trust with the week's rent."

"What do you intend to do now?" I asked him. "What? Now?"

"Yes."

He shrugged his shoulders. "Stay on for a bit, I suppose. What else can I do?"

"You'll lie low and watch points, you mean?"

"My dear Jack, what else can I do? Look at the position for yourself. Here's a man found dead on the moor. The only clue of any tangibility that I can see at the moment is certain reddish marks behind the ears. How they came there, what they mean, and what caused them, God alone knows."

"God and the murderer," I corrected him.

"Yes. I'll give you that," he returned grimly. He repeated my words after me. "And the murderer." As he finished speaking, Anthony walked to the window and looked out.

"Looks pretty dismal," he remarked, "all of it. Can't see very far tonight. Misty! I'm going to bed. Coming?"

"Later on," I replied. "There are one or two things that I simply must do before the morning."

He smiled mockingly.

"Jack's the boy for work—eh! Ah, well—nighty-night. See you at brekker in the morning."

CHAPTER X
SATURDAY, DECEMBER 17TH, 5 P.M.

ANOTHER week went by and the iron grip of the frost was unrelenting. The ice held, on several ponds, for excellent skating. Nothing more had transpired to throw any light on the death of Chinnery. No clue of any kind came to the notice of any of us. Anthony Bathurst, as far as I was concerned, had had an entirely free run. He had drifted in and out of Scarpe at his own sweet will and discretion. I had willingly fallen in with every plan that he proposed, and every activity that he had suggested. I placed no difficulties whatever in his way. He did entirely as he pleased. Some days, on the Tuesday and Thursday, for instance, he had been absent from Scarpe for the whole of the day. That is to say right from breakfast-time until late evening. Other days, he had stayed in until darkness had overtaken the afternoon and then had suddenly decided to go out—to return just before our normal time for going to bed. I gathered, from what he told me, that he had been to see the Squire and had also called on Martin and Sybil Burke.

The day he had called at the Rectory, Verschoyle had been out, but Anthony had left a message and, since his call, had been expecting to hear from the Rector that another appointment had been fixed. I felt in my own mind too, because he *didn't* tell me, that he had had further interviews with Colonel Blount and Dr. Surtees. To say nothing of the policeman, Foxon. On the whole, I thought, Bathurst had not been over-communicative. By the time Saturday came round again, I am sure that I felt very much more like a particularly obtuse "my dear Watson" than that worthy himself ever did.

Blount had arranged for the inquest on Chinnery to be adjourned. I called Anthony's attention to this fact and he nodded. He opened not his mouth. For my own part, I spent my days much as usual. The Polglose ministered to our wants and I did the various jobs of work on the farm that I usually did, and which were necessary for me to do, while my cousin watched and waited. It would be strictly true and accurate to say that the death of Chinnery remained as big a mystery as ever. He had died on the moor, but what had taken him to the spot where his body had been found, nobody could discover or understand.

About five o'clock in the afternoon of the following Saturday, that is to say fifteen days after Verschoyle's dinner-party, A.L.B. returned to the farmhouse at Scarpe after having been out nearly all the day. I was routing out some old papers when he came in, but pushed the job away from me directly he arrived. I locked them in the drawer in front of me. I wanted to talk to him. I had a definite reason for this.

"Something that I should have told you before, but I forgot it," I said. "We can have it out while the Polglose is messing round with the dinner. Can't think why it didn't occur to me before. Sit down and I'll pour you out a beer while you're waiting for grub. It was thinking of Foxon that reminded me of it."

As he sat down, I noticed the queer look on his face. But I was so full of what I was about to tell him that I let it pass without any audible comment.

"You remember Blount cracking at me last Sunday evening, don't you? In the mortuary at St. Roseworthy?" He nodded. "About your moonlight patrol, do you mean?"

"Yes. When I met Foxon for the first time. At a place not over-far from Priestley's Quarry. You will remember that I had told you previously about it. Well, that night I met Foxon on the moor I've a strong idea that I was followed. In the words of the 'thrillers', my footsteps were dogged."

"Good Lord! What gives you that idea?"

"I *heard* the footsteps. Oh—consistently. I tested them, too. Every time I stopped, they stopped. Every time I restarted, the same thing happened with these uncanny steps. They restarted. And it was near Priestley's Quarry, don't forget."

"Sure it wasn't Foxon himself?"

"Absolutely. He was actually standing at my side once, when we heard the noises, which ruled him absolutely out of it."

"See any sign of anybody?"

"Not a glimmer. Kept my eyes glued into the darkness ahead, behind, and all round me. Nothing doing."

He eyed me curiously. "Why do you include 'ahead', if you thought you were being followed?"

His question took me aback rather. "That's funny," I said. "Do you know—I hadn't thought of it in that light. I see what you mean. But now I come to think of it, the steps didn't seem to come from any one direction *all the time*. On the contrary, they seemed 'round me' towards the end of the time. It may sound utterly ridiculous, as I describe it, but there you are."

He pondered deeply over my reply.

"The moor's an eerie place at night, Jack. It's not 'ordinary'. If I didn't know that before I came this time, I know it now! I should say I do! The sun sets before four o'clock these afternoons, and before you know where you are a strange mixture of darkness and mist descends upon you and blots out most of the landscape. Then you can't see much, it's true, but, on the other hand, you can get to places unobserved that you otherwise couldn't get to. Cuts both ways, you see, like most things in this transitory life of faith, hope, and fear. By the way, who owns that stone-built house about half a mile beyond Priestley's Quarry?"

"A man named Vincent. Retired army surgeon."

"Know anything more than that about him?"

"I've met him. Once or twice. At Copeland's and at Verschoyle's. Getting on now. Over seventy, I should think. But he's been here years. Somewhere about twenty, I should say."

"What sort of a bloke is he?"

"Silent. Says very little. Gives you the impression that he's upsides with the world generally. Invalid wife, I believe. At any rate, she seldom shows herself. Can't remember the Vincents ever entertaining."

"Interesting. I see that he's a J.P. and a County Councillor, too, like Chinnery was."

"Oh? Oh yes, probably. Nearly all the big heads round here are. It's all they had to do years ago. As I said, he's been in the district for a good spell. But why are you enquiring about him?"

"Put it down to general curiosity, Jack. It's always uppermost with me. Now answer me another question, if you can. Who owns the big red-bricked house on the corner that leads down to St. Roseworthy? The one with the white gates and the drive."

"That's Captain Shelley's. Bysshe Lodge. A war case. One arm went at Ploeg Street. He's our 'pukka Sahib' of these parts. Married

Lady Rachel Madgwick that was, and settled down here, I believe, soon after the war. He himself lives a very retired life. But his wife, Lady Rachel, takes an active part in most things. Socially, purely socially, she might be described as 'the life and soul of St. Crayle and St. Roseworthy'. Not much goes on round here that she hasn't a finger in the pie."

"How old would she be?"

"How old? Oh, late forties, I should imagine."

"Attractive?"

"H'm, in a way, perhaps. Not beautiful. Not even pretty. But with personality, my lad. Not a doubt about that. Everything she touches, she gives an undoubted impetus to. Most certainly a woman who counts. Especially in a district of this kind."

"So truly rural," he mocked. "'The lawyers looked glum and talked statistics, eh, of *"crime passionel"* in rural districts!' I wonder! Ah, well, so much for Lady Rachel Shelley. I've a strong idea that she and I are fated to meet. Fate wouldn't be so unkind as to keep us from one another. Two glamorous personalities like ours must have a meeting-point somewhere." His eyes twinkled with mischief. "Here's Mrs. Polglose with dinner ready, Jack. I can do with it, laddie. And that comes from my heart."

I joined him in the dining-room. Polglose's soup was always good, but her St. Germain was particularly so. As we sat down, my cousin harked back to our previous conversation.

"So our Lady Rachel has personality, eh? That indefinable quality based upon the unique life of the individual. The combination of the three attributes of consciousness, character, and will. We talk glibly nowadays of 'inferiority' complexes and 'superiority' complexes. Don't we mean rather just 'negative' and 'positive' personalities? Wouldn't those descriptions be nearer the mark?"

"I'm inclined to agree with you," I remarked. "It seems to me that all real progress must come from the development of personality."

"Yes, Jack. There is an impelling, almost magnetic force in this gift that, for want of a better word, we call 'personality'. Expressed in such an exquisite variety of ways."

"How do you mean?"

"Well—let me put it like this. Can't we construct what we may each consider a gallery of perfect human achievements? Take two of the arts alone. No more than two. Music and literature. Rupert Brooke's *The Great Lover*; Mendelssohn's *Spring Song*; Shelley's *Cloud*; Henley's *Invictus*; Francis Thompson's *Hound of Heaven*; Kipling's *Recessional*; 'The Prayer of Humble Access in the Communion Service of the Anglican Church'; Dean Milman's Passion Hymn, *Ride on! Ride on!* Haven't we, in each of these, a facet of the jewel of sheer, blazingly-brilliant personality? I think so, Jack. Marvellous. Instances of sheer and exquisite beauty, where the human mind almost sheds the necessary imperfection that so sadly hampers it and, as a result, impinges on the Divine."

I nodded at his words. I thought that I saw what he meant, and said so. He went on:

"Yes. That's true, Jack. Personality must be found in and fashioned from the best. From the things that have passed through your mind at its best. Dawn in the sky and a tempest at night. Running water. The pageant of the year. Earth, after the benison of rain, with the moon riding high in the sky. Any mother with her young. You can't make a God unless you love him first."

Thus our meal passed. A.L.B. was always inexorably artist. Positive in vision. Sure and exact in the application of technique. Scornful, like all other artists, of any standard below perfection. We came through the stages of dinner to our coffee. Mother Polglose brought it in to us. Anthony, by a look from his eyes, made her understand immediately, beyond any risk of doubt, that her coffee was fit for the highest gods. Nobody that I had ever met could do things of this kind like Anthony Bathurst. I watched him closely. With the simple curiosity of a man, watching the game that he plays himself, played by a better player. There was perplexity now in his face. Together with some degree of hesitation. I came to the point.

"What's the trouble now?"

"Trouble? Oh, the lines of this damned Chinnery picture are all wrong. The pattern isn't plain anywhere. I find it impossible almost to trace the lines clearly. A man frozen on a moor. Clues? Real clues? None. Indications? Almost the same. Marks behind the ears, footsteps in the dark, and 'projections of evil'. Precious little straw, laddie, towards the making of even one satisfactory brick. Trouble—you say! I've no doubt that my face 'bewrayeth' me. If I can't *start*, Jack, how in the name of goodness am I going to finish? Answer me that and I'll be indebted to you for all eternity. There you are. There are *my* cards on *your* table."

I made no reply. For the reason that I could see no answer to his statement. I felt that his contention was unanswerable.

"Seen Mrs. Burke this week?" he asked me, with a quick turn of the head.

"No," I replied. "If you ask me, you've frightened her away."

"Why? Was she a frequent visitor here?"

"Used to drop in fairly regularly, I suppose."

His next words surprised me.

"I should like to have a chat with her. I've an idea that it might prove profitable."

"How could it?"

"Well, she knows nearly everybody round here, and she's a woman. Being a woman's a great help, sometimes. Next to Lady Rachel Finger-in-the-Pie, she fills the bill in this district as the *knowledgeable* woman. That's a fair point, isn't it?"

"Quite. If I run into Sybil during the next few days, I'll let her know what you want. She'll probably pop round to see you."

"Good for you, Jack."

The words had scarcely left his lips when my telephone bell started to ring. I walked across the room to answer it. As I did so, for no reason that I can explain, a chilling fear clutched at my heart.

"Hello," I said quietly. As I had half expected when I rose to answer the bell, the caller was Sybil Burke. I listened to her. The coldness at my heart grew more intense. I heard her out without interruption, and then thanked her for having taken the trouble to ring me.

"I'll tell him, Sybil. I'll tell him at once," I said. "He's in here with me now. Sybil, my dear, this is terrible. What horror's behind it all?" I listened to her answer. "I'll come and see you in a day or two. Perhaps tomorrow. *Au 'voir*, my dear." I turned from the instrument. As I replaced the receiver, I saw Anthony Bathurst gazing at me with startled eyes. He lost no time in putting his anxiety into words. "What's the trouble, Jack?"

"The Squire," I answered, my voice a trifle unsteady. "Copeland. Mrs. Burke tells me that he has been missing since nine o'clock last night."

Bathurst stood up from his chair and stared straight at me. The room seemed colder than ever. I shivered. Anthony sat down again, staring in front of him, saying not a word. I thought of Copeland and of how he had mocked at Martin Burke's story.

Chapter XI
MONDAY, DECEMBER 19TH, 10 A.M.

Colonel Blount paced the room with uncertain step. His features showed unmistakable signs of strain. He liked to take things easily rather more than most men. Not that I would apportion him blame for that. Captain Ronald Shelley stood with his back to the fire-place. Anthony Bathurst and I were there in attendance. Blount had sent for my cousin, asking him to go along for a conference, and I had taken the liberty of accompanying him. It happened to be my first visit to Bysshe Lodge, and both Anthony and I were disappointed to find that our prospective hostess was not there to receive us. Shelley was a tall, dark, lantern-jawed fellow who looked a hard rider, very fit, thank you, and in every way a man who thoroughly knew his own mind. Blount questioned him again.

"You say, Shelley, that Copeland left here on Friday evening shortly after nine o'clock. That's so, isn't it?"

"Yes." Shelley's words came crisp and curt. "He went early. Dinner finished about half past seven. My wife was anxious for him to stay longer, but Copeland insisted on taking his departure."

"And you say that he left on foot?"

"Yes. He walked."

"That was unusual for Copeland, surely?"

"It would be. But there was a perfectly sound explanation for his walking. His car was in dock. He arrived a bit late and told us so when he first came in. I don't know what the actual mischief was. He didn't say. But it must have been pretty troublesome because he said he hadn't been able to locate it. I offered him the use of my car, but he laughed, thanked me, and said that he hadn't half a mile to go."

"How far had he to go exactly, Captain Shelley?" The question came from Bathurst.

"A little under half a mile, if anything."

"Would he have had to cross the moor at all?"

"No. Approaching the front of his place, there was no need for him to touch Constanton Moor."

"Thank you, Captain Shelley."

"There you are, you hear that, Bathurst," said Colonel Blount. "As a matter of interest, I asked Shelley the same question."

"I can say this," I volunteered, "you wouldn't have got the Squire on the moor at night, since the death of Chinnery, for all the wealth of the Indies. He was dead scared. Told me as much himself at my place the other day."

Blount frowned at me for the interruption, but I didn't care two hoots about that. Anthony Bathurst rubbed his top lip.

"Another question, Captain Shelley, if I may?"

"Certainly, what is it?" Shelley still stood by the fire-place, straight-lipped and stiff-backed.

"Who was present here during the evening of last Friday?"

"Guests, do you mean?"

"Everybody. Bar the servants, of course. I won't trouble about them for the time being."

"My wife and I. The Rector, Martin Burke and his wife. Copeland, Dr. Surtees and his wife, Clement Vincent and his wife, and two friends of mine from town. By name Relton and Ladbrook. All my guests remained in the house when Copeland left it."

"Copeland was alone?"

"Yes. His two daughters were invited, but they were unable to come. They've been away for some time in the South of France, and the elder, Norah, has come home with a bad throat, I believe. . . ."

Anthony Bathurst turned to Colonel Blount. "You observe, Colonel Blount, that this gathering, like that of the previous affair at the Rectory, a fortnight ago, was on a Friday? Fridays, you know, are proverbially unhappy."

"Interesting—no doubt," snapped Blount, "but nothing in it. How can there be? Personally, I've no time for superstition."

"We don't know about these matters," returned Anthony, good-humouredly, "and that's all we can say about it."

Captain Shelley became severely practical. "What's it all mean? First Chinnery, and now Copeland. Makes a man feel deuced uncomfortable. I can understand most things, but this sort of thing beats the cocks. I'm not an artist, and equally I'm not an investigator. I can ride a horse, shoot a bird, and hunt a fox. Despite my damned infirmity. But this business—well, I reckon I'm a passenger when it comes to weighing it all up. So leave me out."

"Well," said Anthony, "though I may quarrel with two of your tastes, I won't argue with you concerning the complexities of the problem. Or with your final statement."

"Damned good of you," retaliated Shelley, uncompromisingly. He glared at Bathurst.

"Don't mention it." This from Anthony imperturbably. He went on: "But tell me this, please. How was Copeland during the evening?"

"How was he? Well—come to that—I wasn't with him a great deal. There was better companionship here than Copeland's. My wife would probably be able to tell you better than I can. But, if I *had* to answer, I should say 'not *quite* his normal self'."

"That's interesting. In what way? Could you put a name to it? Think carefully, please. It may help a lot, your answer, *and* possibly save other lives."

Shelley's white collar gleamed against his swarthy skin, like snow in the sun. His lips curled disdainfully. He looked A.L.B. straight in the face. I made the mental note that he looked every inch a soldier, but probably was cursed with a devil of a temper, which occasionally over-rode his better judgment.

"You mean that?" he flung at Bathurst.

"Most assuredly, Captain Shelley. Shouldn't have taken the trouble to say it if I hadn't meant it."

"You think that Copeland is dead, like Chinnery?"

"I'm very much afraid so."

Shelley's lips were prim. A dull red suffused his neck.

"I think, if you will pardon my saying so, that you are inclined to look on the worst side. Personally, I can see little use in anticipating trouble."

"The Irish have a saying, Captain Shelley, relative to the weather on the seventeenth of March—St. Patrick's Day. If it be fine, they say that 'the saint has turned up the right side of the stone'. If it be a bad day, vice versa. In this case, the worst side has already been turned up. Therefore, I am left with but little option with regard to anticipation. Is my meaning clear?"

"You mean that—?"

"I mean that Chinnery is already dead. We *know* that. In that respect we have left the realm of conjecture for the territory of fact. Therefore, by deduction, I fear the worst for Copeland."

"You can't translate everything into terms of Chinnery."

"I am not doing so. Certainly not everything. The likeness between the two cases, though, is sufficiently startling to make one consider them *together*, rather than separately. Surely you will concede me that point?"

"Death is always like itself. It must be. The conditions of death may be similar, but that doesn't prove that the causes are always allied."

Anthony shook his head. "You are arguing round the matter, if you'll pardon my saying so. The value of evidence is trebled when it is accumulative. In the year 1897 Sherlock Holmes, having vacated 221B Baker Street, proposed to devote his declining years to the composition of a text-book, which would focus the whole art of detection into one volume. He didn't. The world was the loser, gentlemen!"

There came a period of silence. Blount eventually broke it. "Well, gentlemen, all this talk isn't getting us anywhere."

"Unhappily," returned Anthony Bathurst, "it's all we can do at this stage of the case. Talk! What do we *know*?"

"Not a lot, I admit. Copeland left this house about ten minutes past nine on Friday evening and hasn't been seen since. I've had inquiries made all round the district. At every railway station and at every bus and coach stop. Nobody resembling Copeland has been reported as having been seen there. It was just the same with Chinnery. There's another precaution that I'm going to take, though. At once."

"What's that, Colonel Blount? Would you care to tell me?" Anthony scratched his cheek as he asked the question.

"I'll make no secret of my intentions. I shall have the moorland by Priestley's Quarry closely watched. Patrolled almost. Night and day. In case—your pessimism is justified, Mr. Bathurst."

There was a touch of irony in the tone of Colonel Blount. Anthony shrugged his shoulders.

"Please yourself, of course, Colonel Blount, and it's presumption on my part to offer advice, but I'll make you a present of a piece of information. Copeland's body won't be found near Priestley's Quarry. I'd go bail on that."

"Mr. Bathurst is very certain of his statement," contributed Captain Shelley, with a soft and suave emphasis.

"Yes," drawled Anthony in reply. "Extraordinarily certain! So certain, in fact, that I'll venture once again into the dangerous realm of prophecy. I'll say, here and now, that Priestley's Quarry is the last place on earth where we may expect to find it. Now, gentlemen, shoot!"

I took a hand. "You mean that the murderer—"

I was summarily interrupted.

"Murderer!" snapped Captain Shelley. "What rot are you talking now, Clyst? For God's sake let's preserve our sense of values."

I gestured impatiently. I was in no mood to argue the toss with any of them. I should have found it difficult to refrain from downright rudeness. They made my blood boil with their damned complacency and self-satisfaction. My cousin could bandy words with them if he liked. I wouldn't waste my time with such a procedure. He interpreted my impatient inclination as I had intended him to. He took it upon himself to answer Captain Shelley's intervention.

"The word that my cousin used, Captain Shelley, was 'murderer'. You heard him quite accurately. Does it occasion you undue surprise?"

Shelley smiled sarcastically. But again there was suavity in the smile as well as sarcasm. He raised his chin to speak. He stood there in his breeches and gaiters, and the breeches had arching thighs which were to his thin knees like the curves of two crescent moons, set horns to horns.

"As I have said, I am no investigator. The trade has but little attraction for me. As I imagine it would have for any gentleman.

Paul Pry has never been a hero in my gallery. But I have sufficient intelligence to appreciate facts. And I understood from Dr. Surtees that Chinnery died from entirely natural causes. I heard from our good friend the doctor no sensational hint at murder." The words were delivered with cutting inflexion.

Bathurst was in at him like lightning. "'Natural causes' is a comprehensive statement, Captain Shelley. We shall all die when our time comes from 'natural causes'. But the question will still remain as to how those 'natural causes' are brought about. What it is that causes our lungs to stop breathing or our heart pumping! Clyst was absolutely right. Chinnery was murdered."

"That remains to be proved, Mr. Bathurst. Until that proof's forthcoming, we will agree to differ." His face was blank and bland. He obtained little satisfaction, however, as a result of his bold attack. That feature of combativeness always suited Anthony Bathurst down to the ground. He saw the flush come under the swarthy skin and the cold glint in Shelley's eyes.

"Oh, I know," replied Anthony. "None better. But, don't worry, it *will* be proved. Take it from me. That's why I'm going to spend Christmas between the parishes of St. Crayle and St. Roseworthy. There's going to be a 'chiel' amongst you, taking notes."

Captain Shelley stroked his buckskins and twisted his mouth. I knew that he had a vast store of experience behind him. He possessed a charming, able wife, a substantial income, and an assured social position in the district where he had settled. In fact, all his life, I reckoned, he had managed to have everything that he seriously desired, even though on some occasions, perhaps, he had been forced to exert himself to get it. These conditions should have brought him to a state of "wariness". I could see that "this fellow Bathurst" annoyed him, but he had sense enough, I guessed, to realize that Bathurst would have to be reckoned with at a pinch. I gave Shelley a certain credit for intelligence, you see.

"To me," he said at length, "this all smacks rather of melodrama. And I'm perfectly willing to admit that I'm not so conversant with the 'theatrical' as Mr. Bathurst doubtless is."

It was evident that Blount didn't like the direction that matters were taking. He was afraid, I felt sure, that Anthony would resent

Shelley's attitude and that the situation for all of us would become highly embarrassing, and the atmosphere acutely charged. After all, we were in Shelley's house, which you will admit made a difference. But, just as Blount appeared to have committed himself towards a diversion, towards even reconciliation possibly, the door opened quietly and Lady Rachel entered. I will describe her.

She was undoubtedly what most people would call a "handsome woman". She had high colouring, fine carriage, and large black eyes. She was ample. Some there might be who would have called her fat. To the fastidious, her arms and hands were too big. They approached the masculine. But her neck and bust were superb. She was not a tall woman. Despite her full colour and flashing black eyes, she was reputed to be of an easy and placid temperament. The countryside had decided that she could nearly always be relied upon for a "comfortable opinion" on most subjects. She rode daily, and played golf as well as a professional. Played lawn tennis too, with less skill but a great deal more sportsmanship than most of the prominent figures of the lawn-tennis world. Her cheeks were a lasting advertisement for the healthiness of the country around Bysshe Lodge.

The chief feature of her, perhaps, or the most worthy of mention, was that although she looked as though she might be shrewish, by a piece of good fortune, over which she had had no control, she wasn't. Her nose was a trifle retroussé. Her lips mocked you. A friend of mine, who met her constantly, used to say that an impertinence from her always seemed mellowed directly afterwards. She had a bright, inconsequent way of probing you to the very depths, and must have been well courted before she burnt her amorous boats and finally accepted the one hand and heart of Captain Ronald Shelley.

She came to us happily. Her brisk entry at this moment cleared the air for all of us. When she saw the company assembled in the room she turned white, and then the pallor faded and she went redder. I knew, having lived in the district for the years that I had, that she was accustomed to a great deal of deference from the ordinary circle of her acquaintances, and I think she realized, or at least was agreed within herself, that something had happened that was going to undermine and probably destroy that deference. There was always the likely chance, too, that she might become the victim of her own rather flamboyant personality.

"Two people here whom you haven't met, Rachel," opened Captain Shelley fussily. "Anthony Bathurst." My cousin bowed. "Jack Clyst, almost a neighbour of ours. Scarpe Farm, you know. My wife, Lady Rachel." I supplemented my cousin's bow with an awkward one of my own.

"Good morning," she said, not awkwardly. "I've had to think very quickly. I suppose you're calling on us because of this dreadful news concerning the Squire. I don't know what things are coming to these days. Positively awful, isn't it?" She addressed the question in a general way, but she looked directly at Colonel Blount as though expecting the answer to come from him. To her, no doubt, he was a dignified figure, for he so obviously represented the forces of law and order.

"It's a great worry to me," returned Blount. "Despite all I do, I come up against the blank wall every time. And blank walls to a man in my position are disconcerting. One can only build on hope."

She nodded. "Yes. I realize exactly how you must feel. Sort of helpless and hopeless."

Her husband intervened. Rather autocratically.

"I was telling Colonel Blount before you came in that perhaps Copeland wasn't quite normal when he was here with us on Friday evening."

Before Shelley could fully develop what he had been about to say, Anthony Bathurst cut in.

"By the way, Captain Shelley, you didn't *describe* Copeland's 'unusualness'. Do you remember, something or the other transpired and we went off at a tangent? What was it exactly that you did notice? Could you tell us?"

Captain Shelley glanced in the direction of his wife.

"Well," he answered slowly, "I'd say that Copeland seemed just a little 'excited'. It's not the best word, I know. It's not really the word that I want. But it's the only word of which I can think at the moment. What would you say about it, my dear? I would value your opinion." Captain Shelley made the direct appeal to Lady Rachel. I watched her carefully. She took some seconds before replying. Then she slowly nodded her head.

"Yes. I think that I know what you mean. I noticed something about the Squire that isn't usually in his make-up. But I wouldn't have described it as 'excitement'. At least—I don't think that I should." She paused with her head a little on one side.

Anthony had a question for her here. "You wouldn't call it 'fear', I suppose. Lady Rachel?"

She shook her head decisively. "No! Definitely *not* 'fear'. And not 'anxiety'. Not 'apprehension'. Now what can I call it? I'm sure that if I . . ." She paused in thought.

We waited for her. She appeared to be so obviously searching for the truth of the matter that we tacitly agreed amongst ourselves, as it were, to allow the quest to go on, unhindered. Eventually she came to the expression of an opinion.

"The best word, better than my husband's word 'excitement', would be 'nervy'. Not 'nervous', you understand. There is a difference between the two words. By 'nervy' I mean that condition that gets hold of an artist just before a public performance. When I was doing 'stage' work, years ago, I used to suffer from the very same feeling myself. When you wait in the wings for the cue that brings you on to the stage for the first time in the play. Yes—that's the word—'nervy'."

"Thank you, Lady Rachel," declared Anthony Bathurst almost fervently. "What you have said is extremely interesting. I know exactly what you mean. It is statements like yours of just now that clear the air for us, and make our work so much easier. Don't you agree with me, Colonel Blount?"

"Oh yes—quite. Thank you, Lady Rachel. I must certainly associate myself with Bathurst." Blount became almost effusive in his gratitude.

"I want you to realize, Rachel, before we go any farther," added Captain Shelley, "that Mr. Bathurst here is taking up a position that, maybe, you don't quite understand. He is talking in terms of 'murder'. Despite the information that came to us from Dr. Surtees, Mr. Bathurst, and Mr. Clyst as well, refuse to consider any other possibility. I think that you ought to know these facts."

"Why, Ronald? I don't quite follow you. What difference does it make to me?"

Shelley shifted uneasily. His wife's calmness was in strong contrast to his own disturbed condition. Things hadn't gone as he had anticipated.

"No difference, of course, my dear. No real difference. How could it? I merely made the statement that I did, in order that you should know just how we stand and be able to answer accordingly."

Lady Rachel turned to Anthony. "Why are you so certain that we are confronted with the forces of evil, Mr. Bathurst?"

He replied to her with dead seriousness.

"My reason and my intelligence tell me so, Lady Rachel. Something took Chinnery from his homeward path a fortnight ago. On a night when to be out on the moor would have been no man's wish. On a night when 'mine enemy's dog, though he had bit me, should have stood beside my fire'. Chinnery, mark you, at the end of it all, was found dead. With two red marks behind his ears."

Lady Rachel toyed with a ring on her left hand. I could see that the magnificent stone was a ruby.

"But it's—not possible! Who would want to harm a man like Mr. Chinnery? Why, he was—"

"I regret that at the moment I can't tell you that. Or even why the wish was there. But I am certain that somebody *did* want to, and, moreover, translated his wants into reality."

He rose, and Colonel Blount followed suit. The latter spoke.

"I don't think we need detain you any longer, Shelley. And you, Lady Rachel. Many thanks for your hospitality and for all the information that you have given us. In a case of this kind every little helps, believe me."

We bade Captain Shelley and his wife good-bye, and Bysshe Lodge became its normal self again. As we travelled back to Scarpe, Anthony made but one contribution that touched the case. "I wouldn't have missed that," he said to me, "for the world."

I don't know that I agreed with him.

Chapter XII
TUESDAY, DECEMBER 20TH, 8.30 P.M.

By EIGHT o'clock on the following evening, no news of any kind had come through. The position as regards the death of Chinnery was unchanged. The situation as to the disappearance of Copeland was also unchanged. There came not a breath or a whisper concerning either man. Much to my annoyance, Anthony Bathurst had kicked his heels indoors all day. You would have thought that murder and sudden death were the two happenings that were farthest away from his thoughts. Towards half past eight in the evening he actually talked round and descanted, if you will, on the subject of cheese.

"My dear Jack," he opened, "if you ask me, cheesemaking is a lost art in this country. In the book of *Husbandrie*, Master Tusser says, 'Bambarie cheese shall goe for my money.' You see, he placed it above such famous cheeses as Cheshire, Gloucester, Wiltshire, or Somerset. Note that! But where can you get it nowadays?"

I quoted him the old Somerset proverb: "If you wid have a good cheese and hav'n old, you must turn 'n seven times before he is old."

He went on with his impeachment. "Do you make goats'-milk cheese in this part of the country, Jack? Why, even in the Celtic period, goats were kept for butter- and for cheese-making, and they continued right through the Roman occupation. In the Tudor period, however, goats were valued at much less than sheep, and don't you forget it! But, from the Norman Conquest to the Black Death, goatherds were appointed amongst the village officials. Who's the goatherd of Scarpe at this day? Got one? I'll lay tens that you haven't."

"Nary a one, Anthony. I'll tell you why. You can tell when they're near. Goats aren't popular in these parts."

"No. I know they're not. I've looked for one in vain. Yet I've read that goats give three times as much milk as sheep. Even so, goats are eclipsed. Hey ninny, nanny! Not so on the Continent, Jack, my son. Oh, no—very much the reverse, in fact. Look at the number of goats'-milk cheeses that you can find over there. In France you have your 'chevret' and 'chevrotin'. In Italy, your 'formaggio di capra'. In Germany your 'Ziegenkäse' and 'Gaiskäsli'."

"Never tasted one of them, and don't know that I want to."

"You haven't? Then you're the poorer. You've hardly lived, my lad. What about Mont d'Or, Maconnais, Saint Claude, Saint Marcellin, Poitiers, Lamothe, and Gratairon. To say nothing of the German Altenburger, Koppenkäse, and Riesengebirge, or the Norwegian Hvid Gjedeost. Yes . . . every one of 'em is as good as gold. And those marks behind Chinnery's ears, Jack, in my opinion, were burns." This was Bathurst, *in excelsis*. His tangents were remarkable. He dropped into a chair, his cheeses behind him. "Burns?" I echoed. "How burns?"

"Don't know. Can't think why. But still—burns. You couldn't be struck by lightning and die of cold very well, could you, Jack?"

"Aren't the effects of extreme heat and extreme cold very similar?" I suggested. "I seem to have heard something of the kind."

"This bloke, Chinnery, was frozen stiff, Jack. We can't shut our eyes to that fact. It's vitally important. Foxon's words, and he *found* the body, remember, were actually, 'he's frozen stiff'. Surtees' P.M. discovered nothing to excite the slightest comment. So I've heard since. Therefore, where are we?"

I purposely made him no answer. Rather, in these meditative moods, would I let Anthony Bathurst have his head. If you did that consistently, before long you were bound to get somewhere. Suddenly he sprang from where he had been sitting.

"Game for a stroll, Jack? What do you say?"

"Where?"

"Oh, round and about and along. All the way and back again. I'll tell you what. Why not have a look at the moor by moonlight? That idea is rather attractive. Up the Baskervilles! Fancy your chance against a spectral hound?"

"I'm game," I replied curtly. "Though I shan't be sorry that you'll be with me. Two's most distinctly company on the moor of Constanton in the moonlight." We attired ourselves for the outdoor weather and, walking hard, came at length to the edge of the dreary moorland. I brought him to the spot where Chinnery had said "good night" and left me to go to his death. The wind of winter still swirled across Constanton Moor and lashed our faces with whipping cruelty. The cold night air thrust its icy fingers round my loins and I shivered more than once. Every now and then, when the wild wind served, I could hear the dull noise of the leaden sea in the distance.

"Well," I said sharply to my companion, "what do we do now? Catch our deaths of cold or what?"

"Deaths of cold, Jack? Or of cold evil? Which? I wonder. Let's cut across over there for a little way. I've an idea in my head."

He strode off relentlessly and I followed him. "Nobody about," he said, after a while. "That's good."

It was a clear night. The clearest that we had had for some time. The stars hung from the sky like shining lamps from an ebony ceiling. A very different night from that misty night when I had ventured out alone. We strode on in silence. I could tell that my cousin was thinking hard. Our steps crunched on the cold, crisp, frost-topped grass. Within a few minutes, however, he broke the silence.

"Tell me, Jack," he said, "when we come to the place where Chinnery would have left the track and turned for home."

"A few yards from here," I answered. "Just to the right. By going that way he cut off a corner. You'll see what I mean in a minute. There you are. Look over there. Those lights are the lights of his house." I pointed over to my right. "You can understand now what a little distance he had to go."

Anthony nodded. "Yes. That explains a good deal. More than I can say. There isn't a lot in his walk if he'd gone straight home."

"Half a mile."

"No more, I suppose?"

"No. Chinnery put it at half a mile himself when he refused the offer of a lift in Copeland's car. He knew, no doubt."

"Yes. I remember you telling me that. Now I want you to do something else for me, Jack."

"Give it a name, and I will."

"Tell me exactly where *you* first heard the footsteps on the night that you met Foxon and thought that you were being followed. I want to scout round a bit when you get me there."

I made him the promise that he required. We walked on again for some distance. I kept my eyes strained in the darkness for anything that I might recognize in the nature of a landmark. Eventually I realized that there was nothing upon which I could rely, and I came to the conclusion that I should be forced to trust the judgment of my remembrance. I waited until I thought I saw my chance. Yes! This was about the spot.

"Here," I said. "Just about here. It's difficult though, to say, within a few yards or so. It's moderately dark tonight, but the time before it was not only damned dark, but misty as well. Still—I'm pretty sure I'm about right. This is the place."

"Walk slowly," remarked my cousin. I obeyed him. We walked on slowly together. All was as silent as the grave. As far as I could, from my position beside him, I was watching the expression on Anthony Bathurst's face. More than anything else, he was listening. But no sound came to reward the effort of his ears. Suddenly he clutched my arm and we both halted in our tracks.

"What was that?" he whispered.

I had heard nothing and said as much. Anthony shook his head at me impatiently. "Ssh," he whispered again. "You're wrong, listen! I'm certain that I heard something." Neither of us moved a step. We waited. But no sound came to us over the dark moor. "Come on again," whispered Anthony. "For a little way. I want to try an experiment."

We walked on again for about another twenty paces. Then a cold fear clutched at my heart. I heard the sound of the footsteps this time quite plainly. As on the previous occasion they seemed, to my ear, to be coming first from the left-hand side, and then from all round me. I looked at my cousin, and he looked at me. At a quick sign from him we broke into a run. The footsteps accelerated also! I turned to look behind as I ran, but there was nobody to be seen.

"Keep going, Jack," cried Anthony, "and don't stop until I tell you to."

We passed the place where Foxon had come into sight during my previous adventure and the line of dark bushes towards which he and I had run, now showed on our left. Bathurst was a pace in front of me. He ran hard for the clump of bushes, like a three-quarter going hell-for-leather for the line, and I ran with him. "With me! Run straight for the bushes!" panted Anthony. We reached them almost together. I thought that I saw a strange shadow flung across them. Just as I had when Foxon had been with me. But again I was doomed to disappointment. When we burst into it, and the growth gave way to us, the clump of bushes was empty! Anthony and I stopped and looked at each other with blank faces.

"Queer," he muttered. "I heard the steps and I could have sworn that I caught a glimpse of somebody or something lurking in here. Moving backward and forward. Don't you agree, Jack?"

I grinned at his chagrin. I couldn't help myself. I knew what I had experienced before, in a similar manner, and I knew, therefore, only too well how he felt now. I told him in greater detail of what had happened to Foxon and me on the previous occasion.

"Deuced queer," he repeated, "say what you like about it. Unless my eyes absolutely deceived me, I saw a dark shadow move somewhere about here. I naturally concluded that it was somebody using this clump of bushes as a screen, either as a hiding-place, or to watch us."

"I saw that shadow," I declared. "And what's more, I saw it before. Foxon swore that he saw it too."

"So there are at least three of us, Jack, who think in the same way. Let's walk back," he suggested. "I may hit on something to account for it."

We retraced our steps until we came to the track that bore away to the left towards the house of the lights where Chinnery had lived. Here my cousin halted.

"You know, Jack," he remarked, "the land all round here on this side of the moor is pretty well level, all things being considered, isn't it? Different altogether from the other side of the path. The side where Chinnery's dead body was found. You'd agree with that statement, wouldn't you?"

"Oh—yes, undoubtedly. But what about it? What's your point?"

"Transport, old son! Transport! Don't you see what I'm getting at? Get your brain busy. Although traces of wheels may be difficult to find, a car could be used on this side of the track without very much difficulty. Whereas it couldn't on the other. Not a hope! Significant, you know, say what you like about it."

"I suppose it is, though I confess that I hadn't thought about it. It hadn't occurred to me."

"You see, Jack, it's like this. Part of our problem is to find out *where* Chinnery was between the time he said good night to you and the time when his body was discovered. He must have been some-where, mustn't he? Even assuming that he may have been dead during the time. Now Foxon is as certain as a man can be that Chinnery's body had not been on the moor for very long before it was found. I've questioned him twice about it and he's emphatic on the point. I can't shake him."

"All the same, he might be wrong. He *might* have missed it. I don't see how he can be absolutely certain over a point like that."

"It isn't likely, though. Don't forget that he was patrolling part of the day as well as by night. And there were several others on the job as well as Foxon, remember."

"That makes a difference, I admit. Yes—the balance is all in favour of Foxon's statements, I know; but—and it's a big 'but', mind you— the moor isn't the size of a bowling-green."

"True for you, Jack." I saw him grin cheerfully and rub his cheek with the back of his hand. When we came to the road again he asked me a question that surprised me.

"How far from here to Copeland's, Jack?"

I considered.

"Copeland's place is almost exactly four miles from the Rectory. Now the Rectory is about a mile and a half from here going towards St. Crayle. I should put Copeland's place therefore at about two and a half miles distant. I shouldn't be much out."

"Two and a half miles," he repeated. "H'm. Getting on for three-quarters of an hour's walk. What do you say? Are you game to do it now? I'd very much like to call there."

"Don't mind me," I said, "where you are, I want to be. But tell me, why are you so keen on going to Copeland's?"

"There's nothing like seeing a thing first hand, Jack. Nothing like it at all. Copeland's quite a different man from Chinnery. Therefore, from *some* points of view, his death may be a different proposition. I should say that the two men, as men, had little in common. Why, then, are they coupled in tragedy? As I feel certain that they are."

We were swinging away along the road. I made no reply.

Anthony came in with another question:

"How old would you put Chinnery at, Jack?"

"Anything from fifty-eight to sixty-five. Men of his type are diffi-cult to judge in that way. He was thin and spare. With a stringy neck and a huge Adam's apple. Call him sixty-two."

"And Copeland?"

"Oh, considerably junior to Chinnery."

"How much?"

"Well, there again, it's a shot in the dark. Say forty-two to fifty. Call it forty-five."

"Seventeen years Chinnery's junior! As much as that?"

"Every bit, I should say, but what's your point with regard to the age?"

"Nothing really. Just packing the two men up, as it were, in the right parcels." He paused but continued again almost immediately. "Chinnery married. Copeland a widower. That correct?"

"O.K., big boy," I gave back to him.

"Chinnery no children. Copeland two girls. Right again?"

"Keep on," I said, "and I'll mark you up with one hundred per cent."

He laughed merrily. We were now making a good pace along the road.

"How old are these Copeland girls? Just what one would expect?"

"Yes. I would give Norah, that's the elder, about three-and-twenty, and Christine about twenty."

"And Norah has a bad throat while Christine is sweet and twenty. Trip it gently, pretty sweeting. Journeys end in lovers' meeting. I wonder now! Copeland a ladies' man by any chance?" He flung the question at me. I thought of what I knew of the Squire.

"No," I replied. "In my opinion, for what it's worth—definitely not."

Anthony Bathurst eyed me shrewdly. "You can't always tell, you know, from outside appearances."

"Agreed on that. But you asked me and I answered you."

For a time he seemed satisfied and kept to silence again. We tramped on, our steps ringing clear on the frost-bound road. Every-thing was still touched with the finger of the frost. The hedges, the grass, and the tops of the gates, that here and there divided field from field. We came to Copeland's house in splendid time, considering everything. As we approached the white gate that crossed the drive, I said to Anthony, "Going in, then?"

"You bet, old son, if I can get in. Why do you think I've walked all the way? To give my liver a shake up? Not this child. Not in these trousers. Ring the bell and see what the fairies send you."

I walked up and rang the bell in the porch. There came no answer. We waited. I looked at my cousin enquiringly. "Ring it again, Jack. Why not? Persistence is a most commendable virtue." I rang the bell for the second time. Again we waited. Again it evoked no response. "A third time, Jack, if you please. You know the luck that proverbially attends upon the third time. Bank on it now."

I rang the bell for the third time. Happily, Anthony's prognostication was correct. A maid in a black dress and with a white apron opened the door to us; my cousin stepped forward and gave her the necessary explanation. She listened and then puckered her brow as though she were puzzled. Eventually, however, she said, "Come in, sir, and you too, sir," and that was good enough in all conscience, and just what we wanted. We entered behind her and at once stood in the brilliantly lighted hall. Anthony enquired of her with his eyes. She understood and we were ushered into a room that was undoubtedly used as the library. Over the fireplace was a full-length portrait of a beautiful and charming girl. Dressed in the clothes of ten years or so previously.

"If you wait here for a moment, sir," said the white-aproned maid, "I will tell Miss Christine and she will come to you."

The girl slid out of the room and we were left to look at each other. My cousin winked at me shamelessly.

"Not a local girl, Jack," he said in a low tone. "Did you notice the way that she spoke? Must have come from the London district, if I'm any judge."

I nodded. "I'm not surprised at that. Copeland wasn't too keen on local products in any direction. I've heard him give vent to that opinion many a time. In fact, it was a pet hobby of his."

We heard steps in the hall outside. The handle of the door turned and a girl came into the room. She was unusually attractive, and I could see that the girl whose picture was above the fire-place was her mother. The likeness between them was too remarkable for anybody to miss. Although I had known Copeland pretty well for some time, and had seen his daughters driving in the car, I had never actually met the younger of them face to face. With her sister, she had been abroad to a finishing-school for some years, and had returned to St. Roseworthy but a short time prior to the opening of this story. Thus was Christine Copeland as Anthony Bathurst and I faced her on the evening of Tuesday, December the 20th. When she spoke, her voice was low and musical.

"Mr. Clyst and Mr. Bathurst." We murmured our corroboration. "Please take a seat. My sister wishes me to apologize to you. She is far from well. A bad throat. The doctor fears a quinsy. Is there anything that I can do for you?"

Anthony was at his best.

"I am sorry about your sister, Miss Christine. I hope that she will soon be better. The mention of 'quinsy' draws from me a flood of sympathy, for I have suffered similarly. I have come to ask you about your father." She gave a startled gasp. "Do you mean that you have news of my father?"

Bathurst shook his head. "I am sorry. No. I have no more news for you, Miss Copeland, than you already know. I saw Colonel Blount this morning, and I regret to say that all of us are still completely in the dark. But that doesn't mean that all hope has been abandoned. You mustn't despair. For a moment. Hence my visit to you tonight."

The girl shook her head vaguely, as though she were at a loss to understand.

"I'm afraid that I can't tell you very much, Mr. Bathurst. My sister and I have been abroad for some time. The result is that we have been out of touch with things and know very little of the district here and still less of the majority of our neighbours. We *were* to have dined with the Shelleys on Friday evening. Lady Rachel has been very kind to us. But Norah had a bad throat, through all this frost and fog, and my father thought it would be safer for her not to go. So she stopped at home and I stopped here with her, just to keep her company. Isn't it all curious? If Norah hadn't had the bad throat, we should have gone to Lady Rachel's and come home with Father and then he would be here with us now. What little things count in this world!"

"Yes. As you say, it's the little things so often that make all the difference in life, Miss Copeland. But don't take yourself to task over it unduly. We can't understand the real reason why things happen, and, because of that, all conjecture as to what might have been or what we might have done is useless, and gets us nowhere. Will you answer some questions, if I ask them of you?"

"I will do my best, Mr. Bathurst."

"Thank you. I knew that you would. To your knowledge, had your father any enemies, Miss Copeland?"

She replied simply. "As far as I know he was good friends with everybody. He was a likable man. Still, as I told you just now, I haven't lived here very much. But I have never heard him complain of any trouble or anything. And I think I should have, had there been any. What else was there that you wanted to ask me?"

"Your father's life before he came down here, Miss Copeland— where did you live before you lived here?"

"In London. My father was born in Glebeshire. After my mother died, we moved away to London. I think the place here had too many sad memories for my father. He said that it had. That made him move away. But only for a time. His native county called him again, as Norah and I always thought it would. He had made a lot of money in business, you see, by this time, and was able to please himself. He sold up very profitably, and we came back here to live."

"And you and your sister have been abroad?"

"Yes. To school. Father insisted upon that. First to a school near Brussels, and then to another in the South of France."

Anthony's next question startled me. "What did your mother die of, Miss Copeland?"

Her eyes expressed doubt. "I don't think that I ever heard. The exact trouble, I mean. She was ill. For months. But I wasn't much more than a little girl at the time so that I haven't a very clear remembrance of it. It was a terrible blow to my father, though, I believe, when she died, and it took him a long time to get over it. It seems to me, now that I look back, that an evil spirit must have vented its spite on us. First, my mother to die so young, and now my father to disappear, as he has, in the prime of life. What have we done to deserve it all?"

Anthony and I each made appropriate expressions of sympathy. Then he continued his questioning.

"Since your father has been missing, I suppose that no correspondence has come for him, or to you or your sister, that has, shall we say, puzzled you?"

Christine Copeland shook her head decisively. There was no hesitating about her reply.

"No, Mr. Bathurst. Nothing has come. In fact I don't remember that a letter of any kind has come to the house since Friday evening."

"Your sister wouldn't have had anything of the kind, I suppose, and not have told you? That isn't a possible happening?"

Another shake of the head, equally decisive. "My sister has been indisposed all the time. I should have taken a letter of that kind up to her, had there been one. I should have been bound to see it. It would have come to me before her."

"It would. I see. Thank you."

Christine Copeland crossed the room and came to stand facing the two of us. "Mr. Bathurst," she said, "I want you to hide nothing from me and to tell me the absolute truth. Do you think that my father is alive." She put her hand on his arm.

Anthony looked at her gravely. "Frankly now, Miss Copeland?"

She nodded bravely. "Frankly now, Mr. Bathurst." As she spoke her lips were firmly set, but there had been a quiver on them that the girl had been forced to conquer. Even Anthony hesitated to reply to her.

"Frankly, then, I am very much afraid . . ." He stopped.

But the girl would have none of his temporizing. "Please finish what you were about to say, Mr. Bathurst. *I* am not afraid. I would rather know the worst than just go on fearing it. It's the suspense that wears me out. You are very much afraid that—that . . . ? I'm waiting for you." Her eyes held her query.

"That your father is dead." Every spoken syllable was eloquent of his sympathy. That's a feeble way of attempting to describe it, but I can't think of a better. Christine Copeland took the blow splendidly.

"Yes. I was afraid so, too," she whispered, almost to herself.

"But you mustn't take what I say for granted, Miss Copeland. All that I have given you is but my opinion. I have no case definitely built up, mind you. There is always the chance that I may be wrong."

"I know what you're basing your opinion on," she gave back to him. "You're going on the death of Mr. Chinnery, aren't you?"

"I must, Miss Copeland. To a great extent, that is. How can I possibly ignore it? It is a signpost of significance."

She nodded. "Yes—I was afraid that you would say that. Both my sister and I have felt the same as you do. Ever since Father didn't come home on Friday evening we have been dreadfully worried. After all, though, why *should* the two cases be the same? What connection has my father with poor Mr. Chinnery? I can assure you, Mr. Bathurst, that I know of none. I am completely puzzled about it."

Anthony Bathurst shrugged his shoulders.

I made a contribution myself. "If I had to describe it, I should describe it like this. They were friends of a kind, that's all you can say about them."

"Yes, Mr. Clyst, I know that. Sometimes when my father wrote to me when I was at school in France, he mentioned Mr. Chinnery by name. Just in a social connection. They were bound to meet a lot, seeing that they lived so close to each other. He would tell me that he had been out to dinner somewhere and Mr. Chinnery had been a guest. As he might refer to Mr. and Mrs. Burke, for instance, or the Rector, Mr. Verschoyle, or to Captain Shelley and Lady Rachel. I believe I'm right in saying that Mr. Chinnery has been here and that my father has visited Mr. and Mrs. Chinnery."

Something seemed to come to Anthony out of the girl's statement.

"Were all these references to Chinnery just general?"

"Oh—quite."

"You don't remember your father making any *specific* statement about him? Anything? It doesn't matter how trivial it may seem to you to be."

His efforts were destined to failure. Miss Copeland wasn't able to remember anything of the kind. My cousin rose. From the glance that he threw in my direction, I thought he desired to end the interview. But I was wrong in my assumption.

"I like your house, Miss Copeland," he said rather eagerly. Almost boyishly, if one could use such a word in connection with Anthony Bathurst. The note of enthusiasm in his voice was definitely easy for me to recognize.

"Yes?" she returned.

"Yes. I like it immensely. Much more than I like most houses. It's a real country house, of the kind that I've always wanted to have myself. Been looking for one for years. I only wish that my visit had coincided with better conditions."

"It is a nice house," she ventured. "I like it too. Father has had many offers from various people who've seen it, and having seen it, have wanted to buy it. But he has always refused to sell. He has said to Norah and me many a time that he hoped to end his days here." The tears showed in her eyes as she uttered the last sentence.

Anthony nodded casually. As though he hadn't noticed her distress and the matter, generally, were a mere commonplace one.

"Any of these offers at all recent, Miss Copeland?" he asked her.

"Oh, yes. One of them has come along since the summer. I couldn't say exactly when—about the first week in October, I should think. Had my father taken it, it would have meant a big profit for him. But he wouldn't budge. He said he couldn't understand why anybody should offer such a big price for it. Norah and I pointed out to him what a splendid offer it was, but he was a man who always knew his own mind. People say that's the chief reason why he was so successful in business. He wouldn't move an inch from a position that he once took up. The house was his and he intended to stop in it."

"How many rooms have you, Miss Copeland? All told?"

"Fourteen. Several bedrooms that are never used. Or scarcely ever."

Anthony Bathurst stood there and listened. Then he held out his hand to her. "Good night, Miss Copeland. Don't give up hope, you know." We shook hands with her. She came with us to the entrance to the house. As we walked home, I put a question to him.

"I'm curious. What were you after, Anthony? For I'll swear that your interest in the house was more than ordinary."

His eyes twinkled at me. "This is too bad. Can't I escape your watchful eye, Jack? Didn't you really see what I was getting at?"

I shook my head. "No. I was lost to it. I'll confess that I hadn't an earthly."

"Well, I wanted to look over the house. I should have liked her to have 'shown me over', as the advertising builders have it. But the little lady didn't bite and there was nothing doing. Never mind. There will come a time, some day."

"Why? It struck me as just an ordinary house. Why were you so keen, I mean?"

He walked on for several paces before replying to me. "Call it a 'hunch', Jack," he declared eventually. "Observe, though, before you fall on me with the tooth and nail of relentless criticism that several people consider the place well worth buying. And one—a recent offer, too, was particularly generous. Why the sudden popularity?"

"It's a place that's different from the ordinary. You liked it yourself. Said you would like to have it. You aren't the only judge of an attractive residence, and you mustn't get it into your head that you are."

"No. That's so. It's a biggish place, though, for a man with two daughters. No wife of the house. And no sons, either."

"Copeland was the Squire of the district. Everyone regarded him as such, ever since he came here to live, and it gave him a position. He was looked up to. He wouldn't live in a rabbit-hutch. How could he?"

"Now you've travelled from one extreme to the other. I say 'a mansion', or near enough, and you immediately counter with 'rabbit-hutch'. Is there no middle way, or must the extremes always have it?"

I cocked my head at him. "What was the hunch about? What's sinister about the Copelands' house that makes you want to wander all over it?"

"Don't know, you old worry-guts. Didn't I as good as admit as much just now? Copeland lived in Glebeshire, cleared out to London, and then came back. Although, as Christine told us, the place held sad memories for him. He was born in the county, don't forget, and stayed there until some years after his marriage. Till, I presume, the death of Mrs. Copeland."

"That's about it. That's what I understood from her. And what do you find there, that's strange or even unreasonable?"

"Don't know. I've repeated myself, you see. Cut it out, Jack, for the time being, for the Lord's sake, and let's think of something else.

Let's clear our brains. Where is Copeland? We don't know. But I'd lay an elephant to an eggspoon that the poor devil isn't a hundred miles away from us as we walk along here. And that there are people still wanting his house." He pointed to the sky of frozen glass. With a moon as high as any moon ever rode. A moon like a burnished lamp.

"The year dies hard, Jack. Just like a man. But with this difference. Another year is on its heels, and there's no time lost between the two of 'em. 'Over the earth there comes a bloom. Sunny light for sullen gloom. Warm perfume for vapour cold—I smell the rose above the mould.'" He turned to me whimsically. "Tom Hood, Jack. The Perthshire peasant. More famous for a certain poem in *Punch*, entitled 'The Song of the Shirt'. A poem that brought him a success which, unhappily, came too late."

"'I smell the rose above the mould'." He repeated the words as though he were loth to leave them, as though he wanted them and their perfume to linger.

"You can have your mouldy rose with pleasure. I'd sooner smell a pony of hot Scotch," I grumbled.

He grinned at my sally and then began to whistle. When we came to Scarpe the cold was more intense than ever. Anthony Bathurst agreed with me on the point. I looked at the thermometer that hung in my hall. It had gone down another two degrees.

Chapter XIII
THE EVE OF CHRISTMAS, 6 P.M.

THE Christmas Eve of that year was a day which, having lived it, you would never forget. It is true that no snow actually fell, but the clouds were grey and ugly and pregnant with its promise. The wild birds came in from the sea and sought the hospitality of our habitations. It was the third week of the great frost. The whole of the country-side lay white in its grip. Mrs. Polglose broke the milk in the pails when she wanted it for the morning coffee. I put oil lamps and straw comfort to all our pipes at Scarpe. Anthony waited and watched. This description truly sums up his attitude. He began to call Christmas, for some elfin reason of his own, "Carissimaristmas". He walked by day and roamed by night. But nothing came to him that he considered worthy of being passed on to me.

On the Christmas Eve, he and I were at tea, when we heard the voices of the carol-singers in the porch of Scarpe. They announced that Good King Wenceslas had looked out once again and shepherds tended their flocks. "Sire, he lives a good league hence." I was able to distinguish, amongst the other voices, that of Sybil Burke. I went to the door and found Verschoyle and her, leading some dozen or so enthusiastic members of the St. Crayle choir. The glow in her cheeks made her look more charming than ever. I made monetary contribution and, of course, she and the Rector came in. The choir was dispatched onward to entertain musically other dwelling-houses in the vicinity with the arrangement that Mrs. Burke and the Rector would rejoin them at a certain given rendezvous later on in the evening. Mrs. Polglose was immediately commissioned to make fresh tea and to toast a further supply of muffins. The cold had given Verschoyle's cheeks a glow as it had Sybil's, a glow that heightened the attractiveness, even, of *his* appearance. His silvery hair and his keen-cut features gave him a distinction that was unusual. Anthony Bathurst, when tea was ready for them, with that streak of impudence that had always been his, sought to make him talk.

"It's awfully plucky of you to come round, sir. The carols have a harder job this year than ever."

"How do you mean, my dear fellow?" smiled the Rector, putting down his tea-cup. "Do you mean from the point of view of the collection?"

"As projections of benevolence, sir. Please mark what I say. If 'evil' walks in St. Crayle, why shouldn't 'good' walk too? And, in the walking, join issue with the evil and conquer it?"

Verschoyle suddenly became grave.

"Yes, I see what you mean. That's certainly an idea. I didn't know that you were arguing in that direction. You are contending on the lines of the sign of the Cross striking terror into the hearts of the devil and of his legions of evil. Holy Water idea, and so on! Well, I, for one, wouldn't say a word against the suggestion. It is obvious that good will always be the power that must ultimately vanquish the forces of evil."

"How's Martin these days?" I asked Sybil, more, I think, to turn the conversation than for any other reason.

She shook her head rather despondently. "Much the same, Jack. There has been little change in him since I last saw you. How could you expect there to be?"

"You mean?"

"Why—this second trouble, of course. After the death of Mr. Chinnery, this disappearance of Mr. Copeland. Martin isn't likely to improve under these conditions, is he? Now I ask you?"

Verschoyle expressed his sympathy. "I noticed it at that dinner-party I gave. The night that poor Chinnery went. I mean when he was last seen alive. Your husband was obviously under a cloud then, Mrs. Burke."

"It didn't start then, Mr. Verschoyle, either. I had noticed it long before that. But I've told Jack all about it before, and for his sake I don't want to cover the ground all over again."

I noticed that Anthony Bathurst was watching her. I wasn't sure why this was so, because I had already told him of what Sybil Burke had informed me of her husband. She and I had discussed it together. The Rector evidently noticed his attitude as well.

"So you're still here, Mr. Bathurst?"

"Yes. Still here, sir."

"Waiting, like Wilkins Micawber, for something to turnup? Is that the idea?"

"Afraid things won't fall into my lap like that, sir. A good man makes his opportunities. Can't stand still expectant. Goes round and gets 'em. I still have hopes."

"Perhaps we're at cross purposes."

"I don't think so, sir."

Verschoyle's face grew graver.

"Is it as bad as you imply, then, Mr. Bathurst?"

Anthony shrugged his shoulders. "Chinnery is dead. A man can only die once. There is no bringing a dead man back. And now—" He broke off.

The Rector waited courteously for him to continue. My cousin accepted the situation. "I have met the younger Miss Copeland. It wasn't an easy interview, sir, I assure you. Personally, I find it unpleasant to strike a girl across the soul." Again he stopped abruptly.

"You mean that you told her you feared the worst?"

"I won't contradict you, sir."

During the period of this conversation, Sybil had sat listening with a strained face. The Rector finished his tea, put his cup down with an excess of care, and rose from the table.

"I hope that your fears will be groundless, Mr. Bathurst. I hope and trust that Chinnery will be the only member of my congregation whom we shall mourn on Christmas Day. The other contingency is too terrible to contemplate. If Mrs. Burke is ready, we will rejoin our carol-singers. Thank you, Clyst, for your charming hospitality. It was indeed a fortunate call that we made. Hot buttered muffins have always tempted me."

The Rector shook hands with me. Before he could reach Anthony, however, the telephone bell rang on the table in the hall. By this time I had come to distrust that sound. To associate it inevitably with sinister tidings. I answered it, therefore, prepared to hear news that I dared not put into words, *before* I heard it. It was Martin Burke at the other end. His voice, as he spoke to me, had a tone in it that was definitely unusual. He asked for Sybil. He had heard, he said, that she and Verschoyle had broken their round with the carol-singers in order to have tea with us at Scarpe. So I went back, found Sybil and took her to the telephone. I watched her anxiously as she answered her husband. I saw her face change as I had expected it to. I heard the words of her reply to Martin Burke. I saw her replace the receiver. I did all these things like a man in a dream. She stood there for some seconds, motionless. Then she spoke to me in just above a whisper.

"Jack, they've found the Squire's body."

"Where?" I said, almost breathlessly.

"On Constanton Moor. Not such a great distance from where the other body was found."

"How did Martin hear?"

"From Colonel Blount, so he says. He met him on the way back from the moor. They had sent for the Colonel and he had been up there. Isn't it dreadful?"

I nodded. "When was this?"

"About an hour ago, Martin says. He 'phoned me as soon as he got home."

"We must tell the others," I replied. "Will you come with me, Sybil?"

We went back to the others. Verschoyle was standing by the fire waiting to go. His overcoat was on and he held his black soft hat in his hand. Just as he had been standing when I had called Sybil Burke to the telephone. He looked as though he hadn't moved a muscle. Anthony was sitting, smoking a cigarette with nervous, uneasy movements of the fingers. His eyes caught mine as I entered. They held an unspoken question and I knew what the question was. I nodded to him. I wasted no time over my announcement.

"Martin Burke has just 'phoned. He 'phoned to Sybil. He had heard that she was here. He has met Colonel Blount this afternoon. Copeland's body was found on the moor about an hour ago."

A stab of pain crossed Verschoyle's face. Anthony Bathurst sprang from his chair.

"What? Again on the moor?"

Sybil answered him. "Yes, Mr. Bathurst. Not a great distance, my husband tells me, from where Mr. Chinnery's body was picked up."

Anthony repeated the words with which she had begun her last sentence. "Not a great distance? Were they your husband's actual words, Mrs. Burke?" She nodded. "I wouldn't *swear* to that. But that was the meaning that he conveyed to me."

"Christmas Eve," said the Rector quietly. "How dreadful for all of us, Besides Mrs. Chinnery, there are now those two poor girls waiting for their father to come home. It's difficult for us to realize all that they must feel. Oh, my dear people, what is this appalling thing that has come to our lovely countryside?"

He put his black hat down and sat in the chair nearest to the fire. It was obvious that he, too, like so many others, was beginning to give way under the strain. Anthony stood again, for a moment or so, irresolutely. Then he turned to me impetuously. In the movement there stood the real Bathurst. The determined, resolute, purposeful man. The man that all the girls loved, the quick-thinking, quick-moving, agreeable personality.

"I'm going, Jack, at once. I fancy that there may be work for me to do. You stay here with Mrs. Burke. The incredible happening has come to pass. What about you, sir? Staying here or coming along with me?" This question was to the Rector.

Verschoyle looked at him strangely. Much of his native assurance, that normally stood him in such good stead, had gone from him. The death of Chinnery had been trial enough, but this second affair, coming so closely on its heels, disturbed him so much that he felt life to be submerging him. Anthony Bathurst's questioning grey eyes were upon him. The Rev. Edward Verschoyle saw himself, for a fleeting second, cowering behind the sharp-edged blade of Fate. He could not fall back upon the reputation of his benevolence. Or upon his aesthetic nerve. Or upon the academic enrichments with which he had been pleased to invest himself. His normal way of knowledge and understanding was of little use to him now. In a manner, it had become out of date. At last he found words to answer my cousin's question.

"I would prefer," he said quietly, and with much dignity, "to stay here. For a time at least. Then I will escort Mrs. Burke back to her home. I brought her out. It is only right that I should take her back. I owe that to my friend, Martin Burke."

"Very well, sir. I think that I understand how you feel about things." Anthony looked closely at the Rector.

Verschoyle had no more words for him. Anthony Bathurst went from the room with long strides. We heard him close the front door. We felt the cold come in from the outside. There was silence. Then Verschoyle spoke. "Though I walk through the Valley of the Shadow of Death . . . I will fear no evil."

He stopped. Silence reigned again.

Then I heard Anthony's steps . . . going away from Scarpe. Towards the moor . . . where Chinnery and Copeland had been destroyed.

CHAPTER XIV

THE EVE OF CHRISTMAS, 10.30 P.M.

THE Rector of St. Crayle, together with Sybil Burke, left Scarpe soon after eight o'clock. I saw them to the door. When I opened it, to let them out, a white mist had come once again to join hands with the relentless frost. The Rector and Sybil had each run true to type during the remainder of the time that they had spent with me. Sybil had been quiet and restrained, and a little disinclined, as it were, to trust herself very far in any direction. Especially as regards conversation. Verschoyle had surrendered himself, even more than before Anthony left us, to a power that he obviously regarded as so entirely superior to himself that he had no control over it. He had sat in his chair with his thin lips pressed together. Speech had been scanty with him. "Religion," he had said in reply to a remark from Sybil, "is a habit of mind. It can't be taught to people. I learned that very early in my priesthood. We are all deeply religious when an unspeakable danger threatens us and our own resources are taxed beyond their limits. I'm a parish priest and I ply my trade. But I know the clear value of sincerity."

I watched the two of them go away from my house and I saw the white mist lick hungrily at their faces as they passed from my sight at the bottom of the Scarpe garden. After that, I sat by the fire and waited patiently for Anthony Bathurst to return. This happened at ten-thirty. When he entered, he at once issued orders.

"Pour me out a stiff Scotch, Jack," he said curtly. "I'm chilled to the bone. God, but it's a swine out there tonight. Enough to freeze the ears off a brass mongoose. One of the worst I've ever known."

I poured him out the whisky that he had ordered. And waited for him. Waited for him deliberately and upon his pleasure. He was always so damned self-contained when he made up his mind to be.

"It's intensely dark. Jack, out there on the moor. Shrouded in veils of thick mist. And it's all so devilishly quiet. The only sound you hear is the sound of your own footsteps. Yes! I mean that tonight, Jack. Every now and then a pebble swishes, when your foot dislodges it, and the noise it makes is magnified a thousand times to anxious ears.

The dead Vikings should turn in their coffins on that moor, Jack, when the sound has travelled far enough to reach them."

I still waited for him to broach his news. For I was certain that he had some. His grey eyes were fixed steadily on the spaces in front of him. At length my peerless patience was rewarded.

"I've a bit of news for you, Jack. Good news, perhaps, from the main point of view. But all the same, call it what you will, it's given me a hell of a problem."

"*Good* news?" I queried. "It's cheerful to hear you say that, but it's unexpected. What's the *good* news that you've brought back with you?"

He looked at me calmly. "This! Copeland has been brought back from the grave. By a miracle, almost. Another hour or so, out in that cold, and it would have been all over with him. But he was picked up in the nick of time, old Surtees was handy, and they got to work on him almost at once with restoratives. I should say that he's a man with a terrifically strong constitution, and they've pulled him through. So that 'the powers of evil', as our good friend Verschoyle would have it, are at least frustrated."

I got excited. "You see what this means, Anthony? It's marvellously good news. We shall now have something to go on! Copeland will talk! He will tell us things. Things that previously we've been able only to guess at."

My cousin slowly filled his pipe. "Good for you, Jack. That's how *I* saw things. I can go even one better. Copeland has already talked! He has already told me things! I wasted no time over that, believe me, Jack. I showed indecent haste over it all, and I got to him directly after the police had been to him, and he was well enough to be spoken to. Would you believe that I've been at his bedside for over an hour?"

I frowned. "At his house?"

"Of course at his house. Where else would you have him be?" He grinned. "In the Courts of Paradise?" I shook my head uncertainly. I didn't quite know how to answer him. After all, he was right in his statement. I ignored his question therefore, and in place of my reply, gave another back to him.

"What did Copeland tell you?"

Anthony replied quietly. "He's had a rough time, and naturally, so soon after the ordeal, he's not what you would term 'himself'."

"Light-headed, do you mean?"

"A bit perhaps. But not *too* bad that way. Is there a shooting-box on the moor?"

"Yes. About a mile and a half beyond Priestley's Quarry. Why?"

"I fancied that I heard Copeland mention the words 'shooting-box'. Your statement confirms the idea. Copeland's talk is a mass of snatched and almost incoherent sentences."

"Tell me some of them."

"I can remember these. 'Death stalked me on the moor.' 'I stumbled through the cold and darkness, not knowing where I was going.' . . . 'I staggered on blindly.' 'The wind was the height of frozen wickedness.'"

"Poor devil," I muttered.

Anthony shook his head with ominous meaning. "The moor kills, Jack. But not this time, thank God. It's been cheated of its prey. In summer, these moors smile at us, but in the winter they lie in wait, to kill us in their cold and callous cruelty."

I broke in. "You're forgetting that I'm in the dark. Tell me Copeland's story, as you were able to piece it together. You've heard it from him first hand. From the time that he left the Shelleys'. That's the part that I can't fathom. The Lauriston shooting-box is miles out of his way. Also, what's he on the moor for at all?"

"I agree, Jack. *In toto*. This, as far as I have been able to make out, is Copeland's story. By the way, he's not an educated man as you and I would understand the term. You're aware of that, aren't you? So bear it in mind as you listen."

I nodded. "I know all about that. On the other hand, I don't think that he has ever set himself up to be one. He's made money and turned it to advantage. There's no pretence about him. No side at all."

"That's in his favour, I suppose. Here's his story. Pieced together. He left Bysshe Lodge, the Shelleys' place, at a quarter past nine in the evening of Friday, the sixteenth of this month. That confirms what Captain Shelley himself told Colonel Blount, if you remember, when we called there on Monday. Copeland confirms Shelley's story, generally. His car was under repair and had been in dock for some days. He refused Shelley's offer of his own car, he says, because he had but a short walk in front of him and he also says that he thought the walk would do him good. It was very cold, he states (as though we weren't aware of it, too), and there was the usual damp swirling mist that seems inescapable from the moor and its surroundings at this time of the year. Copeland says that he was walking well and was quickly into his stride. Suddenly, he says, he seemed to be enveloped in a sort of eerie coldness. This happened to him without the slightest warning. I questioned him closely about his statement and eventually was able to get him to amplify it. These amplifications which you sometimes get from people help, you know, Jack, no end."

"I know," I replied. "Go on."

"Copeland's amplification was this. He says that it was as though a huge blanket of 'cold' had been wrapped right round him, and there was also, as at the day of Pentecost, 'the sound of a rushing, mighty wind'. He says that, although unnerved, he withstood the power for some little time, and then, completely subdued by it, fell to the ground. As he fell, he says, he heard a shrill cry that came from somewhere close at hand. A cry that he states he cannot get out of his ears to this minute."

My nerves tautened. God—what did it all mean? Burke's story of the three murdered men! Where were we? In England or amongst the devilries of the East? Although my mind rioted, however, I found commonplace words. "What happened after that?"

Anthony Bathurst shook his head. "Ah—there's the rub. Copeland cannot tell me."

"Cannot tell you! What do you mean?"

"Exactly what I say, Jack. *Copeland is unable to tell us.* For the simple reason that he cannot remember any more."

I stared at him in amazement. "Cannot remember any more! How can that be? There's an interval of eight days to be bridged. Where's he been? What's he been doing all the time? Has he been unconscious for eight days? The thing's not feasible, Anthony."

Again my cousin shook his head at me. "Whether it's feasible or not, we're faced with the serious consideration of it because our hands are tied! We can't contradict Copeland. He's the man who has endured the suffering. Nobody else counts."

"But where's he *been*, my dear chap? If he were on his way home from Shelley's place, and he's found on the moor near Lauriston's shooting-box, where's he been during the interval? I know that I'm labouring the question, but dash it all, the doubt of it sticks out a mile."

Anthony shrugged his shoulders. "Well, there you are. There was Chinnery too. You must make of it what you can. Same with me. For whatever we may think of Copeland's little mannerisms, you can't deny that in the main he's a sensible enough fellow. Oh, Lord, I'm sticky all over! All the little theories that I was so carefully cultivating have received the nastiest of set-backs. The shock of their lives! Been jolted right on the solar plexus. Which means that I'm forced to start all over again. And you can take it from me that I'm not sweet on that, Jack, my son."

"Don't suppose you are, for a moment. Well, it's all a sinister, frightening, eerie business. Unnatural. One can cope with ordinary, normal things, like revolvers or knives, or even poison. But this—" I broke off. I am not a fluent man at the best of times and the occasion was far from that.

"It's a deuced long time for a man to be unconscious," said Anthony Bathurst reflectively. "I'm with you there, Jack."

"Was Copeland actually unconscious when he was picked up?"

"So I understood. Surtees reckons that another couple of hours' exposure would have finished him off, and he would have been picked up in exactly the same state as Chinnery was. Lucky break for the Squire, *n'est-ce-pas*?"

"Every time. It means that the thousand to one chance came off. But, tell me. Who picked Copeland up?"

"Whom do you think, Jack?"

I stared at him.

"Six guesses," he threw at me.

I thought for a time. Then decided to venture on a choice.

"I know . . . I feel certain I'm going to be right. Foxon . . . Luke Foxon."

"You've clicked—first time. Fifty cigarettes or a box of chocolates? How *do* you do it, Jack?"

I took his mood.

"It's a gift, my dear Watson," I returned. "My mother could do it before me."

He grinned at me. Then suddenly became grave again. "This cry that Copeland heard, Jack. What do you make of that? 'A shrill cry.' Would you mind doing me a favour?"

"Not at all. What do you want me to do?"

"When I came down the other day in response to your S.O.S. you told me a yarn about a yarn. Remember?"

I watched him carefully. I knew what was coming.

"Go on," I returned quietly.

"I expect you've already guessed what I'm getting at. I'm refer-ring to that yarn that was spun for you, and to you, by Major Burke, at Verschoyle's dinner-party."

"Yes. I guessed right. I knew that you were referring to that. Well—what about it?"

"Tell me of it again. In Burke's actual words, as closely as you can remember them."

I did as he had requested me. He punctuated my recital with a succession of nods, listening right through the story without a word of interruption. When I had finished he spoke.

"'The cry of a stuck pig.' They were Major Burke's words?"

"Yes. I'm sure of that. They made an impression on me."

"Have you ever studied the Yogi idea of trans-migration? That final reunion with a universal principle in which they believe? Instant loss of individuality and immediate absorption into the universal at death?"

"Of course not. What do you think I do in my spare time?"

"We're a scatty crowd, Jack. The more I think things over, the more I realize it. We hang a murderer who kills in the heat of the moment, or who murders for jealousy or revenge, but a wholesale slaughterer who goes to war on an innocent race of people, who bombs women and children, who drops death and destruction on Red Cross hospitals, well—we usually conclude by giving him the rank in history of 'great man'. It won't do, you know, Jack. It won't do at all. We shall be forced to readjust our ideas one day. And the sooner the better." He stared into the fire.

"But don't you think that matters generally work out more or less justly in the end?"

"That the right adjusts itself, do you mean? *A brebis tondue le bon Dieu mésure le vent?* Well, that's a good French proverb and I won't say that France has all the faith of it."

I grew impatient. "The horror of this moor business is getting me down. I have such little confidence, I suppose, in the official police."

"That's your modern complex. You're handicapped by it because you can't get away from it. Notable writers, have, I admit, somewhat humoured our beliefs in the fatuity of the professional detective. But more, I think, to exalt their own brilliant creations, their Sherlock Holmes, Hanaud, Poirot, Inspector French, Colonel Gethryn, Philo Vance, and Ellery Queen, rather than to discredit a singularly capable body of men, which, after all, has a persistent record of success behind it to justify its being. Besides, you and I are here, Jack, and two heads of the calibre of our two are very much better than one. We may yet be successful in placing our offering before a British jury. Those '*probi et legales homines*' to the tale of twelve."

I made no comment on this last speech of his. I was thinking more directly. Chinnery was but a shell. A voiceless thing. And Copeland had had the narrowest escape. Chinnery could speak no more for himself. Could tell us nothing. But Copeland, by a lucky chance, could, and had already done so. Up to a point, that is. I could visualize the thin, weak-lined face of Chinnery making mute entreaty for soul-salvation against the Thing that had hurt him to his body's death. Against the monstrous terror which had trapped and then devoured him. My cousin was quick to discern my detachment. He startled me.

"There's one thing about Copeland that I haven't yet told you."

I looked at him curiously. I wondered what was coming. This propensity of Anthony Bathurst's for holding information back might be dramatic and all that, and effective curtain stuff, but it was devilishly irritating for the man who had it passed on to him belatedly. You never knew quite where you were with him. "What is it?" I exclaimed rather sullenly. "Why don't you spill all the beans whilst you're about it?"

He still kept me waiting. "What do you think it is?"

"Can't think. Too puzzled by nearly everything."

Still he played me. "Try."

I thought. Vainly, for a time, and then the blinding truth flashed into my brain. "Behind the ears?" I whispered hoarsely.

My cousin nodded corroboration. "Behind the ears," he repeated. "You have it in one, Jack."

"The two red burns?"

"Well—hardly. But almost. On this occasion they are pink scratches, rather. Much more like abrasions than burns. I've seen them and that's how I should describe them."

"Are they painful, does Copeland say? Any explanation as to how he got them?"

"I don't think that they can be too painful." He eyed me strangely. An idea came to me, born of his look.

"Why don't you think so?"

"Because I don't think that Copeland *knows* he has them. I don't think he knows that they're there. Because he has never once, I understand, referred to them. I don't feel much doubt on the point."

"Strange," I commented.

"Well, I suppose, after all, that it's understandable. If Copeland has been unconscious, or semi-conscious, that perhaps is the better term, he probably wouldn't have the slightest knowledge that the marks had been made behind his ears. His back might have been tattooed with the Thirty-nine Articles and he would still remain in complete ignorance of the fact. So that when you come to weight it all up, it's not really so strange after all."

I reflected over what he had said and came to the conclusion that I agreed with him. I said as much. Anthony looked at his watch. "I'm going to bed, Jack. And I don't think I'll trouble to hang up my stocking. Somehow the place down here doesn't seem to me generous enough. Father Christmas will give it a miss. In other words—there don't seem too many who are qualified to awake and salute the happy morn."

I knocked out the ashes of my pipe and stood up to face him. "Anthony," I started.

He held up his hand as though bidding me to listen to something. "Hark," he said quietly, "the Waits! What a travesty of things as we know them." I listened for the second time to the voices of the St.

Crayle choir. Verschoyle's was clear above the rest. "See amid the winter snow". Again I shivered. Snow—of all things. My body was low, I suppose. I had been sitting still for some time, my limbs were cramped and the time was midnight. The clock of St. Crayle church struck twelve. I counted the strokes. Clear and vibrant on the December air. I can't remember ever doing such a thing before and I know that I have never done it since. Anthony Bathurst looked at me.

"Christmas Day, Jack," he said. "Unto us a child is born. Peace on earth. But—'to men of goodwill', remember that! I have known the message misquoted."

The shivers possessed me. All round my loins.

"If you ask me," I said, "it gets colder every day."

CHAPTER XV
CHRISTMAS DAY, EARLY MORNING

I WAS just getting into bed on that Christmas morning when there came a tap on my bedroom door. I knew that it must be Anthony Bathurst. So I sang out at once, "Come in."

He was at my side in a jiffy. "Jack," he said, "if you want to have a good look at a thrice-blasted, doddering fool, buy me as the premier Christmas Annual. That is to say—'Help Yourself'."

Not understanding, I sat on the edge of the bed. "What's biting you now?"

"Chinnery! Chinnery's body! We saw it in the mortuary together, didn't we?"

I nodded. "Was it such a thrill that you must come and recite about it at this time in the morning?"

"Oh, don't get stuffy. You might be as dead as Chinnery is, and as Copeland might have been, but for a stroke of amazing luck. Consider yourself blessed."

"*That* idea, that there's somebody always worse off than you yourself, if you only take the trouble to find him, *never* cuts any ice with me. My jaw always aches just as badly and my headache's usually worse. Sorry—and all that."

He grinned at me. "Well, listen to me for half a minute, now, and then you'll understand why I've worried you to tell you how I've been such a prize ass."

"Oh, all right. Get it over. But make it snappy."

"Remember Chinnery's face as he lay dead in that mortuary?"

"Haven't been able to forget it. Why?"

"What was the growth of hair on the face? His beard, for instance. And *remember*, before you answer, that hair grows to a certain extent after death."

It didn't take me long to find the reply to that. "I didn't notice any beard, really. Not what you would call 'beard'. But what's your point? Tell me!"

"Why this! How long did old Surtees say that Chinnery had been dead?"

"He didn't say."

"No. He took a good deal for granted. Far too much, in my opinion. The idea of foul play was anathema to him. When I asked him about the findings of his P.M. he was inclined to tell me very little. I observed that particularly. Chinnery had been on the moor, and, as a result, had died from cold and exposure! That was good enough for him and it should, in his idea, have been good enough for the lay mind as well. As you know, I didn't agree. If my opinion's worth anything, if it hadn't been for the red marks behind the corpse's ears, Surtees wouldn't have bothered about a P.M. at all. Now do you see what I'm getting at?"

I shook my head. "Candidly, Anthony Lotherington Bathurst, I don't. Should I?"

"You should, my son. Even though it's a time when all good people should be in bed. *How* long was Chinnery missing? Now, tell me that."

I thought. "Over a week. Eight days—wasn't it?"

"Exactly. Eight days. And as I said a moment ago, hair, the *growth* of hair, doesn't stop directly the body, as we know it, *dies*. Well, *now* where are we?"

I saw his point and said so. "You mean that Chinnery—"

He interrupted me fiercely. "I mean this. Jack Clyst. No more and no less. Where was Chinnery when he shaved himself or who shaved him? *For shaved, between disappearing and dying, he certainly must have been.*"

Again I shook my head.

"And *why*?" He flung the last question at me almost vehemently. I still could find no answer which I considered would satisfy him.

"I'm inclined to think. Jack, that this is where our cunning murderer has made his first big mistake. But *why*? That's the point that I can't feel sure about. When I do find the clue to that, things will begin to move, believe me. I'll promise you that before anything. Give me a cigarette, will you? And don't be so damned silent. Why button up those ruby lips?"

I found the cigarettes in the pocket of my jacket and handed them to him. Then collared my dressing-gown and put it on. "If you aren't cold," I said, "I am, and I've no desire to get any colder. If such a condition is possible, which I very much doubt."

He walked to the window of the bedroom and looked out. There was a dark, deathly calm. Everywhere. The Waits had come and gone. Again I heard the church clock at St. Crayle striking. Away in the distance across the moor could still be heard the dull moan of the sea. Bathurst came back from the window.

"It is cold," he remarked with surprising cheerfulness, "you're right. I shouldn't be surprised if it got colder. After Christmas, I mean. As the day lengthens, so the cold strengthens."

But my thoughts were not where his were. "Red marks on Chinnery," I said. "Not so red marks, you say, on Copeland? I can't quite understand that."

He came over and sat again on the side of the bed, smoking quickly all the time. "There's just this about it. The marks are not terribly unlike the skin-scorching that's found in a lightning-stroke." I looked at him. He went on, still smoking jerkily and nervously. "Lightning scorchings on the skin very often assume a curious branching, tree-like arrangement, according to the way in which the electric fluid has swept over it."

"I've always thought that the marks you are speaking of were supposed to be lightning photographs of a tree or some other object in the neighbourhood of the place where the victim was struck. Isn't that so?"

He shook his head at me.

"Only popular belief, Jack. Nothing more than that. No scientific basis for it."

"No?"

"No, laddie. The belief is very similar to that other popular creed concerning thunderstorms. That it is unwise to take shelter under a tree during a thunder-storm. As a matter of fact, a beech tree is *never* assailed by lightning. But a lot of people don't know that. In many places in the country they go a bit further and argue it to be impossible for a person sheltering under a beech tree to be struck. So there you are. Make what you can of it."

"Two different men wouldn't be struck at different times in the same place. On the same part of the body, I mean—"

"No," he said thoughtfully, taking another cigarette. "I agree with you there, Jack. The coincidence would be far too amazing."

"Good job we agree about something."

"Yes. A house divided against itself cannot stand. What time will you be up in the morning?"

"Well, that's a bit of a question. Thanks to you, I'm not in bed yet."

"Don't worry. You soon will be, Jack. I shan't keep you much longer."

"That's good of you," I grunted.

"I want to be out fairly early. Will you come with me?"

"Christmas morning?"

"It's already that, Jack."

"It depends. What time do you want to be out?"

"As soon as it's light."

"Why go to bed at all?"

"We haven't yet," he grinned at me.

"All right," I returned. "I've brought it all on myself. I invited you down here. Give me a knock when you're ready."

"Good for you, Jack. I knew that you wouldn't let me down. Cheero, then, and good night." He closed my bedroom door and I got into bed. But it was a long time before sleep came to me, and when it did it seemed that I had no sooner slumbered off than I heard my cousin's tap on the bedroom door.

Half an hour later saw me ready and waiting. Anthony joined me in the hall. I left word with Mrs. Polglose with regard to breakfast and once again we closed the door of Scarpe behind us. The frost still lay heavily upon the earth. The sea, according to what our ears told us, was still calm. Away over where we knew the water was, flocks of sea-birds wheeled and flew. The air was deathly still with that clear cold stillness that is so definitely December's and no other month's. I could hear the church bell of St. Crayle distantly, calling the faithful to their act of worship. As I listened, I heard the bell stop. In my imagination, I saw Verschoyle coming to the front of the altar and giving to his faithful congregation the opening words of the Communion Service. 'Our Father which art in Heaven'. Then a question from my companion broke the trend of my thought.

"How many approaches are there to that part of the moor where the Lauriston shooting-box is?"

I thought. "Only one really, and that's the usual one from the road. Any other way to it would take hours."

"Good," replied Anthony. "That's what I wanted you to say."

"Glad to have been of some assistance."

"Don't mention it," he returned with his usual grin.

We came at last to the edge of Constanton Moor. So far not a soul had passed us. Not even an outlying farm worker intent on attendance at St. Crayle Church. Once again we stepped off the road on to the moorland path. I at once noticed how closely A.L.B. watched the rimed grass. More than once he stepped aside from the path to look keenly at a particular stretch of grass that was coarse and frozen.

"I'm right, Jack," he said. "There's been a car along here and not so very long ago, either. See how the grass is brushed and flat in places, every now and then? Please God we shan't altogether waste our time here this morning."

I made no comment and eventually we came to the particular spot where Foxon and I, and after that, Anthony and I, had heard those eerie, synchronized footsteps. On this Christmas morning, however, no sound of them came to greet our ears.

"You think that Chinnery and Copeland were brought by car?" I questioned him.

He hesitated before shaking his head. "I shouldn't like to be cock-sure about it. Either brought in a car or a car came along afterwards. I fancy you'll find, though, that a car has been employed, shall we say, on the two cases? Certainly on one of them Lucky for you, you don't run a car, Jack."

"Thanks," I returned him. "I shall want you on my side; if Blount and Surtees come along and find me so close to the scene of the murder, I shall probably be arrested at sight. You know the idea—that so many people hold—a murderer always returns to the spot where the murder was committed. Criminal psychology!" Then I became severely practical. "Shan't be sorry when we get back to the Polglose 'brekker'."

"Nor I . . ."

We passed the old quarry of Priestley's. I looked at Anthony Bathurst, but he gave me no sign. So his idea was to go on further. I didn't know that I was prepared for that. We came to a place where there was an old disused mine. One of the ancient tin-mines that had long since ceased to give its ore for the use of man. Anthony walked towards it. I followed him.

"Tresarth's Mine," I said to my cousin. "Not been in use for years."

"It has, Jack," he said almost passionately. "Look there, and *there*!"

I looked and saw the tyre marks of a car. There were two of them. Also the stub of a cigarette. Anthony stooped and picked it up.

"Players," he said ruefully. "Who doesn't smoke Players? Tell me, will you?"

"What's this, then?" I said. "Where are we? H.Q. generally?"

"Don't know, but it makes you wonder, doesn't it?" He stood there touching the ground with his stick. Then he swung round on to me with a question. "How far to Lauriston's shooting-box from here, Jack?" I calculated the distance. "Half a mile—not more."

"H'm. That should have suited them all right. But much farther to the old quarry—eh?"

"From here? Obviously. We've just walked it, haven't we?"

"Yes, of course."

"Going on to Lauriston's now?"

"No. I don't think so. Shan't find anything there, if I do."

"How do you know?"

"Because anything worth finding won't be there."

"Why not?"

"Because, my dear Jack, it will be somewhere else. And if you can find me a better reason than that, maybe you'll tell me." He eyed me quizzically.

"Well, you seem to know," I declared, "so I'll take your word for it." I walked to the edge of the mine again and looked down the shaft. Somehow or other, the depth of it fascinated me. Depths and heights of an unusual measure always have done. Right from the days of my early boyhood. Anthony Bathurst came to the side of the shaft and stood beside me. As I took my eyes away, having gazed my fill, I caught his fixed on me.

"Penny for 'em. What are you thinking of, Jack? I'm interested. What's the bright idea?"

I shook my head. "Nothing much. Heights and the bowels of the earth have a knack of sobering me. Always have had. That's all."

He turned aside. "Hallo! This is interesting. They've left an old iron scaling-ladder there, Jack. Look!" My cousin pointed to one side of the shaft.

I looked and saw the ladder that he indicated. "Does breakfast interest you, Holmes?" I asked him. "Because it most certainly does me." I held my wrist-watch in front of him rather pointedly. He nodded. We turned immediately and began to walk back to Scarpe. For some time he said nothing. Actually he was silent until we reached the road again. Here, naturally, we began to meet people. Many of them coming back from the service at St. Crayle church. Two cars passed us. I had little difficulty in identifying them. The first was Captain Shelley's, the other was Vincent's, the man who had been amongst the company at Shelley's place on the evening that Copeland had disappeared. Shelley and Lady Rachel acknowledged us, Shelley himself with a stiff bow, Lady Rachel with a gracious smile. Vincent, as I've said, I knew but little, and his car swept by us unceremoniously as we stepped to one side and gave it the right of the road.

Anthony looked at me askance as it passed us. "In a hurry—eh? Who was in that car, Jack?"

"Vincent," I replied curtly. "The retired army surgeon, of whom I told you. Clement Vincent."

"Oh yes, I remember now! The chap with the invalid wife, you mean, don't you? He didn't seem to recognize you, Jack. Even on a Yuletide morning. Is that his usual style?"

"Well, I've met him out once or twice, but that's about the lot. He keeps himself very much to himself. We aren't bosom companions, by any means."

"Seventy odd, you said, didn't you? Glad he's been to church this Christmas morning. Seems full of love and charity towards his fellow men, which you and I can undoubtedly call ourselves, Jack. But never mind. He's passed and gone. I've begun to agree with you concerning the attractions of an early meal. When we reached Scarpe we found that the Polglose had surpassed herself. Anthony and I did more than justice to her magnificent efforts. The morning walk had put an edge on each of our appetites. As I was lighting a cigarette to go with my last cup of coffee, I was surprised to see my cousin take an envelope from the breast-pocket of his coat. "Christmas card," I murmured. "What is it, a ship in full sail, snow with a robin red-breast, or distant view of a five-barred gate?" He opened the flap, which I saw had been tucked in, and carefully shook something into the palm of his left hand. This done, he held the something out to me, still on the palm of his hand, for my inspection. I gazed at it curiously. Then I put my curiosity into words.

"What the devil have you got there?"

I had decided that I was looking at what appeared to me to be three light-green hairs.

"What do you think they are?"

"They look like hairs, green hairs. Where from, in the name of goodness?"

"I'd very much like to know. That is to say, from where they came in the original instance." I still stared at the hairs on the palm of his hand.

"But where did you get them?" I asked him.

He looked me straight in the eyes as he answered me. "They came, my dear Jack, from the right shoulder of the dead Chinnery's coat. His overcoat, to be precise. Mrs. Chinnery was good enough to let me look at the clothes that he was wearing when his body was discovered near Priestley's Quarry."

"You went to Chinnery's house?"

"Of course I did. I said that I did. How else could I have got them?"

Somehow or other I experienced a feeling of resentment at his statement and I protested. "You didn't tell me that you had been there. I don't remember that you even hinted at such a thing. That you ever even thought of going."

"Diddums," he grinned at me, "and is he so upset? Now wasn't that too bad of me." But he wasn't making me cross in that way, oh dear, no! I flatter myself that I'm too old a bird to be caught like that.

"It doesn't matter two hoots to me, of course," I said evenly. "I merely thought that we were running this job in a sort of partnership, and that I was being kept conversant with all that you were doing. If I had an erroneous idea, overlook it. I shall know better what to think next time."

Anthony eyed me curiously—almost as though a new thought had found its way into his brain. He made no further remark, however, on the particular matter. Neither did I. Instead, I ostentatiously buried the hatchet with much pomp and ceremony, and asked more questions.

"Can't you find out exactly what those 'hairs' are?" I asked him.

"Oh, easily," he returned. "No trouble at all—but what's the real point behind your question?"

"Well—just this. Do you think that the hairs are the hairs of an animal?"

He lit a cigarette before he replied to me. Even threw away the match, before he found the words that he wanted for his eventual reply to me.

"Do you know any animal that runs about this wicked world with green hair?"

I thought for a time. "Don't think that I do. I can only think of birds. A green parrot. But not animals."

My cousin shook his head at me. "These are hairs, my lad, not feathers! Parrots are barred."

"Not an animal, then?"

"Don't think so, Jack, for a minute. Sorry to disappoint you, if you've a genuine love for animals, and are really keen on the idea."

I grew impatient with him. I consider that I was justified. "Green hairs from what, then? There must be some explanation of their presence here."

"Yes, I suppose there is. If we are clever enough to find it. Which I doubt."

"Have *you* found it?" I questioned him closely. His manner intrigued me. He pursed his lips.

"Don't know, Jack. Yet awhile. Haven't more than the glimmering of an idea. May be right. May be wrong. Probably am. The latter, I mean. But I think this—that those hairs came from the floor of somewhere."

"From the floor of a house, do you mean?" I was incredulous.

"Well, something like that, Jack. Listen, and I'll tell you what I'm thinking. No more and no less. That Chinnery's body *lay* somewhere—prostrate in all probability—before it came to its last resting-place on Constanton Moor. And, wherever it lay, it picked up those three green hairs. All this in strictest confidence, old man. I don't want a word of this breathed round the countryside. It's too important, by far." The emphasis of his last sentence rang out sharply. He meant me to take him in all seriousness. I nodded my promise to him. He carefully replaced the three green hairs in the envelope from which he had previously taken them, and, in turn, put back the envelope within his pocket-book. Then he walked to the window.

"What is it that links Chinnery with Copeland, Jack?" he asked, his back turned towards me.

"Nothing," I returned decisively. "Nothing that I know."

"Yet there must be a connection somewhere," he said meditatively. "*Must* be?"

"Oh—I think so. Otherwise I can't see any other reason behind the two affairs. The wheel of this crime-chariot that we're considering revolves so steadily and so relentlessly, that I feel certain I'm right. First Chinnery, then Copeland! And then, Jack, after Copeland—who next?" He spoke his final sentence with ominous quietness.

I shook my head at him hopelessly. Then shivered. Iciness came to me again and held my loins. "Who next?" It wasn't that I was afraid for myself. Don't think that. It was the uncertainty of it all. The thought that we were gradually coming to our respective personal contacts with the danger-zone. One by one. Who next? Anthony Bathurst came and sat at my side again. He repeated his question. Almost in a whisper. "Who next?"

CHAPTER XVI
OLD YEAR'S NIGHT, 5.30

DURING the next week matters in the two tragic parishes of St. Crayle and St. Roseworthy hung fire. Seven days, but seven days of comparative emptiness. Try as I would, I was unable to rid my brain of my cousin's ominous words of Christmas Day, "Who next?" As I've explained more than once in this history of the horrors that befell our tiny stretch of countryside during that memorable winter, periods of suspense are always far more trying to me than spells of fierce activity, no matter how fraught with personal peril those latter periods may be. I have no doubt that fear of the unknown is one of the oldest emotions to have harried and beset mankind. Right from the early times, when units had become families, and families formed into tribes, I presume that we first began the cultivation of the herd instinct in order to protect our naked, unwashed bodies against preying beasts, such as wolves, and then, after that, having successfully prevailed over the wolves and their kind, by reason of our superior numerical strength, we discovered that a condition of defence was the next step towards us becoming, in turn, flagrantly offensive. I mentioned these thoughts of mine to Anthony Bathurst, and it was the cause of him at once unloosing an attack upon what he was pleased to describe contemptuously as our so-called civilization.

"You call us civilized," he said to me, almost mockingly; "for the love of Mike, don't ask me to be a wholesale dispenser of cynicism. Are you going to insist that we are more civilized than the Greeks round Socrates? Or than the Romans were in Cicero's time? Than the Italians were when Leonardo held sway? Than our own English people who lived as contemporaries of Sir Thomas More? Would you assert such a thing? My dear Jack, if you tell me that we definitely are, you're most unashamedly asking for trouble."

I shook my head. I refused the challenge to argument. Wisely, I think. For in the main, I must confess that I agreed with him.

Blount had telephoned two or three times to Anthony at Scarpe since Christmas, but I had not heard from my cousin that any of these communications was to be considered as important. If it were so, he had kept the news to himself. Although, since the obvious resentment that I had showed over his visit to Mrs. Chinnery, about which he had kept me in ignorance, he had been much more frank with me than hitherto, with regard to his activities generally. Nevertheless there was this point to be considered. He had not told me any more concerning the three green hairs and I hadn't been privileged to see them again. Nor had he, as far as I knew, looked at them himself. He continued to spend his days much as he had spent them prior to the Christmas break. The weather now was a trifle milder and in consequence of this he was able to get out more frequently and, when out, to stay out for considerably longer periods. Although, however, the extreme cold and frost and white fog had gone from us, the local weather experts were unanimously agreed that the change would be but temporary and that the old conditions of severity would return to worry us again ere long. Every time that Anthony Bathurst returned to Scarpe after part of a day away from me, he would return with a thoughtful brow and questions on his lips. On the last day of the month of December, a Saturday it was, he came in about half past five in the evening. I was sitting in the armchair in the dining-room. It had been a wet and entirely miserable afternoon and as a result I had stayed indoors instead of going up to the game at Hawthorns as had been my original intention. There was an attractive fixture there and I also thought there was a reasonable chance of Sybil Burke being there, which drew me more. When he came in, Mrs. Polglose was almost ready with dinner and I was feeling equally ready to eat it.

"Ah, Jack," he said, as he entered, "I have leisure, thank goodness, to interest myself in your neighbours. I am deeply grateful for the opportunity. It was a marvellous kindness, really, for you to thrust this grand opportunity upon me."

I nodded and pushed a chair towards him. He took it gratefully, and I saw at once that his face showed unmistakable signs of tiredness. He ate silently. The evening passed. Eventually, over a drink, I questioned him.

"Been far?" I asked him curtly.

"Fair to middling. Up to all sorts of things if I tell the plain and unvarnished truth. Sea-watching. Rock-scrambling. Grass-searching. Been as far as the coastguard station. Right over the moors for some distance beyond the Lauriston shooting-box. I found a boulder, Jack. Jutting out from all the others. So much of a piece with turf and rock that the sea-pinks had seeded in its roof and encrusted it with emerald tufts. A marvellous business, you know, Jack, when you come to consider it. By the way, whose is that tumble-down white cottage on the cliff beyond the coastguard station? Any idea?"

"Don't know," I returned. "Haven't been so far as that for years. Ask Verschoyle, if you're really anxious to know."

"You've missed a treat, if you haven't walked as far as I have to-day. It's a glorious walk. This cottage that I mentioned has two rooms and a wash-house, below green eaves. I pictured myself as its inhabitant, Jack. My fancy adorned the tenement. I saw myself the hermit of the cliff's edge, companioned only by weather and wind and sea. What a life, Jack! Idyllic. Freedom, unfettered space, and superb promise. The sun came out. The wind was even warm. You know—'All suddenly the wind comes soft, and spring is here again'. I came back over rock and then woodland. The black earth, freed from the tyranny of the frost, oozed black water where I trod. All my walking began to get rough and boggy. More than once, Jack, I was perilously near being mired. At last I came to the ledge near Priestley's Quarry. The ledge that I'll call the 'Chinnery' ledge. Past that mass—a little farther along—of tumbled stones, spiked at their tops as though they had once been giant knives. Know the particular heap to which I refer?"

I nodded my affirmative. I did. Not so long before I had hurt a foot there.

"Near there is that stone-built house of Vincent's. I had a good look round it. I find myself just a wee bit interested in Mr. Vincent. How long did you say he'd been knocking round these 'ere parts?"

"For years, my lad. I can't say how long exactly. But when I came down here to live, he was here and had been here for years. Nearly twenty, I should say, if I had to answer. You didn't meet him on your previous visits at all, did you?"

"Nary a once, Jack. Wish I had. I should probably have learnt more about him."

I grunted. It all seemed to be leading nowhere.

"What's he like to look at, Jack? Beyond that he ain't talkative, and don't like the world, you haven't told me much about him. Give me a pen-picture with your tongue. Don't worry." He grinned at me. "That's all right. I admit to being Irish, quite cheerfully."

"He's a thin, sharp-featured man. Near-sighted, so I've been told, by people who know him fairly well. Wears horn-rimmed glasses. Taken to them in more recent years. When he's dressed for an 'occasion', he wears white spats, I believe. But don't be annoyed with me because of that."

"Seventy-odd, you said, didn't you?"

"Must be—every bit of it."

"Go on. Tell me more. The topographical situation of the Vincent residence intrigues me."

"I shall have to think before I can give you much more. As I've already told you, the old man and I haven't a great deal in common."

"No. So I understand. All the same, put in a spot of thinking for me. It's in a good cause, you know, Jack."

"Well, I'll try, but only a part of this will be from what I've actually *seen*. A good deal more will be from what I've *heard*. That is to say, all second-hand stuff. He's a stiff-shouldered man. Holds himself very erect. Has, I believe, literary tastes. A library much above the average, so I've heard. Nearly all selected, bound, and, I hear on good authority, even read by himself. A lean man. About your own height. Leisurely in all his movements." I paused to ask him a question. "How am I doing?"

"All right. I hope you haven't finished, though. I wanted more personal characteristics than physical indications. See what I mean?"

I started again. "His servants like him. They must do. They stay with him. He's had the same chauffeur, for example, for years. Greatly interested in—what's the word they use nowadays—'civics'. Been chairman of This and That. Guardians and, I fancy, quarter sessions. Took it up after he retired from the army."

"Sportsman?"

I hesitated.

"Don't forget that nearly all this that I'm telling you has been gathered from hearsay. I should call him a sporting patron rather than an actual sportsman. Subscribes liberally to most of the sporting activities in the district. I've seen his name in the lists that are published in the local papers. Drives a car, as you've seen. Never heard of him handling a gun. He's a man who's got 'masked' features. Let me try to explain that more fully. When he, as it were, makes a deliberately measured advance, his movements, as he does it, are more subdued than obviously forward. Got my meaning?"

"H'm. I think so. What's Mrs. V. like? Let me see, you did tell me something about her, didn't you?"

"I told you that she was, or so I believed, an invalid. Very little is ever seen of her. I've been told that when he married her she brought him a little money. I've seen her. Once or twice. But not lately. I've an idea at the back of my mind that there was an accident at some time or the other. She hurt her back in some way. But my memory's pretty vague on the point, so don't bank on it."

"Are they all right together? Fit in amicably, I mean?"

I shrugged my shoulders. "Who can tell? That's a question which I would never presume to attempt to answer. About any husband and wife anywhere. In marriage, you know, there is one who loves and one who allows herself or himself to be loved."

"I suppose you're right, and that I asked a foolish question." He fell to silence.

I looked at the time. My wrist-watch showed the hands at just on midnight. If my watch were right, which I had no reason to doubt, there were but four minutes of the old year to go. I stooped to the side-board to get out another bottle of whisky. I thought of the moor! Of Chinnery! Dead and cold. Of Copeland, cold and not quite dead. Saved, in the nick of time, by the skin of his teeth. Strangely enough, Anthony must have been watching me, and, in some queer way, have fathomed the working of my mind.

"How's Copeland getting on now? Have you heard of him at all during the week?"

I turned to him deliberately. "How did you know?"

"How did I know what?"

"That I was thinking of Copeland?"

"I didn't exactly *know*, but I felt pretty certain that your thoughts were somewhere in that direction. You looked towards the window, and your face, well, it wasn't happy, Jack."

It was at that precise second that I heard the bells, Verschoyle's bells of St. Crayle, ringing out the Old Year and ringing in the New. I walked to the window before I answered my cousin's question concerning the health of the Squire. As I looked out across the moor, it seemed darker than ever. The night had drawn huge black curtains across the dome of the sky. The moor was again shrouded in a veil of mist. Everything around was so exquisitely quiet, except for the chimes of the church bells, that you could hear distinctly, intermittently between their sounds, the Crayle Beck crisping over the smooth shining pebbles and swishing its impertinent way between the great boulders that, in parts, fringed Constanton Moor. I sensed that Anthony Bathurst was standing at the window behind me. With me, he watched the night, or indeed, as it was now, the new morning of our newest year. For some time we remained there together. For an unmeasured time. I could almost hear my cousin's heart beating and could even imagine that I could hear, too, the throb of the pulses in his temples. It was he who broke a silence that to me had become almost intolerable.

"Well, Jack? You didn't answer my question with regard to Copeland. I am still waiting."

As I answered him, the bells of St. Crayle ceased their ringing.

"Copeland? I understand that he's better. Almost fit, in fact. But he's a man with a wonderful constitution. You mustn't forget that. Look at his physique, too. A different proposition from Chinnery. Very different." A sudden thought struck me. Something that hadn't occurred to me before, or, at any rate, something I hadn't mentioned to my cousin. I turned to him. "I say," I said, "will the murderer have another cut at Copeland, do you think? Will that be the next item on the programme?"

Anthony Bathurst turned deliberately and looked at me. I could see the gleam in his grey eyes.

"I consider that proposition to be well on the cards, laddie."

"*Before* 'who next?'" I muttered in a hoarse whisper.

"Quite likely, I think."

I caught my breath at the realization of what his words meant. At that moment, there came something which, if I live to be as old as Methuselah, I shall not be able to forget. Across the moor, clear and horrifying, came a long-drawn-out wailing scream. The cry of a soul in agony. It seemed to come from a long way away, and trail off, as it were, because the distance between it and us was gradually becoming greater. As, for instance, the cry of a seagull impresses itself upon the human ear, as the bird that gives it wheels out to sea. Then, immediately following the cry that we had heard, there came a second cry, which lasted for a much shorter time. This second cry broke off suddenly as though a huge hand had been placed across the throat that uttered it and the sound had been choked at birth. My cousin turned and faced me. I could see that even his nerve was affected.

"What in God's name was that?" I asked him, my voice scarcely under control.

He pulled himself together before he replied to me.

"More trouble, I fancy, Jack." He spoke quietly. "Probably the answer to your question of Christmas Day—'who next?' As things are, we look like having an extremely happy New Year."

A draught from the window caught me and chilled me to the bone.

Chapter XVII
NEW YEAR'S DAY, 12.15 A.M.

I GLANCED at him, and there were both fear and apprehension in my glance. "Your dinner at the Rectory, Jack, has a rare lot to answer for, hasn't it?" He had turned quickly away from the window before speaking. I followed him.

"What do you mean by that statement—exactly?"

"Oh, to hell with it!" he exclaimed impatiently. "We'll call it the inspiration and understanding of Martin Burke, and leave it at that. Come on. Get a move on, for the love of Mike."

"Why?" I exclaimed stupidly. "What for? Where are you going?"

"*We*, my dear Jack, are going on the moor. Now! And this time we'll use my car. For speed and safety. Get your hat and overcoat on at once. Even seconds at this point may be valuable to us."

Almost mechanically, I obeyed Anthony Bathurst's orders. I beat back panic bravely and within a short space of time joined him in the car. Almost noiselessly, we ran on to the road and then, believe me, Anthony trod on the juice. In an incredibly short time we came to the edge of Constanton Moor. He drove the car from the road and fiercely towards the grass-track that I had so often walked in the past. We drove on—blindly almost—or so it seemed to me. At the same tearing pace that we had forced along the road. Anthony was preoccupied and silent. Not a word had passed his lips since we had started out on this wild journey. The dark and forbidding moor country stretched all round us. There seemed no break in it. I concluded, after a time, that we must be perilously close to Priestley's Quarry. The wind was north-west and freshening considerably. The mist was flying before it. The world around me looked dim and silently sinister. It seemed estranged entirely and eternally from happiness and sunshine. Very soon, if we carried on from here, the moorland would become almost trackless. Tatters of torn clouds showed dark across the sky. Anthony flung sudden words at me.

"We travel over bones, Jack."

He startled me. "Whose?" I whispered to him, fearfully.

He laughed and shook his head at me. "Don't worry, old man. Nothing as ghastly as you're thinking. Not on your life. I referred to the bones of ancient Britons that have lain here for centuries. Not to any victim of our local terror."

I nodded my relief. For it is true to say that I was relieved.

"What's your objective?" I asked him.

"Don't know quite. I'm really looking out for *anything*. Any sign or shape or hint of anything. You help me. We heard that cry, didn't we? You heard it as well as I. It came from somewhere on this accursed moor. This, therefore, is the place where we should be. More than that, where we *are*. It's appropriate. Keep your eyes skinned, Jack. Your side of the road. I'll look after my side. I think I'll run her as far as the Lauriston shooting-box. O.K.?"

I nodded again to him to show that I understood.

"There's one thing, Jack," he muttered, as the car swept on, "you've certainly taken me most effectively from the *dolce far niente* and plunged me recklessly into violence and restlessness. There are times when I don't know whether you deserve thanking or not."

"Sorry," I returned curtly.

He grinned. "That's all right. Don't trouble to apologize. It will end in my thanking heaven again for the trivialities of life, and then I shall throw more bonnets over the mill."

We had run into a patch of wet mist again.

"Don't tell me that anybody ever called this 'God's own country', Jack. It must have been a man stirring deliriously in a sun-spattered dream."

I made no reply. Truth to tell, I was in no mood for conversation. He rallied me.

"Silence, my dear Jack, is *not* golden. Don't you kid yourself. It is much closer to the pigs. Stable-companion of contentment. Your silent man is a monstrous egotist. Every time. A man who plays the reciprocal game of conversation most unfairly. Takes but never gives. Allows himself to be entertained, possibly even enriched, at the expense of a companion. And, all the time, is so soddened with self-complacence and satisfaction that he never feels he owes anything in return. Can't stand the fellow at any price. Golden silence—faugh!"

Thus Anthony Lotherington Bathurst on the heels of murder. I sought more practical issues.

"Why exactly the Lauriston shooting-box? I'm not quite sure that I—"

He turned the wheel quickly in order to avoid a heap of stones. The car was now travelling very slowly.

"Because, if we cover as far as there, laddie, we shall then have covered both of our friends' dumping points. Look at it for yourself. Wasn't Chinnery's body found by Priestley's Quarry? We've passed there! Wasn't Copeland picked up near the Lauriston shooting-box? Well—there you are, then."

Of course! I saw his point at once. How utterly unintelligent my question had been! This thought was still rioting in my brain when I saw my cousin's features stiffen suddenly. Although it was now bitterly cold and the mist hanging in mere patches, he purposely had the window by the driving-seat partly down. With the idea, of course, of seeing better on his side of the moor. I watched him with curious interest. He flung back his head and then braked quickly.

"What is it, Anthony?" I cried excitedly.

"Woman," he replied. "Scent, or something like scent. Can't you smell it? You should be able to. The wind is bringing it our way."

He stopped the car, put the window right down and stuck out his head.

"Somewhere round here! Surely you get it. Jack?"

I shook my head. "I'm the wrong side, old man. You picked it up before I did, and it's in your nostrils."

"I'm getting out, Jack. Come with me. My nose is terribly sensitive. I'll lay a million of anything that I'm right. Wouldn't surprise me if a dame has dropped a 'flap-jack' or something of the kind round about. It's strong enough. That's what it smells like to me."

He jumped from the car in a flash and I followed him.

"Round here somewhere—don't you get it now?" he said, sniffing the cold air like a bloodhound.

I sniffed, and, sure enough, I discovered that he was right. There was no arguing about it. Above all the natural smells that came from the moor, there hung this unmistakable scent of a woman's face toilet.

"It's face-powder, in my opinion," said my cousin. "One of the Piver manufactures. They've an aroma of their own. You can tell 'em anywhere. Trifle, I fancy. There's been a whole heap of it spilled somewhere round here, and it happened not so long ago. That's why it's so pungent, even out of doors. Got your torch, Jack?"

"No," I returned, "I didn't bring it. Got yours?"

I saw the rueful grin that spread over his lean features as he shook his head.

"*Touché*, you cunning old swine."

We scouted round for several yards in various directions, but beyond the scent that occasionally appealed to my nose, there was nothing to reward us for our vigilance. After a time, Anthony gave it up and signalled to me to abandon my search.

"Get in the car, Jack. It's no use wasting any more time over it. It's too dark for us, for one thing. We're only beating the air smelling round here. Easier to find a needle in a haystack. All the same, we know what we know and that's this. A woman's been on this moor tonight."

"Yes. Question is—what woman?"

I got into the car. Anthony did the same, leant across me and slammed the door.

"Whom have we within our field of selection?" he asked pertinently. The car stayed there. Evidently he wanted my answer before we got on the move again. I wrinkled my brows at his question.

"There aren't a lot, are there?"

"No. I know. All the better. Whom can we reasonably include?"

"Copeland has two daughters, then there are Mrs. Chinnery, Lady Rachel Shelley, Mrs. Vincent—the semi-invalid." I hesitated. "Who else is there? Oh—I forgot—Sybil Burke, of course."

"They're the women whom we know. And, semi-invalid or not, Mrs. Vincent went to Shelleys' the night Copeland was got at. What about those women we don't know? Anybody else come to your mind?"

"Well—there's Mrs. Polglose," I said hopefully.

My cousin nodded his head with a suggestion of infinite sagacity. "Yes. We mustn't forget her. That certainly wouldn't do." He started the car. "I'll finish the journey to the Lauriston box, as I intended to do when we started. Though I'm afraid, Jack, that we've arrived too late."

We kept our eyes open, as best we could, all the way to the place where Copeland had been picked up a few days before, but with no success. All was quiet on Constanton Moor. I even found myself wondering, as the car sped along, whether the two screams that had hurt my ears had been conjured up by an excited imagination. Although I knew all the time that what I had heard belonged to the realm of reality. My cousin, Anthony Bathurst, had heard them as well. Two people, each in sound sense, are not the victims of deception at one and the same time. Besides, there was that scented moss-patch. Eventually Anthony turned the car for Scarpe again. Once more he had fallen into a heavy silence. I tested him.

"Well, how now? Regrets over a futile and wasted journey?"

He shook his head. "Not a little bit. It hasn't been wasted. Far from it, in fact. But what happened on the moor tonight, Jack? That's the point that's puzzling me. How would you venture to describe it?"

"I haven't the foggiest. Actually I've caught myself wondering more than once whether I really heard those screams or just dreamt them?"

"You heard them all right, laddie. Don't worry yourself that far. And—what's more—you heard a *woman* scream, which, in itself, is an added morsel of information. Also, you have had the evidence of another sense that a woman has been on the moor tonight. Question for you and me—which woman was it? Up to now, an unanswered question." I could make him no reply, and thus it was that we returned to Scarpe.

I was destined to have little sleep that night, and when I awakened from a fitful doze in the early hours of the morning, the question that still hammered at my brain was the same question that had worried me on Christmas Day and throughout the week following. "Who next?"

CHAPTER XVIII
NEW YEAR'S DAY, 11.30 A.M.

ON THIS occasion, however, the problem that I have just mentioned was not permitted to worry me for very long. The following morning broke with rare beauty and promise for the New Year. Anthony Bathurst, as I have indicated, was an extraordinary creature, who was always able to behold in the sun's rising the undoubted proof of a daily miracle. But on this particular morning his attitude in that respect was easy of understanding. It was a white morning again, but the sun of the new-born January was doing its majestic best to gild the white. My cousin beetled into my bedroom while I was fumbling with socks and shoes.

"Frost in the air again, Jack; a terrific calm over the sea. But the sun is up. And as this old earth spins and wheels round that sun, so we are at our best, wheeling round the Sun of our Desire. What do you want to eat? Eggs and bacon, or sausages? The Polglose is up and doing and pushing round a questionnaire."

"Anything," I grunted. "Eggs and bacon'll do for me."

"I knew it," returned Anthony. "It always does. And one day perhaps it will. . . ."

In due time, I joined him at breakfast. He was soon at me again.

"Those women, Jack," he opened. "Those women that we discussed in the car last night."

"What about 'em?" I said, draining a cup of coffee. "I've been thinking this morning of Mrs. Burke."

"Mrs. Burke," I answered calmly, "is the pick of the basket."

"Whose basket?"

"Any basket, you ass."

Anthony rubbed his nose, then crossed and recrossed his legs. He grew more studied in his speech.

"Now, look here, Jack," he began, "don't give me any hole-and-corner business. For the sake of all of us. I like Mrs. Burke, from what I've seen of her. That isn't a lot, perhaps, but enough to put me on the right track for assessing her. She's a beauty. Easy on the eye, undoubtedly, *and* with a head on her! In that head plenty to keep her ears well apart. She's a pleasing proposition in every way. But are you sure that she's your pukka line of country? You haven't told me a lot, you know, and you've left a darned lot to the mercy of my imagination."

I stared at him with the utmost coolness.

"If you're askin' me for a clean breast, my Anthony," I returned, "I'm sold out of 'em. All dirt me."

He scowled at an inoffensive rasher of bacon. "Damn your eyes, Jack. I suppose that you'll tell me that you're a better man for having known her—eh? Or some such anodyne. That the life of a woman, full loveworthy, should be unending courtship? That all she does is to sweeten your blasted existence? Are they the words of the anthem?"

I replied to him doggedly. I couldn't forget that I had invited him down. My blood, therefore, must be on my own head.

"Mrs. Burke is very charming, and sweet, and makes Life more fragrant for me by just her graceful act of living. Beyond that, my inquisitive friend, I have nothing to say."

He regarded me quizzically. "Conquered your beasts, Jack?"

"Perhaps," I said diffidently. "Who knows? Anyhow, they're my beasts—and not yours."

Anthony rose from the breakfast-table and stood with outstretched legs in front of the wood fire.

"Daresay you're right, Jack, when all's said and done," he remarked.

"Thanks," I returned.

He took out his cigarette-case, selected a cigarette and tapped the end of it on his thumb-nail. A sudden idea entered my mind. You see—I had no qualms as to Sybil's safety. My soul was absolutely tranquil concerning her welfare. I had no fears whatever that she had been this latest victim of the moor. I can't explain why I felt like this. Sheer unquestioning Faith is difficult of definition at the best of times. I made up my mind to tell my cousin something. Something which I considered it would do his immortal soul good to know. My voice cut into the silence. I became pompous.

"All this is rather amazing," I opened, "in one way. How things work out, I mean. But Sybil Burke was the person at whose request I brought you down here. I thought, perhaps, that, at this juncture, the information would be at least interesting to you, and, quite possibly, valuable." I purposely kept my eyes averted from him as I supplied the statement.

"Really," he returned at length. "I certainly do find that interesting. It tends to make our problem more intriguing than ever." He paused. To proceed again, almost immediately. "All through, this case, Jack, as it has been presented to me, there have been mysterious and subtle 'propaganda' of a sort at work. Operating unseen, like a leaven, as it were, lurking in the very heart of the affair. Comparatively little of the data that has come to me can be, in any way, termed precise or specific. Every now and then, the surface, which persistently returns to a condition of calmness and tranquillity, is broken. Sharply—even terrifically. As though it were an unnaturally strong hand which held and controlled the hidden wires of murder and sudden death. Follow me?"

He looked up at me sharply. There was a note in his voice which showed me clearly that he was labouring under the influence of a strong, suppressed excitement. An excitement that insisted upon immediate utterance. His breathing had, as he spoke, quickened. "I think I do," I answered him.

I wondered what he would say next. I soon knew. Anthony went on again.

"It's a maddening thought that all we want to know, the key to everything, the explanation of the whole business, can't be so many miles away from us. It isn't as though we were dealing with murders in a big city. Like London or Manchester, for instance. With many thousands of inhabitants. Yet, although the solution simply *must* be within the range of our arms almost, for all we are doing and even look like doing, it might well be on the far side of the moon." His voice changed. "So it was Sybil Burke who sent for me, was it? Or prevailed on you to get me down here?" He stopped short—abruptly. Then I saw a peculiar light come into his grey eyes. "Good Lord— what a superbly consummate ass I've been!"

"What is it now?" I demanded of him.

"Why, just this, Jack. I rather fancy that we shall hear, before very long, too, that another member of our little community that exists down here is missing." He held up his hand, quickly. "No—don't say it. I know what's in your mind. Last night and all that. No—I was on the point of going a step farther. I was about to enter the kingdom of prophecy. Always a highly dangerous procedure, because one can so easily cut such an inglorious figure. Perhaps it was just as well that you stopped me."

He cocked his head at me provocatively. In a second or so, it seemed to me, the tension that he had deliberately created grew so great and so acute that I could no longer sit and await his revelation. He moved away from me towards the door. Intentionally, I think. To free himself, possibly, from the intimacy of the stress of my emotional appeal, which, although not yet translated into words, was plainly there for him to discern.

"Tell me," I muttered. "Tell me the move that you think you know."

His eyes mocked me. His lean face with those steady grey eyes had a knack of staring through you as though you were no more than a winter hedge. There were baffling qualities about this cousin of mine and he had the unusual power of affecting a hundred people in a hundred different ways.

"What I was about to say—partly—was this. That I could put a name to the woman who screamed on the moor last night."

I regarded him incredulously. I could not for the life of me see what it was that he was using as a support for his opinion. I put this incredulity into words.

"I should doubt it. I don't see for a minute what you're basing your opinion on."

Again I saw that slightly mocking look in his eyes.

"I thought I should surprise you, Jack. You should welcome the surprise, though."

"Are you absolutely sure of your point?"

"No, not absolutely. Because I haven't a lot to go on, as you say. All the same, I'm fairly confident I'm right. The woman who screamed last night on Constanton Moor, and who in some way which hasn't yet been revealed to us spilled a whole heap of powder, was Lady Rachel Shelley. Now, what have you got to say to me?"

What could I say to him? Lady Rachel Shelley? But why? He pressed me.

"Well? What comments on that? Am I to escape with the honours, untested and untried?"

"What are you going to tell me?" I gave back to him. "That the powder that was spilled on the moor last night, or whatever it was, was the same scent as the powder that you've noticed Lady Rachel Shelley always uses? Is that the intended proposition? Because if it is, it's as old as the hills."

Anthony smiled and shook his head. "Not on your life, sweet coz. That isn't my line of country at all. I hadn't considered the character-istic scent of that powder for one little instant. I am fully aware that I can't offer you a monograph on the two hundred and twenty-two different varieties of face-powder. Which I know would have been the correct thing on my part to have said."

I attacked. "What made you pick on her, then? You must have a reason for saying what you did."

He walked over to the fire with its leaping flames. "By the old-es-tablished process of elimination, my lad. No more and no less. Don't bother me any more for reasons now. I'll give them to you later." He pushed his hands into his pockets and kept them there. His face took on a strange, childish look. The look of a child who surveys with pride and eagerness something which it has created almost unconsciously and who then suddenly finds that its handiwork is good to look upon. Personally, I wasn't satisfied with any of it. Besides, what progress were we making? I gestured to him. The gesture showed impatience. He smiled at me again.

"Now, don't be harsh with me, my dear chap. I'm not a magician. It's your fault and Mrs. Sybil's—it's the correct thing to include her—for having too exalted an opinion of me. Because I fail to fill the entire bill at once, you're showing signs of being disappointed with me. I point *this* out to you, and demonstrate *that*, but because I can't handcuff a murderer for you, double-quick, pronto, and hand some guy over to the Sheriff, you're beginning to get peeved with me."

I shook my head at him vaguely. "It isn't that, you ass. It's just the terrific doubt about everything and everybody that's getting me down. Who's who, and what's what?"

Anthony walked over and patted me on the shoulder; he looked at me with that curious blend of pride and tolerance which some parents exhibit and share exclusively for an open-mouthed, adenoidal, dull-witted child.

"I know, Jack. I can understand only too well how you're feeling. But the horizon isn't quite as black as it looks, old man. Our murderer has shown us his technique, remember. We've had a good chance to study it and to profit from that study. The crime on Copeland was gloriously eloquent from all points of view. It told us a hell of a lot. Two absolutely identical techniques, you see. So much so, taking both crimes into consideration, that we are justified in assuming, almost in *declaring*, that we are not called upon to deal with two murderers, but only one. Well, that's something, Jacko! Raise your eyes to Heaven and give forth full sounds of thanks. *Sursum corda.*"

Before I could answer him, the situation as it was, had changed. I had half-turned, and in the turning, from the corner of my eye, I caught sight of a figure coming up to Scarpe.

"We have a visitor," I announced quietly.

"Oh—who is it that honours us?"

I could now see who it was. "Mrs. Burke," I said in the same tone of voice that I had used before.

"Ah," said Anthony softly, almost under his breath, "I was right then. Mrs. Burke is the messenger this time. Well—I'm pleased."

I heard the Polglose let her in. I caught explanations from the old girl, and as I walked to the door of the room in which Anthony and I were, it opened before I could reach it and Sybil Burke entered to us. She was dressed in black. Black is an unusual colour for Sybil Burke. She showed in her face, figure, and general demeanour traces of a tension which was perilously close to making her overwrought. But although she was obviously suffering from bruised and jangled nerves, she nevertheless had a control of herself that was bordering on the complete. She came and faced my cousin and me. When she spoke, she spoke without emotion.

"Lady Rachel Shelley is missing, Jack. Captain Shelley has 'phoned to the police. Colonel Blount got on to Martin. He told me to come over and tell you and Anthony Bathurst. That's all." She gave a quick glance round the room and then subsided into the nearest chair. With his recent deduction so suddenly verified, Anthony made no clamant claim to triumph. He immediately gripped the problem and allied himself with the real issue at stake.

"Facts, Mrs. Burke, please. As a matter of fact. I've been expecting this news that you've brought us, all the morning. Or since midnight, to be more precise. Tell me all that you know; *all*, if you please."

She nodded in understanding.

"I'm afraid that it won't be very much. Lady Rachel went to Colonel Blount's last night A bridge party, I fancy, from what my husband has told me. She left there about half past eleven. Captain Shelley's chauffeur called for her in the car. The car has been found abandoned on the edge of the moor. Neither Lady Rachel, nor Ramsay, the chauffeur, has been seen since. There you have the facts, Mr. Bathurst, as my husband had them from Colonel Blount and as he subsequently passed them on to me."

Anthony Bathurst's face was grave in the extreme.

"Thank you, Mrs. Burke." He turned to me. The gravity in his face gave way to a sharp swift glance.

"I'll get the car ready, Jack. You get yourself ready as well, will you? I'm going to Blount's. At once. Perhaps Mrs. Burke would care to come part of the way with us." He turned to her. "Would you? We can easily drop you, you know, Mrs. Burke."

"Thank you, Mr. Bathurst. I shall be pleased to come along with you. Perhaps you might—" She paused, rather curiously. For she had conveyed to me an impression, that was almost a certainty, that she had said something which she had rather not have said. My cousin obviously sensed the same idea. He stopped in the doorway and turned towards her. "Yes? Might what, Mrs. Burke."

Sybil burnt her boats.

"I was going to say that perhaps you could take Martin along to Colonel Blount's with you. That is, if he hasn't gone along there already. I know it's his intention to pop up there some time. He told me so directly after Colonel Blount 'phoned us. Still, you'll see for yourselves when we get there."

Anthony nodded and disappeared in the direction of the garage. For a few moments I was left alone with Sybil. For the first time for many days. She faced me bravely and wasted no time over commonplaces.

"Where is all this going to end, Jack?"

I shook my head at her hopelessly.

"It's like a bad dream." This was the best answer that I could muster. "I am expecting, all the time, to wake up from it, as you do from a dream that has worried you, feeling that all the horrors are imaginary and not real."

She nodded.

"I know, Jack. I know exactly what you mean. I feel something of the same myself. But—you see—I know that all this *isn't* a dream, but a dreadful reality."

I then put a question to her that had been on my tongue for some time. The same question that she had answered before.

"How's Martin these days? Things any better?" She gave a quick glance towards the door through which Anthony had just passed, before replying to me.

"No different from what I told you the last time you asked. Like a man in the toils of something. Something that's overpowering him. He worries me dreadfully. Don't misunderstand that. I mean that *I'm* dreadfully worried about *him*. Not the other way round. I shouldn't like you to get hold of the wrong idea."

I frowned. I still found myself at a loss to comprehend fully this position that seemed to be in existence between Martin and Sybil

Burke. Husband and wife! I never had been able to realize its conditions properly when Sybil had first hinted it to me and I was still no nearer to a clear perception.

"What does he *do* with himself?" I asked her. "How does he spend his time?"

"Aimlessly, Jack. So different from the real Martin that you and I used to know so well. He just wanders about. Can't settle down to anything. Round the house. In. Out. Backwards and forwards. Never gets down to anything for any length of time. Nerves absolutely on edge. You know that he was never like that. Quite the reverse. His work is suffering, of course."

"Do you ever tax him with the change?"

"I have tried to raise the subject once or twice. But to no real purpose. He's always evasive. Evasion, as you know, is not a part of Martin's real character. He always puts me off, though, if I attempt to come to grips with him. Treats me as though I were a child whom he was protecting, at all costs, from a fearsome ogre. . . ."

"And that annoys you—eh?"

"Annoys me? I could *scream*, Jack, every time he does it. Although, probably, I think and hope it's his affection for me that's prompting him. I should realize that fact, I suppose, and be correspondingly grateful to him. But I find it hard to be."

We heard Anthony Bathurst's steps outside the door. He poked his head round the corner.

"Come on. Car's O.K., you two. Are you fit?"

I nodded and got my hat and coat. We were soon away. Anthony drove the car fiercely. Very much as he had driven it in the early hours of the same morning. As there was little on the road, his speed was almost unchecked. He pulled up in front of the Burkes' house. Then turned with an unspoken enquiry towards Sybil. She smiled wistfully.

"Well," he said, eventually, "what about it? Has your good husband already set out, or is it going to be our privilege to take him along with us? Will you find out, Mrs. Burke?"

She smiled at him again.

"Martin is there. I know that. I can see by the curtains and the windows. We have our little domestic codes, you know, Martin and I. If we wait here, he will come out to the car in a minute."

Her words and their implication gave me a sharp stab of jealousy and all the points of Bathurst's inquisition of an hour before came back to me. The stab became a sharper one when I saw Martin Burke come down the garden path in the direction of our waiting car. He nodded cordially, but I noticed my cousin's widely comprehensive survey of him brought about by a Bathurst glance alone. Martin looked white and strained.

"Morning, everybody," he jerked at us. Sybil was quick to explain to him after we had returned his greeting.

"Mr. Bathurst and Jack will take you along to the Colonel's, Martin. Mr. Bathurst offered. I told him that we might be in time to catch you here and I knew that you wanted to go."

Burke fingered his chin.

"Thanks, Bathurst. Good of you. It's quite true that I intended to run along directly my wife returned."

"Good," said Anthony with genial composure. "Ready now, or do you want a hat?"

"I'll get a coat, if you don't mind. What are you doing, Sybil?"

"I'd better get out, I suppose." She looked undecided, and Anthony cottoned on to her indecision at once.

"Why not come along with us too, Mrs. Burke? Then we can make a foursome of it."

Sybil looked at her husband for guidance. I didn't think that he appeared too pleased, to tell the truth, but he conceded the point gracefully enough with the wave of a hand and a smile. Sybil stayed where she was. Martin got his overcoat and we started off again for Blount's place. I had offered my seat to Martin, but Anthony had forestalled him from accepting it.

"You come and sit by me, Burke," he had said, with the full battery of his disarming charm, "then we needn't disturb the seating of the others."

Thus we came to Colonel Blount's house on the morning of the first day in January. The wind in our faces, when we descended from the car, was like a keen-edged knife. Sybil Burke drew her furs closer around her, and I shrank into my clothes. Was it still actually turning colder or merely my fancy?

I THINK that, on the whole, Blount seemed surprised to see us. It appeared that Martin Burke hadn't told him that he intended to come along to see him when Blount had telephoned, and, of course, he knew nothing of Anthony Bathurst's visit. Probably the number of our party, arriving, as it did, on a Sunday morning, was the main cause of Blount's discomfiture. However, he speedily conquered it, or, at any rate, its image, and fell in with matters as they were. Dr. Surtees was with him. I had half expected this, considering the circumstances, and wasn't sorry. The quicker that Surtees got an intelligent grasp of things the better it would be, I considered, for all of us who were concerned. As usual, Anthony wasted no time in getting to the point. He had a clear idea as to what was his job and what was Blount's. To say nothing of the part to be played in the affair by old Surtees.

"Mrs. Burke brought us your news, Colonel. Up to Scarpe, my cousin, Jack Clyst's place. When I heard it, *directly* I heard it, in fact, I decided to come along to see you. Mrs. Burke accompanied us and we picked up Major Burke on the way. That explains everything and hence these tears. Your latest news, I understand, concerns Lady Rachel Shelley, who makes the third in order of our missing people. Now, I want you to do something for me, Colonel."

As Blount had already accepted Anthony and the general position, he couldn't very well go back on that acceptance now.

"Yes?" He pursed his lips. "What is it you want?"

"Full story of this latest development, Colonel. That is to say, everything as far as you yourself know it."

Blount glanced across at Burke, but the latter's face was absolutely impassive.

"Well—I see no objection to your having the story, Bathurst. Lady Rachel was our guest here last evening. She and Vincent and Dr. Surtees. All the time that she was here with us she seemed to be in the very best of spirits. She left here, I should say, as near to half past eleven as you could get it. Her car came for her—we knew that it was coming—and it was driven by her own chauffeur. The man's been in her service for years. By name, George Ramsay. He opened the door of the car for Lady Rachel, she got in—I saw all these things myself—and she was driven rapidly away. To her home, we all of us imagined. That is the conclusion of what may be described as the *first* part of the incident. At two o'clock this morning I was called from my bed by the ringing of the 'phone in the hall. I shoved on a dressing-gown and, of course, went down to see who it was that wanted me. It was Shelley on the 'phone. Speaking from Bysshe Lodge. With the absolutely staggering piece of news that *Lady Rachel had not yet returned home.* Shelley, naturally, was full of questions and worried up to his eyebrows. Understandable questions. What time his wife had left here and so on. He asked all the natural questions that you may imagine a man in his position would ask. I think I told him all he wanted to know that I was able to. As a result, seeing that he had no car available, I threw some clothes on, got my car out and drove to Bysshe Lodge."

"What made you do that immediately?" asked Bathurst.

"I felt it my duty to do so," returned Colonel Blount. He was inclined to be short. He didn't, however, appear to resent the question. "Don't forget that I had two precedents upon which to act. The death of Chinnery and the hairbreadth escape of Squire Copeland. This news from Shelley set me wondering again, and, quite candidly, I was prepared for the worst. I felt that I must act. Must do something! That I couldn't stay in my house and wait to hear that yet another tragedy had overtaken us."

"I think that the Colonel acted properly. Any other procedure would have been unthinkable." This was from Surtees with a snap of his teeth. His eyes held an almost savage look as he made the interjection. It was evident that he had little love either for me or for my cousin. Anthony Bathurst paid no heed to him. He waited, by the most subtle suggestion, for Colonel Blount to proceed with his story.

"When I got to Bysshe Lodge," continued Blount, "I found Captain Shelley in a state of considerable agitation. There was still no sign of Lady Rachel. Or the chauffeur. Or the car. We hung about for a bit and then Shelley and I decided to scout round in my car; because it seemed to stand to reason that there must be some trace of the missing people somewhere near at hand. There was only the distance between Bysshe Lodge and here which the missing car could have covered, or, at least, so it seemed to us. We found nothing, Bathurst, after cruising all round, and at half past four reluctantly gave up the search. I took Shelley home and I came back here. I was dog-tired and only too glad of the chance to get some rest. At half past eight, Shelley came through on the 'phone again. With a piece of even more astounding news this time. Ramsay, the chauffeur, had been found unconscious in a ditch by the side of the road. Between here and Bysshe Lodge. We must have passed and repassed him in my car, but of course he was lying there, his body shielded, and it was impossible to see him from the middle of the road. A farm-hand had found him on his way to work. Ramsay has had a nasty blow on the head, and Dr. Surtees, here, is very much afraid that his skull is fractured. The doctor will supply you with more details of this later on, though, should you care to have them."

Anthony Bathurst nodded.

"Good. I'll ask him some questions later, if I may. Now you tell me, Colonel, please, am I to understand that the missing car has turned up since then?"

I noticed Martin Burke's eyes fixed on Blount as he answered:

"Yes, I can answer that. The car was found abandoned on the edge of the moor path not far from Priestley's Quarry."

There came a hush directly Blount finished speaking.

"I hope it hasn't been moved," intervened my cousin eventually. "There is just the bare chance that it may tell us something. I am beginning to have hopes of the case at last."

"The car is still in the place where it was found abandoned," replied Blount.

"Why are you hopeful, Bathurst?" demanded Martin Burke. "What brings you such a ray of light? I must confess that I can't share your optimism."

"The knowledge, Burke, that we are at last up against something *tangible*. A man with a cracked head! An abandoned car! Real things! And therefore much more acceptable to a humble investigator groping in the dark in the hope that he may look on truth rather than on such nebulous conditions as 'projections of evil-thinking'. That's what I mean."

Blount intervened again. "There is still this point, however. I feel bound to remind you of it. Lady Rachel is missing. There is nothing tangible about her at the moment."

Anthony Bathurst frowned. It was obvious to all of us that he resented Blount's innuendo.

"You said that you and Shelley 'cruised round in your car', between two and half past four, didn't you?"

Blount returned the frown with interest. "Yes. That's right. That was the time. Between two and half past four. Why?"

"Only this. Did you happen to go on the moor?"

"No. The moor isn't a place where you'd take a car, now, is it, Bathurst, in the ordinary way?"

Anthony rubbed his lips.

"No. I agree. But things weren't quite ordinary on this occasion, were they? Haven't been, for some little time now. Nothing's ordinary at the moment. Even you being questioned by me isn't, is it? Only I want to help and you're man enough to realize that fact."

Blount's frown became a half-smile. A.L.B.'s attack had borne fruit.

"Go on," he said simply.

"Thanks, Colonel. I will. Did you go *near* the moor?"

"Yes. Fairly so. At that one point where it comes down almost to the road between St. Crayle and St. Roseworthy."

"Good. Saw nothing?"

"Not a glimmer."

"Heard nothing?"

"Not a tinkle."

"Why didn't Shelley come along with his wife last night to your show? Any idea?"

"Seeing that I was host for the evening, of course I have. Shelley hates bridge. Can't stick it at any price. Never plays. Loathes cards altogether. Lady Rachel often comes here for bridge without him. More often than otherwise."

Martin Burke struck in. "Do you know what occurs to me, Colonel?"

Blount shook his head, but Anthony Bathurst was quick with an answer.

"Yes, Burke. I know. A thousand to one, I'll give you your answer."

Burke raised his eyebrows. "What is it?"

"This." My cousin's voice was sharp and decisive. "Chinnery went to the Rectory. Mrs. Chinnery stayed at home. Copeland went to Lady Rachel's. His two daughters stayed at home. And now Lady Rachel came here to Colonel Blount's and Captain Shelley stayed at home. Now, Burke, am I right?"

"Absolutely, Bathurst. You might be telepathic. I am not sure that you aren't. You have read my thoughts marvellously accurately. That was just as I saw it all."

Anthony's face flushed with triumph. "Thank you, Burke. And none of our pigs had roast beef, did they? Far from it. As I said to Jack the other day—friendly death waited for them, but on these occasions, *not* with a warming-pan."

Here I thought it opportune to put in my own individual spoke.

"But look here, Anthony, what you say is all very well as far as it goes. But it doesn't go, at least it seems to me that it doesn't, quite as far as you want to make it go. See here! In this way. Mrs. Chinnery scarcely ever goes out to dinner of an evening. Especially in the winter, and more especially in extremely severe weather such as we've been experiencing lately. Copeland's two daughters didn't accompany him to Shelley's place for very good reasons. The reasons have already been explained to you. Norah had a quinsy throat for example. And in the last instance, that of Lady Rachel—her husband hates bridge. So that there's nothing sinister or mysterious about any one of the absent partners. On the other hand there's an excellent and entirely sensible reason behind every one of the absences."

I saw Sybil nodding as I finished my statement, as though she were in absolute accord with my words. But my cousin wagged his head and his finger at me.

"Surface reasons, all of 'em, my dear Jack, and the solution to this case of ours will be found below the surface, which makes all the difference. I refuse to consider all surface reasons."

Blount spoke. "The inquest on Chinnery has been adjourned. The coroner, naturally, took the usual course. Do you agree?"

"Oh, quite. Nothing else for it. But what are we going to do now? Before we are faced with another inquest? That's the burning question for us to answer."

"What *can* we do?" This from Blount. There was no reply. He went on. "People are missing. They vanish for a time, utterly unexpectedly, and then, almost equally suddenly, they reappear. One dead and the other as near dead as damn it." He stopped.

"Ergo," continued Anthony Bathurst, as it were on his behalf, "in the meantime between disappearance and reappearance, *they must have been somewhere.* Located. Housed, if you like the word better. Where? And the answer to that last question remains to be filled in by one of us. There's our problem, gentlemen, in the most condensed form possible."

Burke spoke very quietly.

"I agree with all that you have said. You have presented the problem exactly as I should have done if I'd been asked to do it. We have to find out where Lady Rachel is at this moment. We must do so."

Blount came in again.

"That's all very well But how do you propose to do it? I confess that I'd very much like to know."

There was another silence. Suggestions did not come. Blount turned to Bathurst again.

"Well, any proposition to advance?"

"It would be presumption on my part to attempt to teach you your job, Colonel. I'll do all in my power to help you, but—I can't very well lead, can I?"

Surtees grimaced uncharitably. "Hallo, hallo! Change of front, what? All modest and humble?"

Anthony disregarded the remark. He put a question to Blount.

"How's Ramsay, the chauffeur, getting on?" Blount gestured towards Surtees. "Ask the doctor here. He can tell you that better than I can."

Surtees took it upon himself to answer at once. "Well—he's had a nasty crack. A real sock on the skull. But I don't think that he'll go under. His constitution's good and his head's thick. Two important assets that will stand him in good stead. He should pull through. Having made a second examination I don't *think* the skull is fractured. At first I thought it was. If things go as I'm hoping they will, two or three days should see a big improvement in him. As a matter of fact, I'm pleased with him, and the progress that he's already made."

Bathurst came to the point with Surtees immediately. "That's better news, doctor. Pleased to hear it. Perhaps the best that I've heard to-day. You see, it touches both Colonel Blount here and me. Which brings me to a question that I hadn't yet dared to ask you. I'll ask it now. When will Ramsay be see-able? Interview-able? Because after you chaps have done with him I want to have a word or two with him very badly."

Surtees looked enquiringly at Colonel Blount. The latter nodded affirmatively.

"I agree, Surtees. Bathurst's right. You know what I said to you half an hour ago. This man Ramsay may hold the key to a good many things. But he's still unconscious, you said, didn't you?"

"Ay. And likely to be for some hours yet, I should say. But, as I indicated just now, his condition is materially improving. I'll let you know when you can visit him."

"Immediately?"

"Yes. Directly I can allow it safely."

"Thank you, doctor. We'll take that as arranged, then. I'll hold myself in readiness for your summons."

Blount turned to my cousin. "You heard what Dr. Surtees said, Bathurst? I'll let you know when anything can be done."

"That's good of you. And the sooner the better for both of us. If we are lucky enough to get Ramsay to talk—who knows?" He shrugged his shoulders. His shrug was eloquent.

Sybil Burke spoke. I think it was the first remark she had made since we had all entered Blount's house.

"And meanwhile, while you are all talking, what is happening to poor Lady Rachel?" The pregnancy of her remark went straight home and hit us all. Certainly none of us who heard it spoke. Our tongues seemed tied—as tightly as our powerless hands. We were obsessed by the fact that we fought an unseen evil. An evil which we could not bring into the open where we might grip it and choke out its unholy life. The realization of this unwelcome truth staggered us and sobered us. We chafed under this heritage of a burden of hopelessness. All of us, that is, with the exception of Anthony Lotherington Bathurst. On the other hand he embraced quotation.

"Mrs. Burke," he said quietly, "and you as well, gentlemen, there is, we all know, which ever way we look at matters, an evil force arraigned against us. When we find from whence that force proceeds, from what human agency, then we may hope to meet it courageously, fight it and conquer it. 'The lion and the dragon shalt thou tread under thy feet, and save my darling from the power of the dog'." A grey line of light came through the window and touched his hair. The thought came to me, as I stood there and watched, that this shaft of light, for some unknown purpose of its own, had deliberately singled out Bathurst from the rest of us. He was a man set apart. Dedicated to a service. His lips relaxed momentarily into a smile. Just the flicker of a smile. We were all privileged to see it. That faint smile broke the strain for us. The tension snapped. The atmosphere cleared. I felt that Bathurst had drawn a glittering sword against this dread dragon of cold evil. And I had unlimited confidence in him and his powers. Because I knew him of old.

CHAPTER XX
MONDAY, JANUARY 2ND, 3.30 P.M.

THE news came through from Blount, relayed from Surtees, that Anthony Bathurst and the Colonel himself would be able to see Ramsay, the injured chauffeur, at half past three on the Monday afternoon. This particular Monday was that day which has gone down on the meteorological records as the coldest day in this country for over forty years. Unless you kept your body unceasingly active, the blood of you almost froze in your veins. Anthony and I had finished lunch when Blount's news arrived. My cousin was bucked to get it.

"That's very useful, Jack," he said to me, when I told him. "I'll run the car up there and meet Blount outside the hospital." Ramsay lay in the little voluntarily-aided Cottage Hospital at St. Roseworthy. "Care to come along?" he asked me.

I considered the request. Eventually I decided to accept his invitation. We arrived at the hospital a few minutes before the appointed time and found Blount already there waiting for us. He came straight up to the car.

"Surtees is inside. I've already seen Ramsay myself and I'll see him again with you. The Rector's here, too. Come to see Ramsay. He is a man of distinctly superior type and a regular attendant at Verschoyle's church or something. On the communicants' roll. He recovered consciousness early this morning, but Surtees wouldn't allow an interview until now. Oh—and by the way—the matron's an utter bitch. No respecter of persons at all. I cut no ice with her, I can tell you. She's all for Verschoyle. How these nursing women run to the cloth, to be sure. It used to be a uniform—but now! Bitches—all of 'em!" He shook his head dolefully.

He walked into the little hospital, past blue-coated porters and white-smocked attendants.

"Ramsay is in a room by himself. I arranged that when he was first brought in. Thought it would be more convenient all the way round. For him *and* for us."

A staircase brought us to a landing. A white-capped nurse met us and pointed to a door. Blount motioned to us to follow him. Surtees and Verschoyle were by the man's bed as we entered. Ramsay's head was profusely bandaged. Surtees, looking all hot and bothered, had two fingers on the injured man's pulse. At our entry the Rector rose and greeted us. He then walked past us on tip-toe, to the end of the bed, and seated himself in a chair that stood there. His habitual grace of movement was noticeable in every action. From the colour of Ramsay's face, I might have thought that he was dead. He lay on his back. Every drop of blood seemed to have been drained from his cheeks. His eyes were almost closed. But when I drew nearer to him I saw that his breathing was regular and fairly deep. I saw, too, the colour of the man's eyes through the partly open lids. Suddenly the eyes fully opened and he gave Surtees the suggestion of a nod of the head.

"He'll talk for a few minutes," said the doctor. "Get to work quickly, and don't worry him overmuch."

Blount hesitated.

"Ask him to tell us what happened, Colonel," said Anthony. "Let him talk in his own words. Without being questioned, I mean. That may tax him less than the other method."

Blount went to the edge of the bed and bent over the injured man. "Tell us what happened to you, Ramsay. If you can. Take it easy and take your time."

Ramsay nodded again. He understood. He raised himself a little in the bed. To get a more comfortable position, no doubt. We waited for his words. They came slowly.

"I took Lady Rachel in the master's car to Colonel Blount's place on Saturday evening. I had orders to be ready at half past six. The Captain told me that he wouldn't be accompanying her ladyship that evening. It's only about a quarter of an hour's journey and we got to Colonel Blount's house about a quarter to seven. As I escorted Lady Rachel from the car she gave me further orders. I was to bring the car back for her that evening at a quarter past eleven for half past eleven. I made a note of these orders and returned to my own quarters at Bysshe Lodge."

Ramsay paused. His voice had been growing weaker for some little time as he had progressed with his telling, and it was obvious that he would need to be rested. Nobody hurried him. We all of us waited for him again, in sympathy and understanding. There was pain showing in the man's eyes. The minutes ticked by. At length Ramsay drew a long deep breath and slowly began to speak again.

"I arrived at Colonel Blount's for the second time on Saturday evening punctually at a quarter past eleven. I waited until I was informed that Lady Rachel was ready and would be coming out. She came out of the house almost exactly at half past eleven. I know this because I looked at the clock in the car. I helped her into the car, as I always do, and commenced the journey home, at about twenty-two minutes to twelve. It was very dark and cold all the way, as you gentlemen know. The lights of my car were like silver ruts cut in the road in front of me. I passed nobody. I passed no car and no car overtook me. I am absolutely certain of that. All I heard was the melancholy hooting of the owls from the moor, on my left."

Ramsay stopped for the second time. Again he seemed exhausted. But on this occasion the pause was by no means as long as before.

"I had run about a hundred yards, I suppose, past the place where the track across the moor comes to the road and had begun to climb the hill that leads to St. Roseworthy. The car was taking it well when suddenly the light of my lamps picked out 'something' in the roadway almost in front of me. I don't know what it was. For certain, that is. It was a . . ." Ramsay hesitated. Nobody prompted him. For this story, vital as it was to us and to our problem, it was essential that he should find his own words. They came. "It was a 'mass' of something. That's the best description I can give of it. With some sort of a light attached to it. The light, though, was dullish—otherwise I should have seen it before. Must have done. Anyhow, it lay there on the road right in the track of my car, so I shoved on my brakes with a screech, as you gentlemen may guess, and brought the car to a standstill. I got down—felt that I must—told Lady Rachel to sit tight for a moment, and moved towards this mass of flickering 'something' that lay stretched out there on the roadway. I came to it, stooped down over it, I heard a strange shrill cry, and that, gentlemen, is all I can remember, until I woke up not so long ago and found myself in this bed here where you see me now."

Ramsay sank back again on to his pillows, and I saw the veins quivering in his temples. The effort had exhausted him. I had noticed that Blount had been busily making several notes from Ramsay's statement. Anthony Bathurst, on the other hand, had so far made none at all. He looked across at old Surtees.

"May I question him, doctor? Is it all right? I promise you I won't be overlong."

Surtees looked pretty sour at the question. "I can't have the man worried. You must understand that. You can have a minute or so with him. Not more. And when I say 'not more', I mean 'not more'."

"Thank you, doctor."

My cousin moved over to the chauffeur's bed. "Forgive me worrying you, old chap, I know you're rough. But there are one or two things about this that I'd love to know. Do you think you could help me without over-taxing yourself? If you feel you can't do it—say so at once."

A faint smile passed across Ramsay's face. "I'll try to, sir. I'll do my best."

"Stout fellow. What was this cry like—most of all? Was it like anything, for instance, that you have ever heard before?"

Ramsay slowly nodded.

"Yes. Perhaps it was. Like the cry of an animal in pain."

"I see. And all this took place, we can say, I suppose, shortly before midnight? That would be right, Ramsay, wouldn't it?"

"Yes, sir." A faint flicker of humour rippled across the man's drawn features. "The first time, for many years, that I haven't seen the Old Year out. More like, sir, to say that the Old Year saw me out." Anthony Bathurst bent over him and patted him on the shoulder. "Nearly, perhaps, but not quite, Ramsay. And a miss is as good as a mile. Every time and always. You're going to eat many a Christmas pudding yet. To say nothing of a nice mince pie. Dr. Surtees here is very pleased with you. And don't you forget it."

Ramsay nodded to him understandingly. We turned away from the bed, and it was at this moment that I remembered that the Rector was with us in the room. He rose from his chair and looked at the patient. His usual smile lit up his eyes.

"Good-bye, Ramsay," he said quietly. "I'll come and see you again the day after tomorrow. And I'll remember you, too, in my prayers. God bless you."

Ramsay looked up at him gratefully. We filed out of the room, only Surtees remaining there. Blount left us outside the hospital.

"Can I give you a lift, sir?" Anthony asked Verschoyle.

The Rector smiled and accepted the offer.

"Thank you, Bathurst. Good of you. It will be a great help to me."

Anthony started the car. Verschoyle sat next to him. I sat behind them. I heard my cousin address the Rector of St. Crayle.

"Prayer, sir! You mentioned it just now. I'd like an opinion from you. I suppose that you would hold a certain belief in the efficacy of prayer?"

Verschoyle smiled at him whimsically. "Why, yes, of course. As a parish priest in a country district, how could I possibly assert otherwise? But what's behind your question, Bathurst? I'm convinced that there's something. I don't believe that you ever ask a question without a real reason."

A.L.B. was a minute, perhaps, before he replied. I listened carefully. Like Verschoyle, I found myself wondering a little at my cousin's question. Came Anthony's reply.

"You would, I take it, believe even more, then, in the power of mass prayer?"

"Mass prayer?" Verschoyle echoed the words after him. "I don't know that I quite—"

"Let me explain, padre. 'Mass' prayer as against 'individual' prayer. One man prays that a certain thing may happen. Two men join in the prayer. In the end, say, a round thousand people find the same prayer in their hearts and ultimately on their lips. Surely the numerical strength alone sponsoring that prayer must inevitably increase its power? Consider, if you prefer it this way, a thousand people all working in the cause of righteousness. Would not that thousand be a terrific power for potential good?"

Verschoyle nodded emphatically. I could see him plainly from where I was sitting.

"Oh, undoubtedly, Bathurst," I heard him answer. "As our Liturgy has it, 'And hast promised that when two or three axe gathered together in Thy Name, Thou wilt grant their request.' There we have the exaltation of just 'two or three'. Therefore the prayers of a thousand godly, righteous souls must be a terrific influence for benevolence. No other condition is possible to a man with clarity of thought and soundness of vision. But what is your real point in relation to this 'prayer' question? I'm perfectly certain, you know, that you haven't told me all yet." The Rector's eyes almost twinkled.

"I'm developing an idea, that's all, sir." Anthony adroitly swung the car round a corner. "The idea is this," he continued. "If 'massed' prayer be accepted as such a potent influence for good, how about the effects of massed evil? Of massed hatred? If prayer be folded and foundationed in Love, surely a projection of evil, of definitely devastating evil, could be nurtured on intense hatred? The analogy seems pretty good to me, padre. What do you think of it yourself?"

"I find it feasible. Yes . . . undoubtedly so. We pray daily to avoid temptation and to be delivered from evil. That, I take it, must cover such things as the *thoughts* of evil. It must do."

"So that you agree with me, sir, that a terrific functioning of hatred and evil-thinking generally *might*, per se, eventually prove to be a force, the effect of which is absolutely frightening? Yes, padre?"

Verschoyle nodded decisively two or three times in quick succession.

"Yes, I'm with you all the way, Bathurst. Good and evil are two similar forces. Diametrically opposed, of course, but working very much on the same lines. I am one who believes in the personality of the Devil. Perhaps that admission on my part surprises you?"

"No, sir. Not at all. As a matter of fact, my own inclinations are in the same direction."

Verschoyle looked at him curiously.

"There are three of us, then," said the Rector. "Because Martin Burke does as well. I've had the privilege of discussing the subject with him many times in the past. Interesting, isn't it? Burke's a remarkably clever, well-read, much-travelled man. One in ten thousand. We agree, he and I, sometimes, and at other times, naturally, we differ. But we *agree* to differ. Burke's different from the other people round here. Different from Copeland. Different from Shelley and Vincent. Different, too, from poor Chinnery that was. I like Burke immensely. It's a pity that you and he, Bathurst, aren't able to see more of each other."

"Time may even remedy that condition," returned my cousin. "Indeed, I find myself hoping that it will. For, like you, sir, I appreciate the qualities of Burke. But here we are, sir. Here's the Rectory."

He stopped the car and Verschoyle alighted. He extended his hand for Anthony to take. "Thank you, Bathurst. It is good of you to have brought me home like this." He came along to me. "Good-bye to you, Clyst. You and I have seen something happen since you dined here on the evening of December 2nd and you took Chinnery part of his way home. What a merciful dispensation of Providence it is that we aren't allowed to see into the future. Few of us could face it." He shook me by the hand.

"Good-bye, sir," I said.

He turned and walked towards the door of the Rectory. Anthony set the car's head towards Scarpe. We travelled the remainder of the distance in silence. We came to Scarpe. Anthony put up the car. I waited for him in the little low-ceilinged dining-room. I was anxious to hear how his final comments would go. He came into the dining-room and took an armchair by the fire-place.

"Things move, Jack," he said at length.

"You think so?"

"Oh, quite. But for the fact of Lady Rachel Shelley, I could find almost a measure of satisfaction."

"What do we do about Lady Rachel? Anything?"

"God—what can we do. Jack? I'm worried like hell. You don't need to be told that. But what *can* I do? I can't take things entirely out of Blount's hands, can I? I'm fettered. Bound, hand and foot! I've ideas. I'll admit that. But they're so damned nebulous. Just that. No proof. No real conclusive data. Nothing to work on. Glimmerings. It's true that at any moment they may become much more of a certainty. But until then—" He stopped and spread out his hands expressively.

"Where do you find your new measure of satisfaction, then? That was the phrase you used, I fancy? I can't say honestly that I'm able to follow you."

He looked at me almost incredulously.

"My dear Jack, wherever are your brains? Consider the attack on Ramsay. It was necessary to remove him so that our murdering friend could get his devilish claws into Lady Rachel. Well, that conceded, how did they deal with Ramsay? A crack on the head, Jack. Just a plain, honest-to-goodness bang on the napper. One can understand the psychology of a matter like that. Just Roast Beef and two 'veg.'. It's so vitally and essentially different from a death as the result of a 'projection of evil'. Don't you see what I mean? One can take steps to meet and oppose forces the genesis of which are understandable to the human mind, even hampered as it is by limitations and frail-ties. But that other business—well—you don't know where you are with it. In the dark—all the time." Suddenly he changed the subject. "What do you think of the Rector, Jack?"

"In what way—particularly?"

"As a man. Character! The word is inadequate, I know, but it will serve my purpose at the moment. You've known him and been close to him for a number of years so that you should be able to place him pretty accurately."

"I think a rare lot of Verschoyle. And I like him. Not an ideal parish priest, perhaps, from some points of view. But eminently suited to a place like St. Crayle."

Bathurst pressed me. "You interest me, Jack. Why can't you award him full marks as a parish priest? I could bear to know."

I hesitated. I knew in my mind what I meant, but I wasn't sure that I could convey the right impression to Anthony Bathurst.

"Well, I shouldn't describe him as the best of 'mixers', for example. Lower class-people to him are—lower-class people. He can't help making these distinctions any more than you can help preferring Ascot to Alexandra Park or *The Merry Wives* to *The Merry Widow*. These things, being as they are, don't tend to make him a perfect parish priest."

"He dearly loves a lord—eh?"

"Not quite that. Rather, that he likes 'pukka' things. You know what I mean. Damned good form. Old School Tie. Public School. 'Varsity. Lord's. Henley. All those traditional interests which almost all parsons have for a time but which some of 'em eventually learn to chuck away. Verschoyle hasn't learned to. Never will—probably. If I know him aright, doesn't want to. They're too much an inseparable part of him. Have I shown him to you more clearly?"

"You have. And I'm thanking you for the enlightenment." The car drew up before the gate of Scarpe.

Before I got out. I put a question to my cousin, straight and direct. "You worry me a bit, old man. I've an idea at the back of my mind that you suspect somebody. Do you?"

He grinned at my unconcealed eagerness. "Merely suspect—or suspect with definite reason? There's a devil of a difference, you know."

"Oh—either," I replied impatiently.

"So you won't be put off—eh? 'Perseverance as an aid to success.' Well, if you must have it, Jack—yes! I do suspect somebody. And more than merely *suspect*, at that."

"Whom?" I flung back at him.

He shook his head, jumped from the driving-seat and I alighted to join him.

"Who is it?" I demanded again. I felt that I must know.

"No, Jack. Not yet. No names, no pack-drill." He shoved his back against the door of the car, took out his pipe and proceeded to fill it slowly and deliberately.

"I'll tell you a story, Jack. I heard it in Bangkok when I was out there. Four Chinese merchants, I'll call them Li, Pu, Chang, and Lung, bought a cat for the purpose of protecting their textiles, which were stored in a warehouse, from the depredations of rats and mice. They traded separately, but had combined in the hiring of this one warehouse. When they purchased the cat, each one of them took over proprietorship of one paw. The merchant Pu was held to be the possessor of the animal's left front paw. In making a leap one day the cat fell badly and crushed this particular paw.

"When the accident was discovered, a veterinary surgeon was sent for and gave orders that the injured paw should be dressed. Dressings were given day by day, and one evening, when the cat was lying by the hearth, the dressing round the paw caught fire. As a result, the frightened animal, almost wild with pain, rushed all round the warehouse and set fire to the goods, which ultimately were destroyed. Thereupon Li, Chang, and Lung came to Pu, the unfortunate Pu, and said to him this. 'It is you who are responsible for this terrible disaster which has befallen all of us. It is the dressing on *your* paw which has caused the fire and the subsequent destruction of all our goods.

"The unhappy Pu, it is recorded, had no reply to this interpretation of the law. But he was a Chinese, and being a Chinese, he thought that it would be just as well if the point of law raised were confirmed by a Court of Justice. He refused to pay, therefore, and his three former partners brought an action against him. The Court deliberated on the case for several days and learned counsel were briefed by each side. 'Li, Chang, and Lung versus Pu' filled the headlines in all the papers. Eventually, the judge who presided came to this decision. 'I find, after hearing carefully all the evidence and listening attentively to the arguments put forward by counsel for the plaintiffs and for the defendant, that Li, Chang, and Lung must pay damages to Pu for the loss of his goods. I find for the defendant. It was the three uninjured paws of the cat, belonging to them, that enabled the animal to move, run through the warehouse, and to set fire to the store of textiles contained therein.'"

Anthony Lotherington Bathurst put a match to the tobacco with which he had packed his pipe. I saw the message of his eyes over the spurt of flame from the match.

"What do you think of that, Jack? Don't you think it worth recording?"

"Interesting without a doubt—but I don't quite see what it has to do with our case on hand."

"I thought you mightn't. But I'll tell you. And why I inflicted the yarn on you. To show you that the result went in an absolutely contrary direction to that which might reasonably well have been anticipated. Instead of Alpha turning up, lo and behold, they went out and encountered Omega."

I turned—to face one of his quizzical, almost inscrutable, smiles!

"Or, in other words," he continued, "that Oxford won the Boat-race."

The flame of the match died away.

CHAPTER XXI
MONDAY, JANUARY 2ND, 9.15 P.M.

AFTER dinner of the same day, Anthony went out. Mackintoshed, scarfed, heavy-booted, carrying both revolver and hand-torch. I raised my eyebrows when he appeared before me thus equipped.

"What's the matter with you?" he countered. "H'ain't you never seen a night-watchman afore? All ready to start on his 'trivial rounds' and extremely common tasks? What's W.W. Jacobs been doing all these years? Gawd'struth!"

"You haven't a tuft of beard sticking from your chin," I returned, accepting his vein, "so that you mustn't complain if I fail to recognize you."

"Always got an answer, haven't you?"

"Where are you bound for?" I queried him.

"Ask me another, Jack. Where the spirit takes me. That, perhaps, is the best answer that I can possibly give you. Put it like this. There are one or two residences round about the district in which I am beginning to have a certain amount of interest. Also, there is a moor.

By name, Constanton Moor. And there you are. Words and music—one penny."

I saw him slip the torch into the left-hand pocket of his mackintosh and the revolver into the other.

"*Adios*, fair coz. We shall meet at Philippi. Peradventure. Perhaps. Perchance."

Anthony Bathurst waved his hand and was gone. I sat by the fire for a time and smoked. Why hadn't he asked me to accompany him? I found the question a disturbing thought. Of all conditions, I hate most that of being deliberately kept in the dark. The night was incredibly still and quiet. The only noises that reached my ears were those that came to me from inside Scarpe. From the ticking of the clocks. From Mrs. Polglose at her various tasks in the kitchen. From an occasional creak of a board. Scarpe was old. Its history went back nearly four hundred years and constantly the wood of it summoned its pride and sought to remind us of the truth. I smoked three pipes of tobacco before I moved from the chair. Mrs. Polglose eventually brought me in my supper.

"Here's a beau'ful Welsh rarebit for you, sir, and the chayse all running from the toast as you like it to be, sir. What shall I be doin' for Mr. Bathurst?" She put the tray with my supper on the table, then waited for an answer to her question about Anthony.

"Don't worry about Mr. Bathurst, Mrs. Polglose," I said to her. "That will be all right. I'll see to him when he comes in. He may be a bit later than usual, so don't you think of waiting up for him."

She blinked at me through her old-fashioned glasses.

"Don't think that I'd mind, sir. Indeed, I'd be pleased to." The little brown old woman made the semi-suggestion with a persuasive flourish. It was really astonishing the effect that my cousin had on all women. She lingered. I'll swear that it was to hear more of him. At the same time, her face held a look of perplexity. One might almost have said suspicion. She exchanged a glance with the ceiling as I attacked my supper. Words came to her.

"I don't know what's comin' over the place, to be sure. All these tragedies. Now it's poor Lady Rachel."

"Who told you?" I asked her.

"Very nearly all St. Crayle and half St. Roseworthy. Almost everybody." She joined her hands together in a gesture, and then separated them as a swimmer does that cleaves the water in front of him. Her eyes blinked again rapidly, two or three times.

"Is there any good news of Lady Rachel?"

"None, I'm afraid, Mrs. Polglose."

She seemed to make a mighty effort. To bring all her faculties to a central focus, as it were. She studied my face intently.

"What is being done to find her?"

"Colonel Blount and the police have the matter in hand. Rest assured that they will do their best."

She shrugged her thin shoulders in turn with a degree of violence, repeating her comprehensive gesture as of the swimmer.

"The police! Their best! What good do they do?"

"They sell tickets for sports," I ventured with mild remonstrance, "and there are always two at the football ground."

She flashed a look of utter disgust at me.

"I am aware," I said "that I express myself badly. That my paraphrases are obscure. But we must all be patient—and—er—shuffle the cards."

"Lady Rachel Shelley is a lady," observed Mrs. Polglose.

"I know."

"She is not very old, either. And she is married to Captain Shelley."

"Who is a gentleman, eh?"

"Of course. Lady Rachel would never have married anybody who wasn't a gentleman."

"So much the better for both of them, then. A happy marriage, of course."

"They are made in Heaven."

"So I've always heard."

"But you know Lady Rachel and her husband, sir. You don't need me to tell you about them. You have lived here at Scarpe close to them for some years."

"That's very true," I returned gravely. "And yet I feel that I do not really know either of the Shelleys."

"They have many servants. Rich people always do have."

The Polglose made the generalization with superb confidence.

"She came here to this very house not so long ago," she continued.

This startled me, and my flippant mood dropped from me as a cloak is discarded from the shoulders. "Who did? What do you mean?"

"Lady Rachel Shelley did. I mean her."

"What?" I cried. "Are you sure, Mrs. Polglose?"

"Of course I am sure. You were out, sir. So was Mr. Bathurst. I expect that Lady Rachel came to see him."

"Why, indeed?" I demanded, a trifle nettled.

Mrs. Polglose wrinkled her brows. "It is the more likely, I think. Mr. Bathurst is a lovely man."

"But didn't Lady Rachel *tell* you what she wanted? What she had come here for? Didn't she leave a message or anything?"

Mrs. Polglose shook her head.

"Of course not. Had she done so, I should have told you."

"What did you do? Entertain her in the kitchen?"

"Yes. Indeed, Lady Rachel told me *not* to tell you that she had called upon you. That is why I didn't."

"Was the embargo placed on Mr. Bathurst as well?" I was quite aware of the asperity in my tone.

She shook her head again. "I do not understand."

"Good heavens! Did Lady Rachel tell you not to tell Mr. Bathurst that she had called here or was he to be treated differently from me?"

"No, sir. Just the same."

"Oh!" I grunted. "I see."

Mrs. Polglose looked at me a trifle defiantly.

"At any rate, it was undoubtedly for the best that Lady Rachel did come here."

"Oh, indeed? Why's that?"

"We at Scarpe were favoured by it."

"Favoured? What on earth are you talking about?"

"She is of the gentility. Not the same as you and me. The house was saved from a disaster."

"A disaster?" I was amused.

She nodded solemnly. "Yes. The pipes have never been frozen during all the terrible cold weather. Just think of that. They are almost the only pipes in the district that haven't been."

"Mrs. Polglose," I said, "are you really serious?"

"Yes, Mr. Clyst. Indeed I am. I have never been more serious in all my life. The cold would never seize the pipes in a house where one of the gentry had recently visited. I am a Glebe woman, sir. Like my mother and my mother's mother. Glebe is in my blood. I know these things." She faced me unflinchingly, her eyes blinking again through her spectacles.

"And we are in the twentieth century," I remarked. "Can one really believe it?"

"We are, for some things, sir, but not for others. There are some things that don't belong to any one century. They just belong to Time. The pipes were going to freeze here, I know, but Lady Rachel called, and they didn't."

"We must regard her arrival, then, as an act of the Almighty. I rather think that Lady Rachel Shelley must be my long-lost uncle."

"Uncle, sir," mumbled Mrs. Polglose, questioningly. "Well, certainly not my aunt. You may remove the supper-tray, Mrs. Polglose, and not worry any more about Mr. Bathurst. Also we will pray jointly that Colonel Blount's efforts are successful."

"Yes, sir. I understand." Mrs. Polglose saw that the interview was finished and that it was time to take out the supper things.

I sat there, I suppose, for another half hour. Half asleep. The fire was cosiness itself. My chair was beautifully comfortable and I let my tired body relax. Then, I was sharply and suddenly aroused from my lethargy. My telephone bell rang and rang insistently. I pulled myself rather wearily from my chair and slowly made my way towards it. It rang again before I could reach it. I hastened my steps. The voice at the other end cut through peremptorily the moment that I picked up the receiver. I recognized it at once as I listened.

"Is that you, Bathurst? This is Colonel Blount speaking."

"No," I replied. "I'm not Bathurst. It's Clyst this end. My cousin's out. Is there any message that I can take for him?"

"Message?" Blount's voice became even more peremptory. "What time do you expect your cousin back? Any idea?"

"Before midnight."

He almost exploded. Blount at his bombastic best.

"What's he doing?"

"I don't know whether he's gone to a whist-drive, or the Girl Guides' performance of 'The Sleeping Beauty' at the Church Hall." I stuck my tongue in my cheek. "He didn't say when he went out. But it's something of the sort, no doubt. He's a devil for a hectic time."

Blount shouted his response down the telephone.

"Well, tell him this, will you, when he returns? *Directly* he returns. Lady Rachel's body has been found right against Priestley's Quarry. About half an hour ago. By Foxon again, the man who found Chinnery when this infernal business started, and who afterwards picked up Copeland by the Lauriston shooting-box."

I took the shock badly.

"What?" I stammered. "Do you mean—Lady Rachel—dead?"

Blount's voice lost all its aggressive ring. He spoke quite softly. "Dead, Clyst. Frozen! Death from exposure—just the same as in the case of Chinnery. We rushed Surtees to her. There was no hope from the start. She was too far gone when Foxon picked her up. Pretty kettle of fish, isn't it?"

I could scarcely find words with which to answer him. I realized at this moment, perhaps more acutely than I had ever done before, what all this must mean to a man in Blount's position.

"Terrible," I eventually uttered. "I'll tell Anthony Bathurst what you say directly he comes in."

"Tell him the body's been taken down to the mortuary. He may want to have a look at it. In fact, I think he's bound to."

Something in his tone caught me and my mind reacted immediately to the inner meaning that his words held. I spoke hoarsely into the telephone.

"You mean," I cried, "that there are—" I paused.

Somehow or other the rest of my intended sentence stuck in my throat.

"Yes," came Blount's grave reply. "There is a red mark behind the left ear."

My hand shook as it held the receiver.

"Very good," I said weakly. "I'll see that my cousin is told directly he comes in. Good-bye—and thank you for ringing up to let me know."

I replaced the telephone receiver and went more wearily back to the chair from which I had come. In less than the time it takes to record the fact, Mrs. Polglose was at my side. If I hadn't know her too well, I might have thought that she had been eavesdropping.

"What is it now?" I asked her dully.

"The telephone, sir, I heard it ring and you answer it. Is it . . . more bad news, sir?" She twisted her old worn hands in front of her and fixed her eyes anxiously on my face.

"Yes," I replied to her with a simplicity that I scarcely recognized as my own.

Mrs. Polglose drew a deep breath. She almost whispered her next question to me.

"Was it . . . about . . . Lady Rachel?"

"Yes," I said again.

She gave a half-groan before summoning to her aid her ancient fortitude.

"What has happened to Lady Rachel?" Her voice sank again as she waited tense and anxious for my reply.

"Lady Rachel is dead, Mrs. Polglose."

"Dead, sir?" Her eyes were suspicious, almost upbraiding.

I nodded.

"How?"

"Her body was found about half an hour ago. Near Priestley's Quarry. She has been killed by the cold. Just as Mr. Chinnery was the other day."

"Lady Rachel!" You could perceive, if you watched her closely, that she brought herself with difficulty to frame the dread hypothesis—"Lady Rachel has been killed?"

"Yes, I think that's what it comes to. The whole place is in the clutch of evil. There are things stalking abroad that neither you nor I, Mrs. Polglose, can understand."

Her brow became a network of wrinkles. "You mean—witchcraft, Mr. Clyst?"

I shrugged my shoulders. "Frankly, I don't know what I mean. If I did know, I should know more."

The wrinkles increased. She bent her old eyes upon me for a moment studiously. Then she shook her head sapiently.

"No. Even then perhaps you wouldn't. If it *is* witchcraft, as I fear."

I tested her. "According to your argument, when you brought in my supper, Lady Rachel Shelley should surely have been immune from the evil power of witchcraft. How about that, Mrs. Polglose?"

She shook her head again. "No. That doesn't follow at all, sir. The nobility turn evil from the paths of *others*. They have no power to protect themselves. The good they do, the benevolence that comes from them, is used on behalf of those below them—their inferiors. Do you understand, now, what I mean, Mr. Clyst? It's a sort of burden that they're always called upon to bear."

"They save others—themselves they cannot save! Is that your meaning?"

"Yes, sir. You've put it beautifully for me by saying that." She came and stood close to me. "The powers of darkness are terrible. I am frightened of them. The whole place should be sprinkled with Holy Water. That is the only way in which ordinary people like us can cope with them. Be sure of that, Mr. Clyst. It's just a question of good against evil. If the good is properly used it must beat evil in the end—always."

There seemed to me no argument against this last contention, so I held my peace. Mrs. Polglose had spoken entirely without vehemence, indeed without emotion. She had scarcely raised her voice for the effort. There came a dead silence. I looked and saw her turn away. Tears for Lady Rachel Shelley ran down her cheeks. I watched her with silent sympathy as she trudged slowly back to the kitchen. I looked at my wrist-watch. The time showed as half past eleven. The fire was beginning to burn low. I took the poker and prodded it to a brighter blaze. The flames began to flicker again, and I was just responding gratefully to their warmth, when I heard Anthony Bathurst at the front door. In two minds whether to meet him or to stay where I was, I decided on the latter action. I heard him parking his outdoor things in the hall-cupboard and whistling softly to himself as he did so. Then I heard him hum the words of "The Chocolate Soldier" song—"My Hero". "Come, come, naught can efface you, my arms . . . to embrace you." I heard him shuffle his feet on the mat and then the door opened and he came in to me.

"Hello, Jack! Thought you might have gone up to Uncle Ned. God—it's a foul place, this St. Crayle—in the dark! If I've barked my shins once tonight I've barked 'em a dozen times."

"Why not take the car?"

"A-ha." He wagged a finger at me. "Didn't want the car, Jacko. Wanted to go places and see things! Places and things that don't exactly harmonize with noisy cars, with lights and wheels and general car-equipment. See, my faithful Sempronius?"

I nodded to him. "I expected you to say that, so I wasn't disappointed. As a matter of fact, while you've been out you've been wanted. 'Phone call came through for you some little time ago. I answered it for you."

He stared at me. "Who was it, Jack?"

"Colonel Blount," I replied tersely.

"Old Blount? What did he want at this time of night?"

"He had news for you." I intended to play him as long as I reasonably could in return for his single-handed effort during the earlier part of the evening. "News—what of?"

"Lady Rachel Shelley."

The name absolutely galvanized him into throbbing excitement. He couldn't hide the fact from me.

"Lady Rachel? What about her?"

"She's dead," I said quietly. "Our question has been answered—as to 'who next?'."

He came and stood over me. "Dead? Tell me all you know, Jack. And for God's sake, don't waste any more time."

I met the censure calmly.

"I won't. I promised Blount all sorts of things like that. Lady Rachel's body has been found just like the other two were. Chinnery's and Copeland's. Except that she's dead like Chinnery was."

"Where was she found?"

"Near Priestley's Quarry—so Blount says. Again, you see, like Chinnery. The man who was dead! The quarry is evidently the danger-spot. We must remember that."

"When was she found?"

"About an hour and a half ago. I've worked that out as well, from what Blount told me."

"And the cause of death?"

"As per specification. Cold. Exposure to the elements. Frozen to death, I suppose you'd call it." He looked at me curiously as I said this. I wondered why, but I wasn't destined to know the reason until later.

"Where's the body, Jack?"

"Mortuary. On the same slab as Chinnery's was, I expect. Oh, and by the way, our friend Foxon found it again. That's his hat trick. Always in at the death, that man, if you like. Blount told me all this. He wanted you badly, to tell you. I fancy he thought that you'd buzz off to the mortuary to look at the body in double-quick time."

I glanced up at him to see how he was taking it all. "H'm. He thought that, did he? Well—I might—but patience first, please. Never was patience more strongly indicated."

"You think that, Anthony?"

He nodded his head affirmatively but very slowly. "Yes, Jack." Then he flashed another question at me. "Any more to tell me?" His eyes searched my face. "Yes."

"I knew it! The red mark again?"

"Yes."

"Same place?"

"Yes. Behind the left ear."

"Cunning devils. But they'll take one step too many, and then, by God, I'll have them in the hollow of my hand." The lines of his face tightened. He turned away from me. I saw his fist clenched and the veins stand out on his forehead. Anthony Bathurst had picked up the challenge! There was no mistaking that this time.

"What are you going to do?"

He shook his head at me impatiently.

"Do you see how the 'technique's' been varied this time, Jack?"

"Technique?" I repeated.

"Yes! The 'technique of murder'. Look at the 'time' question, for one thing alone."

"The 'time' question?"

"H'm." He nodded. "Exactly. Can't you see what I mean?"

"No. I'm dashed if I can. Show me the way and I'll endeavour to be intelligent."

"Well—look at it this way, Jack. Take the times between the original disappearances and the finding of the various bodies. It's most significant." I nodded. At last I could see what he meant. Anthony went on quickly, to drive home, no doubt, the point that he had made. "It took a week to kill Chinnery and the same time to put Copeland in the valley of the shadow. But it's only taken a couple of days to give Lady Rachel Shelley her quietus. That's the point."

I made no reply to him.

"Why only two days for Lady Rachel and a week for the others? Tell me that, Jack. I'm puzzled. But I've got them! Whoever they are. Either the one—or more."

"How do you know that?" I asked curiously.

"How do I know it? I know it very well, Jack, my boy. I'm as sure of it as I am of tomorrow's dawn." His eyes held a strange, fierce light. "I've been out tonight with a purpose. I haven't been walking round with my eyes shut and my mouth open with my tongue hanging out. Not on your life. Also, my lad, I've been on the moor. Constanton Moor. Not over far from Priestley's Quarry either, as it happens."

I thrilled most strangely to his statement.

"You have!" I cried. "Then you must have been . . ."

I stopped. I scarcely knew what to say to him next.

"Must have been—what?" he queried.

"Not far away from the trouble," I concluded lamely. The gleam in his grey eyes flickered up again.

"Not too far, Jack. As the crow flies. And that's the reason why I said just now the thing I did. The body of Lady Rachel Shelley wasn't lying near Priestley's Quarry at half past nine this evening. I can tell you that without the slightest fear of contradiction. Because if it had been, I should have seen it. Got *that*, laddie? And what it signifies?"

"You're *certain* that you didn't see it?"

He flashed a look of contempt at me. "My dear Jack. What's come over you? I thought you knew me far too well to ask a question of that kind. I was so close to Priestley's Quarry at the time that I mentioned, that if the body of Lady Rachel Shelley *had* been there, then I couldn't possibly have helped seeing it. *Now* do you understand?"

"Where did you get to after that?"

"Over towards the other edge of the moor. In the Lauriston shooting-box direction. I wanted to have a second squint at both places. *Inter alia*, that is. All of which helps me to the confident opinion which I expressed just now, that I know *just* a little too much for our murderer—or possibly murderers."

"Yes—but what you know is only 'general'. It hasn't much particular value that I can see."

"Why not?" His eyes searched my face.

"Well, has it? Look at it for yourself. All that you know, that can be regarded as more than anyone else knows or will know, is that the dead woman's body wasn't in the place where it was ultimately found at half past nine! Can't see myself that that's going to cut much ice."

"With whom?"

"With anybody."

"It will with the man that counts."

"Who's he when he's at home?"

"*I'm* that man! What I found out tonight is going to cut no end of ice with me. And in the words of Long John Silver—'you can lay to that'."

"All right, I'll take your word for it. I know it's a lousy, rotten job, and all that, but what worries me is that we get no nearer to anything that's real. On the contrary, our scanty population is becoming depleted, one by one. In five years we shall be like the Dodo. When I enquired 'who next?' the other night, I little thought what the answer would be."

My cousin was silent. I think that my words had struck home. When he did reply, it was with a shrug of his shoulders.

"You're right, Jack. I admit it. But I haven't Blount's resources, you know. I'm only here to help, quite unofficially. I have only myself ... and ... er ... you. I haven't bags of men and cars that I can throw as a patrol over the whole countryside indiscriminately."

"I know you haven't. Don't take what I said to heart. But what's Blount doing about it all? I tell you straight, my patience is just about reaching exhaustion point. We're all in danger, or, at least, so it seems to me. Every one of us. We're here today, but none of us knows whether he'll be gone tomorrow. I don't like it. Not a little bit.

I haven't the slightest desire to be picked up stiff and stark either near Priestley's Quarry or close to old Lauriston's shooting-box."

His eyes met mine and held them.

"You need have no fear of that, Jack. I shall be here to look after you."

"You weren't here tonight," I retorted curtly. "I could have been spirited away from here without your being a whit the wiser. You can't be on the moor *and* protecting me at Scarpe, you know."

He persisted. "That makes no odds. I tell you, you won't be touched. You're as safe as I am myself."

"How safe's that, to be sure?" I grumbled.

"Safe enough. As you'll see yourself when the job's through and over. 'Dinna fash yersel', mon.' Bank on the skill, sagacity, and subtlety of Anthony Lotherington Bathurst. He won't let you down. Even though there should be other shocks."

He fell to quotation. "'Who are these coming to the sacrifice? What little town by river or sea-shore? Or mountain-built with peaceful citadel. Is emptied of her folk this pious mom? Little town, thy streets for evermore will silent be . . .'" He stopped suddenly and took a cigarette.

"I must go and look at this last dead body, Jack, and then—clear the decks for action."

"When are you going? Tonight?"

"No—curse it. Too dead tired now. Brain dull and stodgy. First thing tomorrow morning. That will be time enough. Still—I must ring old Blount. I must show him that courtesy."

I watched him walk towards the 'phone, and then, as he started to speak, I made my way to bed. Anthony wasn't the only man who was dead tired. They could say what they liked to each other for all I cared!

CHAPTER XXII
TUESDAY, JANUARY 3RD, 11.45 A.M.

MARTIN Burke and Sybil Burke, together with Verschoyle, were with me on the following morning when Anthony Bathurst came back from the mortuary at St. Roseworthy. The three of them had walked over to Scarpe, to see if we had any more news concerning the tragedy of the previous night. I told them, when they came, that my cousin was out. They elected to wait until he returned, whenever that might be.

Verschoyle made himself comfortable in an armchair. He looked at his best this morning. His delicate, strong features, his prominent nose, his well-marked, finely lined jawbone, his clear-cut chin, his humorously cynical mouth, with the delicately chiselled lips, his high yet rather narrow brow, rising above his deep-set eyes, all of them held my attention and attracted me. There was no doubt that Verschoyle was a decidedly clever-looking man. He *looked* an aristocrat. He had distinction. Even without his collar and jacket, most people would have taken him to be what he was. He bore the ecclesiastical impress. He had that indefinable air of the cleric which most people are quick to recognize, though it isn't an easy matter to say from where, or what, it takes its origin.

Verschoyle looked the part of the earnest scholar. There was a rumour in St. Crayle, concerning him, that he had a private collection of hunting-knives and that he had journeyed as far as a Ghetto of Rome, south of the Tiber, during the previous summer, to bring back with him a pair of stilettos that had most certainly not been used in the cause of Virtue. Verschoyle's voice, his speaking voice, that is, was silver-toned. But at times there was a trenchant edge upon it, a general asperity that gave it its claim to character. His singing voice was even better than his speaking voice. It was a tenor, and it was always my opinion that it never showed to better advantage than in the Versicles.

Little was said by any of us until Anthony returned. Sybil looked utterly played out and Martin looked absolutely ghastly. We muttered commonplaces to each other. Verschoyle had taken his chin into his hand as though it had been a beard, and considered us. At last he touched on the subject which was in all our minds.

"You're frayed," he said, "you're worn. All of you. This 'Thing' that has folded itself round our lives is sapping your vitalities. As though it were a vampire or a were-wolf. We must summon all our resources of Goodness, if we mean to combat it successfully."

I saw Martin Burke clench his fists. The action suggested that he was fretting at an imposed condition of helplessness. Sybil half-shook her head. Her husband burst into speech. He had been conquered in the struggle.

"It's a question of Evil," he cried. "Some things, and some people, are evil by nature. I'll say again, what I said before. They *project* evil."

Verschoyle nodded. "I agree with you. I think that you're undeniably right. I told you before that I did."

Burke nodded in response to him.

"Yes. I know you did. Let me illustrate my point. Take orchids, for instance. Those Messalinas of the hot-house! What are they but mauve corruption, with their leering spotted faces? What other reaction comes from them, ever, but one of noisomeness? They bend towards each other. Their faces are evil. They are grotesque, with horrible, misshapen chins. They whisper soft sensuous histories to each other of unknown sin. To mock at everything that *is* not and *has* not its being in their own stench-bed of evil." Martin Burke paused as abruptly as he had started. There was a red flush across his forehead.

Verschoyle answered him.

"Yes, I cordially agree. The picture that you drew is an excellent illustration of your point. I remember a room into which I once found my way that affected me very much in the same manner. There was a couch painted into the semblance of a female figure. Between her arms, there was placed a cushion for the head of the person who rested there. Contorted atrocities from the East, in the shape of ivory figures of strange postures, were almost everywhere. A Liebl hung on the wall. It was of a smoking cocotte. The whole apartment was lewd, and the room seemed to palpitate with a heavy languorous music that made one's senses drowsy. The entire influence was narcotic. I went there with a doctor, on an errand of mercy."

"There is no need for you to tell us that. We knew that, Rector," said Sybil.

Verschoyle thanked her with a smile and then went on.

"There were silver ornaments that would have been in keeping with the garish boudoir of a Parisian *fille de joie*. The carved woman, that I just described, might well have been the couch to which Thais tempted Paphnuce. You see what I mean?"

It was at that moment that Anthony Bathurst came in. A quick step was audible in the hall, the door of the room opened and he entered swiftly to us and with an air of ruthless determination.

"Good morning, everybody," he said quietly. "I'm pleased to see you all gathered round, but I fear that, in the circumstances, you will find me devilish bad company."

Burke's flush spread to his cheeks.

"Really, Bathurst? That's rather a pity. Because obviously we are here out of a desire to talk things over."

Anthony shook his head.

"To come here was a mistake. There is so much work to be done."

"Can't we all help, even if there is?"

Anthony shrugged his shoulders. "In a multitude of counsellors . . ." He turned away and stared moodily out of the window. All of us respected the silence. My cousin came away from the window. He addressed himself to Verschoyle.

"Rector," he said, "you and Burke, I believe, are still definitely attracted by the theory that has been put forward to us of the malevolent activity of an evil spirit? Am I right in assuming that?"

Verschoyle looked across at Burke before he replied to Anthony Bathurst's question. Burke, however, showed neither sign of agreement nor gesture of encouragement. Verschoyle, therefore, took unto himself the responsibility of the answer.

"I believe in the powers of evil, certainly. I believe in the personality of the Devil. I have already told you of these things. Once you admit that, you must admit the other possibilities."

"That's 'general', sir, and if you will forgive my saying so, bordering on the nebulous. Are you of the opinion that these 'crimes', here in this district, which have horrified us and shocked us so profoundly, are the result of the workings of an evil power such as you describe?"

"I do not necessarily assert that to be so, but I am prepared to believe that it may be so. Count me with Horatio." Verschoyle spoke calmly and with dignity.

Anthony swung round on to Burke.

"Well, Burke, what have you to say? You heard what I asked. I'm interested."

Burke twisted his face, as was his habit when pressed for an opinion or for. a reply.

"I agree with the Rector on general principles. I've lived out East, you see. But you know that. It makes a vast difference to a man. When one has had daily contact with the Oriental mind, over a fairly long period of time, one begins to believe in so much that, previously, one would have unreservedly scouted. And it's because of these things that I find myself unable to contradict the Rector."

Anthony Bathurst nodded his head slowly several times.

Again there came a silence. Verschoyle sent a sharp shaft singing into it.

"I take it, Mr. Bathurst, that you find yourself in complete disagreement with us?"

"Not exactly. As regards the existence of 'evil'. We have two deaths on our hands. There is enough proof of that. Proof that we dare not ignore. But I tell you candidly—I would much rather believe in a living murderer than in a baleful banshee."

Verschoyle smiled blandly. "You would, of course, then, look askance at a belief in lycanthropy or vampirism?"

"Not necessarily. That would depend," replied Anthony guardedly.

"On what?"

"Oh—many things. Each case should be treated on its merits."

"Or—demerits," smiled the Rector.

"If you prefer to have it that way."

I heard the wheels of a car stopping outside. Burke looked at the window and the Rector raised his eyebrows. Then I heard Mrs. Polglose admitting Copeland. It was the first time that I had seen the Squire since his narrow escape from death. I was unprepared for the change that had taken place in him since the dinner-party at the Rectory from which point this history began. All his fat, robust boastfulness had gone from him. The old cocksureness and swagger were evidently left behind him for ever. His ordeal on Constanton Moor, even though he *had* managed to escape its direst consequences, had laid its icy fingers on him, and the impressions had remained.

"I heard that you were all here," he said as an opening remark, "because I've been talking to Blount. So I thought I'd come along. You don't mind? God—but this business is terrible! It gets worse. What are we going to do about it, Rector?"

"We must remember one thing, and one thing only. That we are in God's hands. His will must be done."

Copeland made an impatient gesture. For a moment, at least, some of his aggressive egotism returned to him.

"That's all very well, Rector. But I've got an answer to that. And that answer's this. God helps those who help themselves. I like the sound of that a lot better. What do you say, you others?" He appealed to us all with his eyes.

"I'm with you, Squire, for one." The words came from Anthony Bathurst.

Copeland nodded.

"That's the best thing I've heard so far. What's Blount going to do? Any idea? I found him about as communicative as a Bluepoint."

Before Anthony could reply, Verschoyle came into the conversation again.

"Whatever he may do, whatever any one of us may do, we are, as I said just now, in God's hands. Our faith in the ultimate triumph of Goodness, assisted by the Grace of God, must come to our rescue and in time clear away our troubles and defeat our foes. Have we no belief in the Holy Scripture? The Altar of the Holy Eucharist must wipe out sinful deeds and banish them from our midst."

To a certain extent, Verschoyle was showing me something that I had not seen in him before. Anthony became practical.

"Tell me, Squire," he said. "have you seen Captain Shelley this morning?"

"Yes," returned Copeland, shortly. "Why? Why do you ask, I mean?"

"How is he?"

"A broken man, utterly and completely. Taken a very bad knock. There isn't the slightest doubt that he was tremendously attached to Lady Rachel. Much more than I, for one, had ever dreamed."

Anthony nodded. "He can supply us with no additional data?"

"I didn't ask him that in so many words. But I shouldn't imagine that he can. Blount's seen him twice, I believe. That brings me to the question, Bathurst, that I asked a short time ago. What *are* we going to do about things? I, for one, refuse to sit here with arms folded waiting for the next person to be murdered. Especially as it will probably be me." Copeland stuck out his determined jaw and I felt sure that my cousin warmed to him. I was acutely aware that I did, and as the thought came to me Anthony Bathurst made the announcement that brought astonishment to all our hearts.

"At least there's one good point about the whole thing," he said quietly.

"And that is?" asked Martin Burke.

I saw Sybil open wide her eyes when her husband put his question. I shall never forget the terms of Anthony's reply.

"That it's only a matter of hours now before I get him."

His tones were quite quiet. There wasn't a trace or a hint of braggadocio to be heard in his voice. As far as I can remember it was Copeland who put into words what we were all thinking.

"Get whom, Bathurst?"

"The murderer. The Rector's disembodied evil spirit—or whatever it is that he fancies in that line."

Burke shook his head impatiently, as though Anthony Bathurst's remark had caused him annoyance. We all stared incredulously. Verschoyle's lips curled a trifle.

"Why, Mr. Bathurst—why this sudden burst of excessive confidence?"

Copeland looked at Anthony as though he were an object deserving the full flow of human pity. Martin Burke regarded him as he would have regarded a poor, witless soul unable to understand the most elementary principles. Only Sybil and I, in a certain dual measure responsible for his being there in our midst, remained entirely normal. Anthony replied to Verschoyle with the utmost candour.

"Well—why not, sir? Things have cleared so much during the last few days. I may even be forgiven for having 'groped' a little in the past. I was intended to, you see. By the murderer. Now, however, there has come a change, and I'm going to call his bluff."

"What's the change?" asked the Rector.

"What I said! I'm going to call the killer's bluff."

"How?" enquired Copeland.

"In such a way that he won't know it's being called. Which is by far the best way when you're dealing with a killer of this calibre and cunning."

Martin Burke came and faced Anthony Bathurst. "Do you mean to tell me that you know the identity of the person responsible for the killing of Chinnery and Lady Rachel, and the attack on Copeland?"

Anthony returned the searching glance with which Burke had favoured him.

"Yes."

"Then why the hell don't you go straight to Blount and have the scoundrel arrested?" This from Copeland.

"I *could* do that," returned Anthony evenly.

"Then what the hell are you waiting for?"

"Certainty, Squire. Absolute, uncontradictable certainty. I want my suspected person to be much more than a suspected person. I want him to be taken, as it were, *in flagrante delicto*. All wrapped up and with somewhere to go. And that's how I intend that he shall be taken." Anthony smiled nonchalantly.

The Rector stepped forward and shook him by the hand.

"Brave words, Mr. Bathurst. The red badge of courage at last! My heart kindles to hear such words spoken. *Your* murderer! *My* evil spirit! Body does not make the man, Mr. Bathurst. I would have you remember that. Spirit is the man. The colossal importance of the spirit-force in man has never been properly realized. When a spirit leaves the body for ever—owing to that affair which you and I call 'death'—it finds itself on the astral plane. It probably feels entirely weary and, I am sure, speaking for myself, just a wee bit bewildered. But this spirit is still in the form of the body from which it has just flown. Because it is puzzled and has temporarily lost its way, it will be looked after by another spirit or spirits, sent to that astral plane by God Himself, for that special purpose and service. The evil spirit, though, has none of these services or ministrations. It wanders through a No Man's Land, seeking evil. Seeking to 'do evil'. To 'help on' the *cause* of evil. Some of us are clairvoyant. Others are clairaudient. I want you to ponder on, and remember, all these things, Mr. Bathurst."

The Rector let Anthony's hand go. He had held it all the time that he had been speaking. My cousin was as self-possessed, though, as Verschoyle himself.

He replied quietly.

"I will not argue with you, Rector. To me, a murderer must be insane. Murder is so alien to humanity. But he's better off behind bars of a kind. Although the veil may be across his soul, he carries evil in his heart, and in his hands. When that evil is spilled, an innocent person may suffer. A life may be summarily ended. These things are wrong. They should not be. Indeed they *must* not be. I am going to see to that. I am sure that you are with me there, sir."

"I will leave you to contemplate what I said to you. I think that we must understand each other. Any other condition would be incredible."

Copeland, as usual, brought us back to the more commonplace.

"This spirit stuff from the Rector here and the 'astral plane', whatever that may be, don't make a lot of impression on my mind. In other words, that fit my way of thinking and speaking a little better, they don't cut much ice. But when Mr. Bathurst talks in terms of catching a murderer, I come over much more sympathetic. Especially if it's the bloke who nearly showed me the way to Kingdom Come. I find myself extremely interested, let me tell you. So interested, that if he'll have me, I'm out to give Mr. Bathurst a hand."

Anthony smiled heartily at the Squire's enthusiasm.

"I'm very grateful for the offer, Copeland. If I can, I'll make use of it. I can do with all the help that I can get."

Burke came in with a question.

"For God's sake, Bathurst—what are you going to do? Think things over, man, and look where you're going. We don't want another tragedy in our midst. If you *must* go into this fight, as you tell us you must—why then—use Blount and—all the resources of his authority, if you possibly can. But don't go into it single-handed, which I'm very much afraid is your intention. I know you. I know your temperament and your inclinations." He turned impulsively to his wife. "Sybil," he cried, "add your entreaties to mine. Please! Bathurst may listen to you, where he won't listen to me. In a way, I feel to a certain extent responsible for his safety. I know how you were instrumental in bringing him down here." Martin Burke's face was twisted with emotion.

Sybil shook her head very slowly.

"Anthony must do what he thinks best. That is the only thing he can do. I have enough faith and confidence in him not to be afraid."

"But, Sybil—you don't know—" Burke's voice rang out, and then ceased abruptly. We caught our breath. She responded to his mood.

"I know that I don't. I know there are many things about it all which are almost impossible for me to understand. Nothing that you can say, Martin, can make me see that any more clearly. Mr. Bathurst will work out his own salvation. By doing so, he will work out the salvation of all of us who are left here. He has a trained mind. He has the gift of acute perception. He has something else, Martin, even more important, perhaps. He has the sensibility of one who is thoroughly conversant with the mental and physical vagaries of human nature."

As he spoke, I caught Sybil Burke's eyes gazing steadfastly into mine. I caught her mood and her enthusiasm.

"She's right!" I cried. I could do nothing else. I *had* to say what I did. I *had* to declare myself on her side, as it were. "Let Anthony get to work as he wants to," I went on. "Sometimes it's every man for himself, but here it's a case of Anthony Bathurst for all of us."

Copeland came and shook me by the hand.

"By God, Clyst, you're right, and Mrs. Burke is right too. Here's luck to Anthony Bathurst."

"Thank you," returned that worthy, "every one of you."

Verschoyle's voice rang out like a clarion. "We wish you good luck in the name of the Lord."

I caught my breath, and even Copeland seemed impressed.

Verschoyle had the knack of doing things like that.

Chapter XXIII
SATURDAY, JANUARY 7TH, 9.30 A.M.

THE coroner's inquest on the body of Lady Rachel Shelley was adjourned, even as the inquest on Chinnery had been. I fancy that Blount was prompted by Anthony Bathurst with regard to this. But, as was to be expected, our little corner of England began to attract undesirable attention from the daily Press. Such sensational head-lines as "Glebeshire Horror", "The Frozen Fear", and "Death on the Moor" began to appear at the top of columns of most of the morning dailies. Both St. Crayle and St. Roseworthy found themselves well on the way towards the acquisition of most unsavoury reputations. In the two villages themselves, however, little or nothing happened.

Anthony Bathurst seemed inactive. Some people, more imagin-ative than their neighbours, might have described his condition as "ominously quiet", without knowing towards whom, or what, the omen was to be directed. On the following Saturday morning, almost immediately after Mrs. Polglose had cleared away the breakfast things, he somewhat surprisingly began to talk to me concerning the traged-ies. These words were the first words that he had uttered in connection with the moor murders since the occasion when Verschoyle, Cope-land, and the Burkes had been with us. He spoke in this wise.

"Frozen bodies, a red mark behind the ear, car-wheel tracks and green hairs. Not much to build on, John Clyst—and yet I'm defin-itely going to build, and from that scanty material. Also, my lad, I'm going to tell you something which I think will make you sit up and take notice."

"I'm all attention," I answered. "What is it?"

"You remember the morning 'after the night before', when the body of Lady Rachel Shelley was discovered?"

"Quite well. But let's see where we are. Lady Rachel was found at night."

"I know. I expressed myself badly. But morning and night—with afternoon—make up a full day. She was found dead through exposure, wasn't she? What the man in the street would call 'frozen to death'. You won't contradict that, will you?"

"No. That's as I understand things."

"Good. That's established, then. Now, Mr. John Clyst, see here. During the early evening of the night that Lady Rachel was being picked up by Foxon *there was an undeniable thaw*! The thermom-eter actually registered several more degrees of temperature." There was a ring of triumph in his voice as he flung the fact at me.

"Go on," I said patiently.

"Right. I can see I've got you interested this time. That thaw, laddie, continued *all the evening*. Gradually but steadily."

"Which means . . . ?" I interrupted him.

"That I am far from satisfied that Lady Rachel, or Chinnery, or Copeland was the victim of an exposure to extreme cold in such a manner as was generally believed and accepted. Surely Lady Rachel would have—think of the condition of her clothing, for example—"

I broke incontinently into his speech. My excitement had mastered me.

"They were dead before they reached the moor! Surely that's the explanation of it all."

"Looks like it, Jack, doesn't it? Though I'm hanged if I understand it all. I've examined the Shelley car. Picked up nothing from it. There's only one thing left for me now. I'm going to see the job right through. I know enough, I think, to get a real line." He turned away.

"What are you going to do?" I asked him pointedly.

"I'll let you know, Jack, so don't get windy over anything. I want to go to my room for half an hour now."

I'm afraid that I shrugged my shoulders and let him go without further remark. There was never any good purpose to be served from an argument with Anthony Lotherington Bathurst when his mind was set upon anything. So I went through into the outhouse and put in half an hour or so with a saw and a few hefty elm-branches. From these branches I managed to get twenty-two good-sized logs for the fire. I carried eight of them into the kitchen and handed them to Mrs. Polglose for the day's use.

"A fire, Mrs. Polglose," I said, "a roaring, mighty fire of flame! A fire such as I love and which gladdens my heart. We will shut out from our living-room this devilish cold."

She shook her head moodily.

"We may shut out the cold, sir, but neither you nor I can shut out the devilry. The Devil gets into places so easily. The way always seems smooth and slippery for him. Although he's named Lucifer, we're no match for him. I don't know why that should be. It just is."

I thought of Verschoyle and his expressed belief in the personality of Satan. But I made no reply. I could hear Anthony's steps close at hand. I went into the dining-room to join him. He came up to me in a way that I can only describe as curious.

"Jack," he said, "I'm going out now. And I don't know when I shall be back." He held out his hand to me, but averted his eyes as he did so.

"Danger?" I demanded curtly.

"Yes. I'm afraid so. But, as I see things, there's nothing else for it. I *must* call the murderers' bluff."

"*Must* you, old chap?"

"I think so. But don't worry your fat over it. If the worst comes to the worst, nobody'll weep overmuch over me."

"Can't I help?"

"Quite a lot, old man, but not in the way you'd like to, I'm afraid. Not even in the way you may be imagining."

"How, then?"

"By being a damned good soldier and obeying orders."

"Whose orders?"

"Mine, of course. Whose else?"

"What am I to do?"

"That, Jack, you will know later."

I fenced with him. "Why not now?"

"There you go, you see. Just as I anticipated. Questions instead of implicit obedience. Where are we ever going to get on those lines?"

He annoyed me. It's no use my denying it. Rules may be rules, but they're only made to be broken. Orders may be orders—but circumstances alter cases. Surely the position in which he and I now stood brooked no servile pandering to set regulations?

"If not now, then—when?"

"For you to know, do you mean?"

"Yes."

"Just this. Jack, and nothing more. My plans are made. They affect not only you, but also some others. To alter them now, to concede anything to what after all is but a whim of yours, might very well be disastrous. That's why."

He noticed that I was crestfallen.

"Oh, come off it, Jack. I've not signed my death-warrant yet. Far from it, laddie. I've a two to one on chance of eating another Christmas dinner. Even a 'Carissimaristmas' one."

"You have? You mean it? You're not pulling the wool over my eyes?"

"I have much more than an even chance, Jack. Honest Injun. See my finger wet? There you are, then. But you must understand this. My chance is *only* my chance, in those proportions, if my orders are obeyed to the letter. And those orders partly concern *you*. Have I made myself clear?"

"All right," I assented. "I give in. How long's it going to last?"

"How long's what going to last?"

"The suspense. The waiting time. For if there's anything I loathe, it's doing that."

"I know you do. I'm much the same as you are. Most normal men are. If I were certain of the length of time, I'd make you as wise. But I'm not. So I can't, and it's no use my trying to. But tell me this, Jack, what do you know about the calorie?"

"Nothing," I replied promptly, "beyond, that is, its general meaning. Why do you ask?"

"Because the problem of 'cold evil', Jack, is closely concerned with the calorie. It's the name applied to a unit of energy. There are two units which axe called by this name. Did you know that?"

I shook my head.

"No. Why should I?"

"First of all, there is the small calorie, the 'gram' calorie or 'standard' calorie, which is the amount of heat required to raise one gram of water one degree centigrade as regards temperature. But the 'large' calorie is known as the kilo-calorie."

I nodded. "Yes. I do remember that I've heard that. Read it somewhere. Go on. Though, for the life of me, I can't see where all this is leading."

He waved his hand deprecatingly.

"Never mind that for the moment. We'll get on with our friend the calorie. This large calorie, or, as I've just called it, the kilo-calorie, is used in the study of dietetics and physiological processes. It is the amount of heat required to raise one kilogram of water one degree centigrade in temperature. Get that, Jack? Now the number of calories required to carry on the processes necessary for life and normal body warmth, such as the beating of the heart, the movements of the chest in breathing, and the chemical activities of the secreting glands, is, in the case of an adult person of average weight, somewhere in the neighbourhood of sixteen hundred. To carry on ordinary sedentary occupations, an individual requires about two thousand five hundred calories. To perform light muscular work, slightly over three thousand calories are required. For hard, sustained continuous labour, a man requires no fewer than about four thousand calories. Daily, that is." He paused. Then proceeded. "Those calories, Jack, are my most pressing problems at the moment. And that's where this conversation has been leading. Now—are you satisfied?"

I thought that I saw the light. "It boils down to a question of food value, surely?"

"You mean protein, fat, carbohydrates, etc.?"

"Yes. That's it. Why not?"

"Well, some places aren't exactly restaurants, you know."

I stared at him. I failed to comprehend his meaning. He amplified his previous statement.

"The moor isn't, for one."

My eyes opened. "What's the moor got to do with it?"

He shrugged his shoulders.

"That's where they die, Jack. Where they're picked up stiff. Two of 'em already. And very nearly three."

His eyes held a far-away look.

"If three thousand calories are necessary, as I said, for lightish work, and since about four ounces of normal daily food are protein, it means that two thousand five hundred calories are to be supplied by carbohydrates and fat together." He paused again. "Different people treat the problem in different ways. The Esquimaux, for example, make the deficiency up in fat. But the natives of India and the poorer classes of the world in general act differently and make it up in cereals."

"Why's that?" I was endeavouring to follow him.

"For economic reasons, I should say. Cereal food is much cheaper than fat. Though, of course, fat has, bulk for bulk, more than double the calorie value of the carbohydrate. Kean, the famous actor, was a tremendous believer, by the way, in the effect of the calorie, and he took his views to absurd lengths. He would choose his dinner according to the part that he was about to play. For a tyrant he would take pork. For a murderer, beef. But always mutton for a lover. Perhaps, I suggest, to obtain the sheepish look. But more probably a mere matter of digestion. Butter, cheese, raisins, and walnuts have all high calorie values. There you are, Jack. Now you know much more than I intended to tell you when I came in. Good-bye." He held out his hand to me again.

I grasped it tightly. Much of what he had said left me wondering, but I was able to tell, without the vestige of a doubt, that he had a fixed purpose in front of him and would not swerve from the achievement of that purpose unless the odds were cast tremendously against him. I had seen him determined and resolute in the past, but never more so than he appeared to be at this moment. I saw him thrust his right hand into the pocket of his jacket and then a look of relief cross his face.

"What is it?" I enquired.

"Didn't want to forget something, Jack. Can't afford to. It may play a vital part in my plans." He grinned at me in his old cavalier way. I instantly understood his meaning.

"Revolver?"

"Yes, laddie, revolver. And loaded in every chamber. Quite a useful auxiliary to take with me. Because you never know, old son, when you go out on a job of this kind."

I nodded. There was a certain amount of relief for me here. The revolver must make his position stronger, unless things went unnaturally badly with him. As the thought registered in my brain, he turned and left me. I heard his steps in the distance. I little dreamt when, and in what danger, I was destined to see him again!

CHAPTER XXIV
SATURDAY, JANUARY 7TH, 10 P.M.

THREE people telephoned for Anthony Bathurst during the course of that day. I answered all three of them. The first message was from Blount. I told him that Anthony had gone out again and that I didn't know when he'd be back. He cursed at me and was still cursing when I put down the receiver. This happened in the early part of the afternoon, soon after Mrs. Polglose had cleared away the things from the luncheon table.

In the early evening Martin Burke rang. He also wanted to speak to Anthony. His reaction, however, to my cousin's absence was different from Blount's. I told Burke what I had told Blount—that I didn't know when my cousin would be back. He thereupon came through with another enquiry. Did I know where Anthony had gone? Upon my replying that I didn't, Martin Burke seemed to become apprehensive. I thought that I heard him say something to somebody who was at his elbow (Sybil possibly), but I wasn't able to catch the actual words used in this remark. He then asked me if I would get Anthony to 'phone him directly he returned. I countered by the enquiry: "Does that hold good if he doesn't return for a week or so?" His reply this time undoubtedly showed a certain amount of anxiety. "Was I really serious in anticipating that my cousin might be absent from Scarpe for as long as that?" I replied, "Quite." Which brought from him the remark that it all seemed pretty hopeless, then, and it wasn't any good prolonging the conversation, and Martin Burke rang off.

The third person to ring through was Dick Copeland. This happened about half past eight. Much to my surprise, he wanted Anthony to go over to his place that evening. "Not in," I answered, "so you're doomed to disappointment, Dick." His tones expressed genuine regret. "Where is he?" I repeated after him. "I couldn't say. He's out and about and that's all there is to it. But when he comes in I'll tell him that you rang. Even though it takes a week. That O.K.?" "Yes," he returned to me. "That's what I'd like you to do. By-bye, Clyst. I've a tremendous appreciation of your cousin, you know."

He rang off at that, and I, for the third time, replaced the receiver with a certain amount of thankfulness. The night was pitch-black. More than once I went to the window and looked out at it. If Anthony Bathurst were out on Constanton Moor in that darkness and the evil were stalking abroad, God help him! His sole weapons, as far as I knew, were a revolver and an electric torch. Unable to settle down, I wandered from room to room. Eventually I found myself in the little

195 | COLD EVIL

room which I used as my library and writing-room. Idly I made my way to the desk.

From the way that the chair was standing, and also from the arrangement of the various articles on the desk, I could see that Bathurst had been there, and comparatively recently at that. My eye fell carelessly on the blotting-pad that I always kept there on the front of the desk. Across the corner was a note in Anthony's handwriting. I couldn't possibly miss it. His script, noticeable for the remarkably distinct Greek "epsilons", so different from mine, stood out to my eye, almost as plainly as though he had intended me to see it. With a perhaps pardonable curiosity, considering the nature of the circumstances, I bent over the blotting-pad so that I might read what my cousin had scrawled there. What I read occasioned me extreme surprise. The words were as follows:

Query: Clement Vincent due to leave St. Crayle secretly at the end of the week. On no account must this be allowed to happen. Action to prevent it must, therefore, be taken at once.

I don't know exactly why, but reading that added a sense of shock to my surprise. Vincent! A man of whom I had scarcely thought in connection with this business. And yet—a retired army surgeon. A man who had seen service, no doubt, in the far-flung corners of the Empire. How in the name of all that was wonderful had Anthony Bathurst got hold of this piece of news? Again—where was reason in any of it? Vincent was a man advanced in years. Over seventy. What was behind it all? I remembered, as I thought over these things, of Anthony's early enquiry as to who was the occupant of Vincent's house. When he had pointed out to me that it lay about half a mile from Priestley's Quarry. But Vincent had lived in that house, as far as I knew, for over fifteen years. Nearer twenty, perhaps.

Then I remembered something else. Clement Vincent had been a guest of the Shelleys on the evening that Dick Copeland had disappeared and had also been at Blount's when Lady Rachel went there to play bridge. On the contrary, though, he had *not* been at Verschoyle's when the deaths had started. My acquaintance with him was but little. True, I had met him at one or two places, but these occasions had been very seldom. As I have indicated earlier in this story, Vincent's wife was almost an invalid. She had been in this condition for many years, and this fact, no doubt, had been the chief contributory cause to their leading such a comparatively quiet, unsociable life.

I looked at my watch. It was this action that brought me back from the dread of dreadfulness to ordinary everyday matters. Try as I would, I was unable to keep my thoughts off Anthony. Why the hell must he always attempt his tasks single-handed? My imagination conjured up the moor with its rises and its dips. With its rocks and patches of morass. Again I walked to the window. The moon had now partly broken through the black clouds. It seemed to me to peer down on Scarpe like a bright, powerful, vigilant spirit. As far as I could tell from indoors, there was but little wind. I heard an owl hooting in the distance. I thought of Ramsay still lying in the hospital. The trees round Scarpe were dark and unstirring. The moonlight crept round the circle of the outhouses, lighting up the dark ground. Again came the owl's hoot. The eerie sound of it made me shiver.

I walked away from the window and sat down by the fire. I dreaded the thought of the long night that was so soon to come. I knew, without a doubt, that I should sleep but little. I had not been sleeping well for some time, as may be well understood, but now, with this latest escapade of Anthony's uppermost in my mind, I felt that I must refrain from going to bed until the desire for sleep became much more potent than I felt it to be at this moment.

While I was musing thus, a strange sound caught my ear. I sat bolt upright in the armchair and listened intently. All was silent. I settled down again in the chair, under the impression that my ears had tricked me into the belief that I had heard a sound when there had been none. But my comparative tranquillity was short-lived. For again I heard the sound that had disturbed me before. I hastily looked round the room. I could see nothing at all. Immediately, however, the noise was repeated and I realized what it was. Somebody was tapping on the window-pane! I half-rose from my chair, and as I did so I found myself wishing that Anthony Bathurst's revolver was in my pocket instead of being where it was, in *his* pocket. Then, ashamed of my wretched fears, I walked to the window, pushed it open on its fastening-catch, and stared out into the darkness. I distinguished a dark form crouching in the lee of the house.

"Who's there?" I cried sharply. I saw a white hand come up through the darkness. The hand held an envelope towards me.

"Who is it?" I cried again.

"It's all right, sir," came the answer, "it's only me. I was asked to hand you this." The voice was the voice of Luke Foxon.

"Why didn't you come round to the front of the house in the proper way?" I took the letter from him as I spoke.

"Mr. Bathurst's orders, sir. He doesn't want anybody to know that he's communicating with you, sir. Very important, sir."

"Where did you—?" His uplifted hand stopped me.

"Don't talk too loudly, sir, please! You don't know who's about at this time of night. Especially when we know what's been going on."

I took the hint. "Where did you last see Mr. Bathurst, Foxon?"

"On Polchester Station, Mr. Clyst. That was where he gave me your letter. But I can't stay here any longer, sir. Good night."

Before I could properly take in this last announcement, Foxon had turned and slipped noiselessly away into the darkness. I carefully closed the window and, highly puzzled, returned to the armchair by the fire with my letter. I quickly slit open the envelope. The contents were surprising to me in the extreme.

Saturday, noon. My dear Jack. Things are going well. Far better, indeed, than one could have reasonably anticipated. Thought that you would be bucked to know this. I know "whom" for certain and I know "why", which is most decidedly a help in the right direction. I felt pretty sure of my friend when I left Scarpe this morning, but since then certain information which has come to me has clinched the issue! Now for the fierce and final struggle. "Bon rat—bon chat." And rely on my messenger. All the best.—A.L.B.

I frowned, I'm afraid, as I read the letter. But I understood, I think, as the direct result of reading it, that the end of the trail was much nearer to us than I had been all the time fondly imagining. Foxon was one of Blount's officers. I wondered if Blount knew that Anthony Bathurst was using him in this way. Probably not, I argued to myself. Still, what did it matter? To me at any rate. And A.L.B.'s news was reassuring, if nothing else. I decided that I would now go to bed. There was nothing to worry me unduly so far, and the letter had made a big difference to me. So bed it was. As I undressed in the bedroom, I was unable to resist the temptation of going to the window again and looking out. I stood there, I suppose, for a couple of minutes or so. Suddenly my senses tightened! There came two flashes of light across the moor. My eyes caught them distinctly. One! Two! Then, as though in direct and immediate response, there came two more, away from right over in the St. Roseworthy direction. I remembered the scream that Anthony Bathurst and I had heard on Old Year's night. I remembered the news that had come to us subsequently, the death of Lady Rachel Shelley. I remembered the body of Chinnery in the mortuary. I remembered the attack on and the narrow escape from death of Dick Copeland. I thought once again of Anthony Bathurst's challenge to the Evil, and as I got into bed I trembled at the possible result.

What would be the end? How would it affect me?

CHAPTER XXV
SUNDAY, JANUARY 8TH, DURING THE DAY

THE Sunday that intervened passed more or less uneventfully. But it was memorable, from my point of view, in that I went to church in the morning. I am not a man given to sudden "urges", but on this occasion I did feel that I would go along and hear what Edward Verschoyle had to say in his sermon. I must confess at once to being disappointed. To my surprise he trotted out a story of a saint obscure as far as I was concerned, St. Eugenian, and told us, his congregation, of the saint's martyrdom. Verschoyle informed us that January the 8th was the day given to this saint by the Church of Rome. Only the Squire, of my special circle from St. Crayle, was present in the congregation. I walked home after the service and couldn't help contrasting the conditions of the walk with the conditions of the previous Christmas morning, when Anthony Bathurst had accompanied me. We then had met several people. Cars had passed us. The Shelleys' car, for one. Now Lady Rachel was in her grave and her husband mourned for her. She had smiled at us from the car as it had passed us. Ronald Shelley had bowed. Clement Vincent's car had been another that had passed us. Where was Vincent now? I thought of Anthony's message again that Foxon had brought to me, and with that I thought of the phrase in my cousin's handwriting that I had found scrawled on the blotting-pad.

The weather was still very cold, but not quite as cold as it had been at its severest. I realized as I walked along that I had suddenly become utterly lonely. If things that day took their normal course the only person to whom I should speak for the rest of the time would be Mrs. Polglose. I felt for the first time a certain grief for Chinnery, and also, though in a less degree, for Lady Rachel. A lonely path in winter is not the best place to combat sorrow. On the contrary it is inclined to accentuate depression. Crowds and noise and gaiety are the best antidotes to sadness. Human desire is to avoid concentration and self-introspection when one is suffering a sense of loss. I suppose that in reality one becomes a different self after death. And how awful it would be, never to die! Now, however, I was alone. I felt rather terrifyingly alone. There are few terrors, perhaps, quite so abject as this dread of feeling absolutely alone.

Thus I was musing when I came to Scarpe for lunch. Mrs. Polglose entered just as I was finishing.

"You would like coffee, perhaps, sir?"

"Not 'perhaps', Mrs. Polglose—but certainly."

During the afternoon I had a snooze in the armchair and afterwards wrote a letter to a cousin of mine in Marseilles, Vi Meredith. I had remembered, all too late really, that the day was her birthday anniversary, and it was altogether an astounding thought that twenty-two years had gone by since she had been born. To me the twenty-two seemed much more like a mere seven or eight. How Time flies, to be sure!

My next employment was to do the *Sunday Express* "How Much Do You Know" questionnaire, and I found that I fared much worse than usual. I wasn't certain what a "sprew" was and was appallingly ignorant as to the real meaning of the word "Oireachtus". When I totted up my marks for successful answers, I could amass only 62 out of the normal 100 that I usually assess over the full twenty questions. Anything less than 75 per cent I regard as a failure, let me say, and I usually make the 75 without a great deal of difficulty. Tea-time came and then the evening. About half past eight the more important incidents of the previous evening repeated themselves. I congratulated myself that I had stayed indoors instead of walking over to the Burkes' or Copelands'. Once again I heard the light tap on the window and I opened it to find Foxon there just as he had been on the previous night. He handed me up a second letter and spoke softly.

"Evening, Mr. Clyst. From Mr. Bathurst again. You're to read it at once and to tell me that you understand."

I nodded and opened the envelope. This second communication from my cousin read as follows:

Sunday morning. My dear Jack. All goes well still. Things are moving rapidly and as far as I can see at the moment there should not be any great delay in bringing matters to a successful conclusion. Certainly two or three days from now should settle the issue. Please remember this. "Trust Foxon". Trust him implicitly, and if there comes a time in the very near future when instructions come from him to you, and not from me, spend no time in weighing their "pros and cons" when that time does come. Act decisively and immediately—as he will instruct you. Just as though the orders were mine. Obey him to the letter. Yours hopefully, A.L.B.

Having read the message once, I read it again. The writing was a little unsteady for Anthony's, but I wasn't too disturbed thereat because I didn't know under what conditions the note had been written. I saw Foxon's face searching mine for the reply which my cousin, no doubt, had told him to bring back from me, without fail. So I nodded my acquiescence to him.

"Tell Mr. Bathurst that I understand, Foxon, and will do exactly as he says."

"Right, sir. That's good." Foxon touched the peak of his cap and disappeared.

I went back to my chair. So things were actually moving. I referred to the letter again. "There should not be any great delay in bringing matters to a successful conclusion." What was Anthony up to? How much more comfortable in mind I should have been feeling if he had taken me into his confidence and shown me the board with all the pieces on it. My thoughts were very much on these lines when I went to bed, but I slept, in the end, better than I had anticipated. The cold was beginning to relax its grip. Gradually but unmistakably. Was the evil of it also passing from St. Crayle and the country round St. Crayle? In the morning I was destined to receive part of the answer.

CHAPTER XVI
MONDAY, JANUARY 9TH, 10.22 A.M.

I BREAKFASTED in the morning, gave Mrs. Polglose certain instructions to relay to my two farm-hands and then made up my mind that I would pop up to Burke's and have a word with Sybil and Martin. I was just about to leave Scarpe when who should blow in but Dick Copeland. He looked as big as ever, possibly, but his cheeks were pale and his eyes uneasy.

"Jack," he opened at once, "where's Anthony Bathurst? Is he back yet?"

"Not yet," I replied.

He stood and stared at me. Then blurted words. "Heard the latest?"

I had been looking unconcerned, I suppose, for he immediately followed up his previous remark with, "Jack, old man, I'm serious. Have you heard this morning's sensation?"

I shook my head. The knowledge that I had Anthony's letter in my pocket fortified me somewhat against the worst.

"No. What's up now?"

"Vincent's gone!" he replied. "Disappeared—just like the others! My God—I'm afraid, Jack! They'll come for me again—I know they will. And this time they won't make a mistake. They'll get me. Where *is* your cousin?" His teeth were almost chattering.

"Pull yourself together," I said to him. "They've had you once and you beat 'em. You're made in the likeness of a man. Don't forget it."

All the same, his news had shaken me. How far was Anthony Bathurst's latest move responsible for Vincent's disappearance? Knowing what I did, I was bound to connect the two facts. Dick Copeland continued his miserere.

"Vincent's over seventy. Old. Worn! Side-whiskers and a little tuft of beard. Where shall we find *his* dead body, Jack? An old man like that. In the winter of his life. None of us is safe from this deadly spell. Only your cousin can save us, I'm convinced of that. Will he be back here today?"

"I don't know, Squire. And that's honest. But tell me more. Where did you pick up the news about Clement Vincent?"

"It's all over the place. Mrs. Vincent communicated with the police early this morning, I understand. It's on all fours with the others— Vincent hasn't been home all night."

"Where was he? I mean this:—was he out anywhere last night, do you know?"

"Haven't heard, Jack. Nothing beyond the bare news that he's missing. I can't go through it again, Jack. What I went through before. Not for all the gold of the Indies. That awful deadly coldness! It choked the breath from my body. And that devilish cry before everything faded out for me." He paced the room. I could see that I had to deal with a thoroughly frightened man. His face, his eyes particularly, told me that plainly and clearly. What could I say to him?

"You see," he said again, "the people that have died have all been so different! Take Chinnery. An inoffensive, easy-going fellow. Never made an enemy, I suppose, all his life. Then Lady Rachel. A benefactress all round, if ever there was one. Now Vincent! Who'd ever want to harm poor old Vincent? And in between those three, the swine, whoever they are, have had a crack at me. What have I in common with those others? Nothing whatever! It's damned absurd, Jack. It's so absurd that I'm beginning to think that it's not a *human* agency at work. I'm inclined to agree with Burke and the Rector."

I rallied him.

"That's a complete reversal of your original position, then, Copeland. Talk about a come round! I shall never forget how you laughed that evening at the Rector's dinner-party. Scepticism? It wasn't in it. Find me a stronger word. You were the worst of all of us."

He smiled, but with an effort. For Copeland—it was a sickly smile indeed. My thoughts went back over the events of the past few days.

"It might well be," I remarked, "that there is more in this Vincent business than meets the eye."

The idea appeared to startle him.

"How do you mean?" he enquired.

"Oh, I don't know. A thought occurred to me—that was all. That perhaps the Vincent disappearance might *not* be on all fours with the others."

"Jack," he said, "what do you mean? You get me down. You're hinting at things."

"Well—look at it like this—suppose Vincent *hasn't* been 'got at' like the others? Supposing that other considerations have been the cause of his vanishing? You know as well as I do that people are lost sight of every week. In various parts of the country. They aren't *all* picked up on Constanton Moor."

"No, I know they're not. But the coincidences of our case are pretty strong, you know. I hope your theory's right—but Jack—" He shook his head sadly.

"You never know," I returned. "Men turn out very differently from our ordinary notions of them. Vincent's an excellent example of that contention. He's been in the district for years, but nevertheless how little we really know of him. Look how he's kept himself to himself. Never mixed much with any of us. We accept him for what we *think* he is, whereas in reality he might prove to be something entirely different."

He nodded as I finished speaking.

"It's possible, I suppose, but hardly likely. More probably the whole place is cursed, as I tried to say just now. I wish to God I knew where Bathurst was, but as you say you can't tell me, it's not much use my waiting here on the chance of him coming in, is it?"

"Not the slightest," I asserted cheerily.

What a complete metamorphosis this was of the cocksure Copeland whom I had known! What a spot of unholy fear will do to a man, to be sure!

He accepted the situation.

"I'll get along then. Seen Burke this morning?"

"No. I was thinking of going up just as you came in. Why?"

"Nothing. Only I may go along there later on. It's a comfort to me to have men like Burke and Verschoyle near me. I like both of 'em. And you too, Clyst, of course. No need for me to mention that, I know. You three are all so different from each other. And different from Shelley as well. Can't stick Ronald Shelley. Never could. Don't know why. Just can't. Sorry for him, naturally, as things are. Damned sorry. Know what it means to him. Lady Rachel was a thunderin' smart woman. They tell me he's a broken man. Shouldn't have expected that—but that's what they tell me, and I'm inclined to agree from what I've seen of him myself."

"I'm not surprised to hear it. Lady Rachel was extraordinarily *able*, and a man usually misses an able woman. Especially if she's been his wife. He probably relied on her in a good many directions, and now she's gone he feels the draught. I'm not a bit surprised."

Copeland waggled his big head.

"Still, he's a 'cocky', superior bloke at the best of times. I always reckoned that she was a damned sight too good for him!"

"All the more reason why he misses her," I remarked sapiently.

"That's one way of looking at it, I suppose. Well, cheerio, Jack, thanks for putting up with me. The chat's done me no end of good. I hope that Vincent's all right and that we shall have good news of him before long. Good-bye."

Dick Copeland shook hands with me and cleared out. During the remainder of the morning I did little. I can't remember a time when I have felt more unsettled. Blount called in to see me just before lunch. Surtees and Ronald Shelley were with him. They confirmed the news that Copeland had brought me earlier in respect of Vincent. Like the others who had preceded him along the avenue of death, he had vanished into thin air. The Colonel, as you may guess, had called with the primary purpose of seeing Anthony Bathurst.

"Nothing doing," I replied to his enquiry. "Sorry and all that, but I can't help you. Bathurst's away, as I told you on the 'phone. And I don't know for certain when he'll be back. In other words, the situation is unchanged."

"Yours is, maybe, Clyst. But mine isn't. Vincent's gone now. Oh well, if Bathurst isn't here, he isn't here. All the talk in the world won't alter that fact."

Old Surtees grimaced at me and spoke savagely.

"What's the matter? When he was here he didn't exactly set the rivers on fire. Plenty of talk and theorizing. Little else. Chinnery. Copeland. Lady Rachel Shelley—and now Vincent. Goodness gracious!"

This nettled me.

"You ought to shout, Surtees, I must say! You've done such a mighty lot yourself, haven't you? Still, there's nothing like sheer effrontery to push a man on in this world. No wonder you're such a howling success."

But he had a nature that was always pachydermatous. He just grinned at me and showed his big teeth.

"Thought that would sting you, Clyst. There's nothing like the truth to make a man wince. That's one thing at least that my profession's taught me. Come along, Colonel Blount."

Blount nodded. With a final, "Let me know when Bathurst returns," he gestured to Surtees and they left me.

The rest of the day passed uneventfully. I had a walk in the afternoon, but met nobody. I had hoped to encounter Sybil, but my luck was out. I took the path which I thought would be the most likely one for her to use, but didn't as much as catch a glimpse of her. Eventually I turned back home, heart heavy and spirit brooding. I had dinner at the usual time and was just settling down to a pipe and a spot of old liqueur Scotch when the bell went, as one might say, and the seconds were definitely out of the ring. I heard a noise behind my chair and turned hurriedly to see what caused it. What I saw, although it shouldn't have done, gave me a sense of shock.

My hands trembled and I could almost hear my heart thumping against my ribs!

Chapter XXVII

BEHIND my chair stood Luke Foxon. He came and faced me. His face was set and strained. He had no time to waste on preliminaries.

"Mr. Clyst," he opened, and directly he spoke I could tell that he was labouring under the influence of a strong excitement. Some natures show the crises which affect them much more than others. "I beg of you," he continued, "to act immediately. Mr. Bathurst is in danger. Grave danger. I know it, although I have no conclusive proof to offer you now. Trust me and be guided by me, as you promised Mr. Bathurst you would be yesterday. Is that O.K., sir?"

I remembered Anthony's letter and my promise and nodded to him. "Trust Foxon. Trust him implicitly."

I rose from my chair. "What am I to do?"

"Go to Colonel Blount's place, sir. At once. When you get there you will be told what to do next. And also, Mr. Clyst, will you please bring a revolver?"

I was determined to test him. "Why are you so completely in Mr. Bathurst's confidence?"

"And not you, sir? Is that what you mean? That's all right, don't you worry. You see—I'm so much better placed than you are, Mr. Clyst, to help Mr. Bathurst. Just a question of opportunity and convenience, sir. Now is everything straight?"

"So straight, Foxon," I replied, "that I shall be at Colonel Blount's in less than half an hour. That suit you?"

"Very good, sir. Then I'll say good night."

Foxon turned quickly on his heel and disappeared as silently as he had arrived. I little thought then what the circumstances would be when I was destined to see him again. I shoved my things on, cap and heavy coat, saw to a revolver that I knew I had knocking about somewhere, told Mrs. Polglose that I was going out and that she was not to worry over the time of my return, and then started off for Blount's.

Blount was waiting for me when I arrived, and, as usual these days, Dr. Surtees was with him.

Blount was cordiality itself.

"Glad you've come, Clyst. Been waiting for you. God knows what's doing, but I've promised your cousin that I'll back him all the way. And that explains nearly everything. I've been expecting some summons such as this for a day or so now. Are you fit?"

"What for? Where are we going now?"

"Don't know quite. But I've heard from him since he's been away, and since I 'phoned you—and I've more or less given him permission to use Foxon as and how he wanted him. But there's one thing that is certain—we're going for a car-ride. Come on, the car's waiting."

The three of us walked out to the waiting car. I saw that it was a big powerful police car. The blinds were drawn. Also, I could see nobody in the driver's seat.

"You are armed, Clyst? I take it that you . . ."

I nodded and patted my pocket. We got in the car. Surtees sat on the seat in front, next to the driver's. Colonel Blount and I sat at the back. I was directly behind Surtees. I saw a dark figure climb into the driving-seat, but was unable to distinguish who it was. Away we went at once. To travel in silence for a long time. I was by no means certain of the direction which we were taking. After a time the car began to lurch considerably and I judged that we were either on the moorland track or close to it.

"The blinds are drawn at your cousin's request, Clyst," said Blount. "He must have a serious reason for it."

I had been attempting to see something of where we were and the way that we were taking, but it was quite a hopeless proposition and I could make out nothing. Occasionally, just through the chinks, there came the yellowish blur of a light when we were passing it— that was all. Now and then I hazarded a remark in order to break the spell of the monotony of the journey, but Blount answered only in monosyllables and the spark of conversation died down almost as soon as it had flickered up. I looked at my wrist-watch. We had been running for seventeen minutes. I had scarcely registered the thought, when the wheels of the big car began to jolt terribly and I knew for a thousand to one that we were somewhere on Constanton Moor. Judging by the time that we had taken, we must be well beyond Chinnery's house and even farther on than Priestley's Quarry, that is if we had come straight along the way that I knew, and had not turned off anywhere. Then the car lurched and jolted more than ever. One more violent lurch than the others threw me against its side, and I heard Blount give way to a muttered curse. I could tell that the pace was slowing down. Eventually the car stopped. Blount opened the door and got out. I quickly followed his example. I could see Surtees just ahead of me, and in front of him the man who had driven the car here. Surtees turned suddenly and put his finger to his lips. I understood. We were not to be conversational.

As far as I could tell, we were on the moor, but there was a light showing from a house about a hundred yards or so to our left. It was dark, wretchedly cold, and raining slightly. Blount gestured to us, and we moved forward. I know that for a time we moved over coarse grassland. I should say that we walked straight ahead for about a hundred yards. Then the man who was leading the four of us stopped. Surtees did likewise. I followed his example and my ears told me that Blount, behind me, had done the same thing. When you come to think over things of this kind, it's amazing how quickly "understandings" are effected. Without previous planning, I mean. You take your cue from the next man and, unconsciously almost, achieve, without the least fuss or bother, an organized unanimity that has only intelligent spontaneity as the foundation stone of its organization.

By now the rain was falling more heavily, and my knowledge of the locality and its general weather conditions and tendencies made me feel moderately certain that we were in for a drenching night. This anticipation made the prospect much more unattractive from my own individual point of view, as I loathe rain rather more than the next man at the best of times. Then something happened. Surtees turned to me—he was game, I'll say that for him—and showed me unmistakably with a movement of his arm that he was handling his revolver. I took mine from my pocket and grasped it firmly, fully determined not to be caught napping in this particular direction, at all costs. We moved forward and made a half-turn to the left. I was soon able to distinguish the rough outline of a fence of sorts. Of wood. Broken badly in one or two places and obviously needing repair in many parts. It seemed to me, from the hazy glimpse that I was able to obtain of it, to enclose a piece of ground, in size about sixty feet square. I saw the man who was leading the four of us strike off again at a tangent and start to cross towards a point that I judged to be almost the middle of the sixty feet square that I have just described. There was hardly a sound as our light feet trod the longish grass. Surtees waved me forward with a quick movement of the hand, and the three of us who had been bringing up the rear went up together and joined the man who had been in our van. To my surprise, as I joined the circle I saw that this man was none other than Luke Foxon himself.

As Blount and I joined Surtees and him, Foxon put a finger to his lips, much as the doctor had done, and produced an electric torch from his overcoat pocket. This he flashed on to the grass around us. The beam of light soon picked out what he sought. For I saw a square slab of stone about the shape and size of a flagstone some dozen yards or so in front of us. The grass that surrounded the stone was thick, but by no means as long as most of the grass that we had trodden. The inference was obvious. Foxon beckoned us forward again and we gathered round him more closely.

When I came right to the edge of this stone I saw something else. In the centre of it was a ring. By which, plainly, it could be lifted from its bed of grass. Foxon looked towards his chief, as though seeking instructions as to his next procedure. Blount nodded twice briskly. Foxon took a scarf from his neck, straightened it out and then looped it through the ring of the stone. He pulled with the scarf and I saw the stone lifted from the grass and then stand almost upright on its edge. Foxon's actions all the time were noiseless. He bent over the edge of the aperture that the moved stone had disclosed. We three others clustered round him. But I was unprepared for what I was to see next. The opening was not unlike the manhole that the ordinary sewer-cleaner of a big town is called upon to descend for the purpose of performing his daily duty. Against one side there was an iron ladder flush against the brickwork of the opening. I could see its rungs plainly as I looked down into the hole, but I wasn't able to count them, because my eyes couldn't follow them right down to where the ladder finished.

Blount gestured to Foxon, busy again with his scarf, and I knew instinctively what the gesture meant. We were going down there. All of us. Blount showed his revolver to Foxon and the latter nodded, to show, no doubt, that he understood his officer's orders. Then Foxon threw his leg over the side of the opening and commenced to descend the ladder. He gradually disappeared from sight. Not a sound reached us from below. Then the doctor swung his leg over the side as Foxon had done, and followed his predecessor down the iron ladder. He went and I immediately followed in my turn. It was a rougher job than I had anticipated. I counted each rung as I left it behind me. There were no fewer than twenty-two of them. When my feet touched the ground again I found myself in a subterranean chamber which struck me at once as being icy cold, and, but for the light from Foxon's torch, would have been pitch dark. Surtees and Foxon were by my side. In a few moments Colonel Blount came down the ladder and joined us.

Our backs were to the wall, the same wall against which stood the iron ladder, the use of which had brought us there. Facing us, I saw, from the light of the torch, a square receptacle, in shape and size very like a cage. Except for the fact that in a cage one expects to find bars. But this, except for a kind of wicket-gate on the front of it, was filled in and therefore self-contained all the way round. Away to the left, I discerned an opening in the wall which faced the cage. Probably a door, I thought, leading from this subterranean chamber to a house or building of some kind. Where we really were, I hadn't the slightest idea. Had I been asked, "Somewhere on the moor" would have been the best definition that I could have supplied. I seemed to have lost all sense of direction. I strained my ears in an effort to hear any sound that might come from the outside world. I could hear nothing. Foxon came and stood next to me. Blount edged away from Surtees and put his lips close to my ear. He whispered words, but his lips were so close to my ear that I could hear him without the slightest difficulty.

"There mustn't be any talking. Also I don't want us to show too much light. I'm going to tell Foxon to mask his torch a bit. Is that clear?"

I nodded and then in turn put my lips to his ear.

"Yes. I understand all that. But what's the idea? What are we waiting here for and how long? It's enough to freeze the ears off a brass monkey down here. I tell you straight, I doubt if I can stick it for long. When do the Polar bears come out?"

Blount turned away from me and, at a gesture from him, Foxon covered the light of his torch. All was silent. The four of us stood there in semi-darkness. The atmosphere grew colder and colder. I wondered where Anthony Bathurst was while all this was going on. Every now and then Blount would whisper a remark to one of us, as a rule to Foxon. I should have loved to have stamped my feet, but I knew that to put the idea into practice was out of the question. I buttoned my coat right up to my chin, pushed my hands into my pockets and huddled myself as far as I could into the warmth of the big storm collar with my back pressed against the wall. By putting my wrist-watch to my ear occasionally I could hear it ticking, but it hadn't a luminous dial, so that I was unable to tell the passage of time.

In this way, twenty minutes or so, I suppose, must have gone by. I was just resigning myself to dying by frozen inches when my ear caught a slight sound. I knew that I hadn't been deceived, because I felt Foxon, standing by my side, stiffen. I expect that I was even more aware of that fact than Foxon was himself. Yes! I was right! The sound came nearer to my ears. It was the sound of a footstep, I decided. Footsteps of *somebody*! A man, I judged, who, for some reason, was approaching this underground death-trap in which we were all standing. Blount sent a message of one word along our line of watchers. "Revolvers." My hand closed on the butt of mine. Thank God! Action at long last!

By this time the sound of the approaching footsteps was clearly audible. I knew, praise the Saints, that the moment of action for which I had been waiting could not now be long delayed. The half-light from Foxon's torch could no more be seen and we stood in an inky well of frightening darkness. I heard a clicking noise away to my left and I sensed at once what it was. The person who had come was opening the door of the chamber where we were. I was right. I heard the door swing open and I could tell, in that strange indefinable way that one *can* tell these things, that somebody had entered through the door and was standing but a few yards from us. I flattened myself still further into the wall at my back. Instinctively. I judged that a man's figure walked from the entrance door towards the cage affair, a matter of three or four yards. From the spot of light that played in front of him, I guessed that he was using an electric hand-torch similar to the one that Luke Foxon had. But inasmuch as he kept the light in front of him all the time, I was unable to see who it was.

Then there came another noise and in the beam of light I saw a hand fumbling with that part of the cage-like structure that I have previously described as a wicket-gate. The lock of this seemed to slide back and at once the gate arrangement opened. The beam of light from the man's hand picked out the interior of the cage for me. I saw a place of strange smooth shining walls . . . glistening walls . . . walls that looked almost unreal . . . and then my eyes, following the questing light, picked out, also, a huddled heaplike form recumbent upon the floor.

The man who had opened the door of the compartment and who stood looking in, laughed. It was a wild, mocking, but frightening laugh! Although mine is only a lay opinion, to my ear there was an unmistakable note of hysteria in it. It rang through this eerie place discordantly, and turned my heart almost to the coldness that my body knew. The laugh was followed by a fiercely-triumphant cry and the words: "Vincent! The last of my bag!"

The figure, shapeless almost, with hunched shoulders, still lay there motionless. I felt Foxon's elbow pressed into my ribs. The movement was as eloquent as though he had spoken actual words to me. My muscles tightened, even though my heart had now come into my mouth. I was just able to see Blount move forward towards the cage, silently but rapidly. His revolver was drawn. I moved forward, too. Foxon was still on my immediate left. His breath was coming in short, sharp gasps—and I, like the fool that I was, didn't know the real cause of his vital anxiety. Suddenly the light flashed out from Foxon's torch and the man on the threshold of the cage, who had been gazing at the prostrate form that the cage held, turned like lightning to meet its remorseless glare. Like a flash his hand went to his pocket just as Blount's voice rang out.

"Up with your hands, or we shoot!"

At that moment I saw the man's face for the first time that evening. My shock and my surprise were such that I cried his name aloud!

The echo came back from the walls of the chamber and almost beat me in the face. I sprang forward. But I was dazed, and without knowing why I did it, I cried his name again!

CHAPTER XXVIII
MONDAY, JANUARY 9TH, IMMEDIATELY FOLLOWING

As I cried his name for this second time, his revolver beat Blount's by the fraction of a split second, and I heard Foxon give a smothered curse as the bullet smithereened the torch he held and ploughed a deep red furrow in his wrist. We were now in complete darkness. I heard Surtees and Blount plunge forward as cattle will in fear, but our assailant fired again twice and literally buffeted his way towards us. Blount and Surtees were swept aside by sheer impetus and a fierce blow to my chin sent me staggering. The man who attacked us knew the conditions of the place so much better than I did, and therefore had all the advantages. Although I was desperately afraid of hitting the wrong man, I recovered my balance and fired as my assailant flung himself from me, but my bullet must have gone aside, for he broke clear. Before I could stop him, he was at the foot of the ladder that I knew would take him to the top and possible safety. I turned and caught his leg, but he swung round viciously, flung his torch in my face, thrust me aside, kicked at me, and hurled himself up the ladder.

All this happened in the space of a few seconds. Foxon picked up the torch that had been thrown at me and ran to Vincent within the cage. He flooded the place with light. For, luckily, the torch in its fall had suffered little damage.

"Bring him along, Foxon," cried Blount. "Don't give him the brandy unless he asks specially for it. Get him moving about."

"Supposing the stone falls?" asked Surtees.

"It doesn't matter," I said, "the other door's open. Look behind you. Whatever he does, he can't close that. He'll waste his time if he attempts to push the stone back."

"You and I, then, Clyst," said Blount. "After him. He's only a few seconds' start. Let the doctor and Foxon attend to the poor devil whom we've just snatched from death. Take him out the other way."

He sprang up the ladder and I followed him. We saw a running figure in the distance and then we heard the noise of a car being started.

"It's not ours, Clyst," said Blount again. "Thank God for that. It's coming from the wrong direction. Our car's over there. He won't live with it. With ordinary luck, we've got him in the hollow of our hands."

We raced hard for the powerful police-car. I followed Blount. Without him, I doubt if I could have found my way to it. It was the work of a few moments to reach it, start it and turn it towards the other escaping car, the lights of which we could see about three hundred yards ahead of us. Blount swung the big car on to the moorland track and without a second's hesitation trod on the juice. We roared ahead. The car swayed from side to side and all the time neither of us spoke. I had little words, for my thoughts wholly possessed me. Our big car had all the advantages; and it could be but a question of time before we ran the other down. We ate up the distance between the two cars relentlessly. As we drew closer and closer, my hand closed again on my revolver. My heart raced perilously. To think that I knew the truth . . . the dreadful—almost paralysing—truth!

Blount drove on inexorably. The quarry was ours. There was no possible chance of him escaping us now. Then, as though by a sudden gesture of an evil spirit, the situation changed. A shot rang out in front of us, the car that we followed, like a wild animal, seemed to leap almost, and, uncontrolled, left the rough track of moorland, ran on for some little distance, lurched like a living thing, plunged forward and turned over on its side. As we came up with it I heard Blount wildly cursing, and I pulled the body of the driver from the overturned vehicle. He was quite dead. . . . There was a little hole in his temple through which the bullet had entered and I looked for the last time on the face of a man whom I had known so well. The deathly pallor of it showed so, upturned as it was to the darkness of the sky. Dick Copeland, the Squire of St. Crayle, had made no mistake with his final shot . . . if only for the fact that he knew at last the game was up!

"The best thing he could have done—the swine," growled Blount, as he looked down at the body. "And but for Bathurst, I doubt whether we should ever have got him."

I stared at him blankly, for I was still wondering. There was so much, as far as I was concerned, that needed explanation!

Chapter XXIX
MONDAY, JANUARY 9TH, TOWARDS MIDNIGHT

WE THREW a coat over the dead man's body and left him there on the unfriendly moor. It was Blount's decision, and what he said in regard to this went, as far as I cared. Blount drove back along the way that we had just come.

"I think I know where the turn comes," he muttered. "Keep your eyes open for it, will you, Clyst?"

I nodded and, guiding each other, as odd turns here and there presented themselves, we came again to the place where we had parked our car before. We alighted and Blount began to run. I followed him. Somehow I was afraid that there was more danger still to be faced.

"I want to see how Clement Vincent is," he cried to me. "That's what's troubling me."

I could well understand his anxiety. We came again to the square of grass that covered the stone leading to the underground vault or whatever it was. Blount disregarded it and ran across to the left. Then I began to see better where we were. We were about a hundred yards to the rear of Copeland's house. When we came round to the front and to the door, it was Surtees who admitted us.

"All right! Don't worry yourselves. We've got him round. Just in time. Foxon's worked like a Trojan. Where's that other monster from hell?"

The terms of Blount's reply surprised me, though I admit that I couldn't think of any better, or, under the circumstances, any more apt.

"Gone to his own place," were his words, "and arrived there none too soon, believe me." He stopped, to go on again at once. "Take me to our last patient, thank God. I think, Clyst, that I can say that this time, with complete confidence."

Surtees beckoned to us.

"This way. The two girls know nothing, so far. The bad news can wait. They're in their bedrooms. I told them not to worry and that somebody had been found ill on the moor whom we were forced to bring in here for assistance. That their father was helping us and wanted them to stay in bed. Best thing I could say in the circumstances, don't you think so?"

Blount nodded.

"I quite agree, doctor. You couldn't have done better."

We followed Surtees into a room on the left. The warmth of the room was a benison to us after the coldness that we had known. The fire on the hearth was a sight for the gods. On a divan arrangement, in front of the fire, lay a man. He was as pale as death. When I looked at him, I could scarcely believe the truth that my eyes told me. For here lay my cousin, Anthony Bathurst, but with side-whiskers, pointed beard and glasses, and wearing clothes that belonged to the wardrobe of a generation ago! He grinned at me weakly as I entered, and tried to flap a fin.

"Hallo, Jack! Behold the decoy out of cold storage. Best Norfolk bird! It was a risk, but it came off, thank God!"

I shook him by the hand.

"Can you talk?" I asked him, "or must we wait for explanations?"

He looked askance at Surtees. The latter nodded to him reassuringly.

"If you feel you can, Bathurst, it's O.K. with me. But for the Lord's sake, if you feel the strain's too much for you, knock off at once."

Anthony grinned again.

"What was that awful place?" I asked.

"A refrigerator. Exactly that. Nothing more. Nothing less. Just the same as a cold storage chamber. For freezing humans, not Argentine beef or Canterbury lamb. Just an apparatus for cold-blooded murder," he chuckled.

Blount and Surtees joined me. We gathered round him.

"He told me he could get it to 273 degrees below zero. In time. He boasted about it. Thank God he didn't."

"But how did he get you there?" I exclaimed incredulously. "Whatever happened? What were *you* doing about it?"

"I knew he wanted Vincent, so I forced his hand. Vincent was the last one he needed for his collection. I told Vincent how things were and sent Vincent to him with the news that he (Vincent) was leaving the district for good and had come to say good-bye. Vincent, therefore, a little later, was walking back home across the moor. I *knew* the murderer would snap at the chance. He did. But friend Vincent had gone the other way, and he got me in his net instead, plus Vincent's 'externals', clothes, beard, horn-rimmed glasses, etc. I flatter myself that I made a very good retired army surgeon. Anyhow, in the dark this evening I passed muster, which was all that mattered."

"But what's it all about?" demanded Colonel Blount. "What obsessed the maniac to run such a campaign of wholesale slaughter in a village district like this? Just blood-lust, and wanton cruelty, or what? Sadism, all over again? I confess it all amazes me."

"No. None of these things. He *had* a motive," said Anthony Bathurst quietly, "a motive that to him had become the overwhelming passion of his later life. That motive was one of the greatest of all human urges. I refer to the world-old motive of 'revenge'."

Anthony paused.

I think that every one of us stared at him.

"Revenge? Revenge for what?" Surtees was the speaker. " What harm had anyone of us here ever done him?"

A.L.B. took out his pocket-book and carefully selected something therefrom. He passed it to Blount. I saw that it was a newspaper-cutting. Surtees and I read it over Blount's shoulder.

On Wednesday last, July 22nd, at St. Roseworthy Petty Sessions, before Christopher Chinnery (in the chair), Lady Rachel Shelley, and Clement Vincent, Esq., Irene Lois Whitmarsh, married woman, aged 22, of Thisterrol Cross, Stapleton, was charged with stealing a lady's frock valued at £5, the property of Samuel Stone, draper, of Polchester, on the 9th of July last. Defendant, after evidence had been given by Det.-Constable Jennings, maintained that a terrible mistake had been made. She urged that she had no intention whatever of stealing the article, but had merely taken it from one counter of the shop towards another, before intended purchase, so that she might be able to see the colour better in conditions of superior lighting. Addressing the accused, the Chairman said that the Bench did not believe a word of the story, which had obviously been concocted to suit the occasion, and that she was not only a thief, but an accomplished liar. He and his colleagues were determined to put a stop to this practice of stealing from shopkeepers and the accused would be sent to gaol for a term of one month. Whitmarsh fainted in the dock when sentence was pronounced and had to be given medical attention.

Blount looked up in amazement. "But I—"

"Yes! Revenge!" said Anthony. "That's a cutting from the *Polchester Recorder*—something like fifteen years ago. There you have it. The full story. Consider the names. Chinnery, Lady Rachel, and Vincent. Mrs. Whitmarsh was Copeland's young wife. His real name was Whitmarsh. She died soon after coming out of prison. He dedicated his life to the purpose of avenging her. Went away from the district, made money, bought property here, came back as the man you all knew—Squire Copeland. He had his 'refrigerator' specially constructed and the underground chamber made and prepared to take it. His house was on the moor. It took him years to build the entire apparatus, but his victims were literally at his finger-tips and he could afford to wait until his plans were complete. It had a touch of cat-and-mouse which rather suited him."

I nodded. I understood.

Anthony went on.

"The Rector's dinner-party turned the scale. Brought him to action-point. Burke's story, I mean."

I nodded again. "Yes. Copeland's plans were all perfected and he suddenly saw how he could dump the bodies on the moor in weather such as you were experiencing, after his machinery had frozen them— and who would there be amongst us to suspect murder? Burke's story gave him the idea of putting the red marks behind the ears. Another touch this—that would divert the issue. When his victim was dead, he heated something—the prong of a table-fork, perhaps—and produced the mystic mark that was like a scratch. The idea of 'projected evil', as put forward by Burke, suited him down to the ground. Where before he had been wondering, *now* he saw the way clear."

Blount cut in.

"That was a clever blind that attack on himself. Especially coming second in the list of outrages."

"Yes," returned my cousin. "He realized, you see, that whereas Chinnery's death would be *accepted*, the others that he intended to follow up with would necessarily bring the matter to the pitch of sensation. Things then would undoubtedly be much more seriously looked into—so that if there *were* 'suspects', he would remove himself from that area by being so nearly killed himself. And I'll tell you how he managed that, if you'd care to hear."

"By all means," replied Colonel Blount.

"When he left Shelleys' that night, after the bridge-party, he walked across country to Verrinder. The walk would have taken him about an hour. In spite of your enquiries, Blount, he *did*, I think, take train from there to Polchester *via* St. Crayle. There's one at 10.29. He lay low in Polchester for some days. His next step was to purchase a cheap car. In it he came back to the moor in the darkness of the night, ran the car down Tresarth's disused mine, because he obviously didn't want it found there in the morning, and then lay on the moor waiting to be picked up. It was a bit risky, but he was a strong man and he took care not to be there too long. Also he knew the patrol was out and chose a spot where he was certain to be found. He saw to the scratch on his ears, and, of course, had a perfectly astounding story for us, when he 'recovered consciousness'. But there were ear-marks and cigarette stubs near the mine. I found them and showed them to you, Jack, remember?"

I did remember and nodded to him.

"Copeland's story was devilishly clever. He reproduced *all* Burke's stuff, but adroitly avoided all reference to the marks behind his ears! On the grounds, I suppose, that they had been inflicted whilst he was unconscious, and that, since he hadn't seen them, by reason of the position, he therefore would know nothing about them. Damn' smart, that, gentlemen!"

"How did you get on to Copeland in the first place?" I asked.

"He made a bad mistake. The only one, really, that he did make. Bad one, I mean. When he attacked Chinnery on his way home from Verschoyle's party, he laid him on the floor of his car. On a green rug. The green hairs that I took off Chinnery's coat came from where his body had lain on that rug. I watched for days for a car with a green rug. When I saw a green rug in the Squire's car I began to think. And I thought to such good effect that I got to work on Copeland's general antecedents. Things began to point in Copeland's direction. Remember how his daughter told us he had refused fancy prices for his house? Of course! This murder-mechanism was installed there and on the point of fulfilling its purpose. Then, my London agent, whom I had put on to the Copeland 'early days', reported that he had got on to something. He had traced Copeland's business career right back to the days when he had left his native Glebeshire to start in London. He had eventually come across the name of 'Whitmarsh' in a deed of assignment, and further investigation, fortified by an early photograph of 'Richard Whitmarsh', brought out the information that Whitmarsh and our Copeland were one and the same person. Armed with these facts, I hammered at the Whitmarsh end down here in Glebeshire. Eventually an official at the Polchester Police Court remembered the name of Whitmarsh as having come under his notice in some way or other. Ultimately he produced for me that news-cutting at which you have just looked."

"You were 'home', then, of course," said Surtees.

Anthony smiled contentedly.

"Chinnery, Lady Rachel, Vincent—Justices of the Peace—all of them, *and* the 'motive', all ready for me in a row, and piping hot. When I found his ringed stone almost hidden in the grass at the back of his house I could see almost everything."

"Why did he keep Chinnery in the refrigerator so long?"

"I think that he killed *him* very gradually. Tortured him, Gloated over him, if you like. Chinnery was his first victim, don't forget. And the man who had whipped his innocent wife with his tongue as she stood in the dock. He shaved him after death, too, remember. To give the impression, I fancy, that Chinnery had been staying somewhere in an ordinary capacity. Any more ends want sealing up?"

"Yes." The intervention was mine.

"Those synchronized footsteps that we heard. I've puzzled my—"

"You need not, Jack. The explanation is simple and entirely natural. That particular place on the moor has a natural 'echo'. I've tested it and proved it. Think, man! Synchronization! Or almost. A noise—and its own echo! The shadows we imagined. Quite an easy thing to do in that peculiar light."

I nodded.

"Another point, Anthony. What was Martin Burke's trouble?"

"Ah—well, I'll answer that question in this way. Burke is *susceptible* to evil. He's sensitive—telepathic, if you like. Copeland's presence near him affected him, although he couldn't have explained the reason of his being affected. When that man fell into the sea from St. Crayle harbour and was drowned, I'll lay a pterodactyl to a ptarmigan that Copeland was in the immedite vicinity. Not connected with the incident, but approximate to it. Get me?"

"Yes, I think so. Martin will be all right now, I suppose?"

"Go and see him. He's bound to be. And Sybil." He smiled at me. There was raillery in the smile.

Blount interposed with yet another question.

"How did you fix things with Foxon after I had lent him to you?"

"In this way. I arranged that if I didn't appear in a certain spot on the moor each night, he would know that *Copeland had me*. The first night I missed he was to act on the instructions that he had received from me. I had told him about the stone in the long grass. He was to bring you fellows so that you could see for yourselves, beyond the vestige of a doubt, that Copeland was the man you wanted and could be taken almost red-handed. Luke Foxon was one of the best all the way through."

"How long could you have lasted in that refrigerating chamber?"

"I don't know. But I had an electrical heating apparatus attached to me, round my waist, which would have helped me to resist more than the ordinary person could, and I had fed intelligently for some time previously. I had even lectured Jack here on the value of the calorie. Every little helps, you see."

"Did he put you straight in there?"

"Carried me there straight from the car, where he had flung me when he took me on the moor. I couldn't struggle too much, as a

222 | BRIAN FLYNN

'three-score-year-and-tenner', could I? He bound my feet and hands with ropes, but he took these off when he slung me into his icecream outfit. He was so certain that it was Vincent whom he had that he never really inspected me. No doubt he used the same methods with Chinnery and Lady Rachel Shelley. Although in the latter case he attracted the chauffeur's attention by a trick. Possibly a white sheet tied round his body."

"Did he tell you why he was doing all this?" asked Blount.

"Oh yes. Came and parked himself outside the cage. He told me what I, as Vincent, had done to the girl he loved. In a way, I felt sorry for him. He loved her so much, you see. Then he informed me how I should join the other two who had sat on the Bench that memorable day all those years ago, and how cold I'd be before I burnt in hell. Oh, yes, he read me the Riot Act all right, don't you worry."

"I don't think we need to any more," I said quietly. "Thanks to you."

"Neither do I," said Anthony, "and thanks to me—my grand-mother!"

"*Our* grandmother. We're cousins," I reminded him.

"Did you ever meet her? She smoked a clay pipe."

"She swore like a trooper, I know that. And wasn't too concerned about marriage certificates."

"You surprise me! I was her favourite grandson, though. At least, Mother always said so."

"That was to get you off to sleep. Dope!"

"Think so? Shouldn't be surprised myself. Shan't want any tonight. I shall be the 'Big Top' itself."

His eyes showed what he was feeling.

I answered him.

"You will? Don't be too cocksure! You never know. The Polglose is waiting for you at Scarpe. She'll wake you up, my lad, if I'm any judge."

But this time I received no reply.

For the best of reasons. Anthony Lotherington Bahurst was fast asleep!

THE END